SURPRISE CEO

IONA ROSE

SOME BOOKS

Publisher: Some Books

ISBN: 978-1-913990-51-0

AUTHOR'S NOTE

Hey there!

Thank you for choosing my book. I sure hope that you love it. I'd hate to part ways once you're done though. So how about we stay in touch?

My newsletter is a great way to discover more about me and my books. Where you'll find frequent exclusive giveaways, sneak previews of new releases and be first to see new cover reveals.

And as a HUGE thank you for joining, you'll receive a FREE book on me!

With love,

Iona

Get Your FREE Book Here:
https://dl.bookfunnel.com/v9yit8b3f7

ADELE

I felt terror.

But at the same time, my blood was simmering with excitement.

Tonight was the night.

I was sure of it, and I was also incredibly close to just exploding and telling him to get it over with.

I could see he was just as nervous as I was.

For one he was wearing a jacket, and although it was just a basic corduroy, his actually wearing one was still unusual enough to indicate today was going to be a special occasion. It was my birthday, and thus far I'd had two birthdays with him and he had never bothered with a jacket. There was the well-worn short sleeved dress shirt underneath which was most definitely nothing special, but I ensured to ignore it so I could appreciate the elegance he seemed to want to sport for me today.

He however couldn't stop fiddling with his collar, despite the absence of a tie to irritate him and then there was the tiny fact his eyes hadn't quite been able to meet mine for more than a second at a time thus far into the night.

All of this served to torture me, and I prayed he would soon say what he wanted so I could return to some semblance of normalcy; a steadily beating heart, an acceptable degree of clarity for my future, and really just an appetite healthy enough to allow the enjoyment of my saffron risotto and carabineros prawns.

"Why did you choose this restaurant?" I asked.

He froze, and without realizing it, his gaze stayed on me for more than a second this time around.

"I thought you wanted to come here," he said. "You've been constantly mentioning this place over the last couple of months."

He was right, and my heart did a little flip at his attentiveness.

It was another confirmation.

I was most definitely going to get engaged tonight.

"I do, and I did," I blushed as I brushed my shiny blond hair over my shoulders.

It revealed the pale, delicate curve of my shoulders, thanks to the very deliberate choice of the halter neck, satin, olive green dress my co-worker Melinda had insisted I borrow from her closet.

"It's a special night," she'd said. "And you're both going to take pictures after you say yes. These pictures are going to be forever so you should look smoking hot in them."

I'd rolled my eyes. "I've been with the guy for two years. What's left to be blown away by?"

Still, I'd accepted the dress and especially now, appreciated how flattering and feminine it made me feel, clinging to the soft curves of my body and exposing just the right amount of side cleavage.

"Well, I listened," he said. "So here we are."

"Thank you," I replied and scanned his strangely, tight face. He seemed so tense. "You're the best Andrew."

"I have something to tell you," he said. "But I can't seem to decide whether to say it now or to just wait till after dinner."

Finally.

"Now is best," I responded, and set my fork down. "Let's get it over with. We can continue eating afterwards. The prawns will taste even better afterwards."

I laughed, but noticed he wasn't exactly as excited as I was.

His expression tempered, and then he drained his glass of wine.

"Adele," he called. "We've been dating for about two years now right?"

"Yeah," I replied, completely attentive.

"Well, um... I think we've had a great run so far."

My heart leapt into my throat.

"Yeah... I think so too."

"I really don't know how to say this," he said. "And I don't want to hurt you either. I just really want you to understand."

All my excitement instantly ceased, and in its place was a chilling dread.

"W-what do you mean?" I asked, now much too afraid to assume.

"I think we should take a break."

"What?"

At his words, something slammed so hard into me I felt my balance topple. My high heeled encased feet were still on the floor, but it didn't seem like my soul was still inside my body. Instead it seemed as though it was floating overhead and watching this nightmare as it unfolded. He wanted us to take a break. I had to have misheard him right?

"W-what do you mean?"

He released a heavy sigh. "I want us to see other people. Just for a little while."

I frowned at him. "What the fuck do you mean by *'you want us to see other people just for a little while?'*"

He seemed perplexed as though he couldn't understand why I wasn't comprehending his request.

I felt a deadly calm, so I folded my arms across my chest and glared at him. "You're breaking up with me?"

"No! I mean... it's just a break."

"So you're taking a break *from* me."

"No, not from you. From dating... the relationship."

I couldn't believe him. "What?"

He sighed and picked up his wine glass, and it was only after bringing it to his lips he realized it had already been drained. So he placed it back on the table and met my gaze.

I couldn't prevent it then. Tears stung my eyes and it made me even angrier. This was the man I had given the last two years of my life, body, soul and heart to. Tonight, I was sure he was going to ask me to spend the rest of his life with him but instead he was breaking up with me? I wanted to kill him.

It took every bit of strength inside of me not to erupt so after forcing myself to take deep breaths, I took my trembling hand off the table.

"Why?" I asked. "Did I do something wrong?"

"No," he was quick to refute. "It's me. I just... I just need some time to myself."

I was even further confounded. "I only see you a couple of times a week."

His lips parted but no words came out.

So I waited for him to gather the balls to tell me the truth.

"Adele, let's not make this more difficult than it has to be. People grow apart and break up all the time."

"Ah," my mouth fell open. "So this is not just a 'break.' We are breaking up."

He was struck dumb then.

To be honest I couldn't say I was completely surprised. The passion had slowly fizzled out of our relationship over time but I had never been too concerned about it. That was normal wasn't it? All around the world and between couples, that fiery desire and desperation for the other was supposed to cool down to a warm acceptance and enjoyment of the other person's constant presence. Was this not how it was meant to be? So what the fuck was going on?

I looked away and took in the magnificent tropical oasis decor of the restaurant. Its warm ambience and assortment of flowerbeds had caught my eyes from the moment I had first caught wind of it on an online review by La Liste for being the most favored spot for proposals by women. Hence my desire to someday visit here with the piece of trash sitting before me, in order to perhaps obtain a proposal for myself too. But now, he had forever ruined this place for me, and it was such a shame because the magnificent gardens surrounding us were quite the occasional sight to behold.

From now on, I would always and only be able to remember this place as where I was all too elegantly dumped.

"Why didn't you just say this to me over the phone or at home... or something? Why did you fucking bring me here, and force me to dress up just so you could humiliate me?"

"Adele, I don't want to humiliate you."

"Then why did you fucking bring me here?"

My tone had lost control and at the near yell, heads all around the restaurant turned towards our table.

This of course embarrassed him.

"Calm down," he said through gritted teeth and I wanted to throw something at him. Before I could stop it the tears rolled down my cheeks and I turned my face away. I rose to my feet then and it was so forceful my chair tumbled back and fell to the ground. I didn't care. I began to step over it but then he jumped to his feet, the glasses and ceramic on the table rattling.

"Adele," he reached out to me but I recoiled like a snake.

"Don't you dare touch me... you piece of shit."

I could barely catch my breath. I snatched my purse, fury both at him and myself scorching my insides and stormed out of the restaurant.

My hand shot out to hail a taxi without even seeing one. My sight was too blurred by the tears.

"Adele," he soon caught up to me and I instantly turned. I continued to walk down the street and past its throng of people, unaware of where I was heading. I just didn't want to see him, or worse have him see my disconcerted state and the pain he was currently putting me through. I tried to reign in my emotions but I just couldn't because I pitied myself. I had lowered my standards in the first place for this trash and he had still for some reason found the audacity to dump me first.

"Adele!" he called out and suddenly appeared before me. "Please stop. Let's talk about this."

I was seething. "Andrew, get out of my way. I don't care about you or your explanation. I just want you out of my sight and out of my life."

He stopped then, which also forced me to stop so I wouldn't run into him.

"Wow," he said with a sadistic laugh. "This is it. This is our problem."

"What?"

"You," he said, and I was taken aback. "You are our problem."

I couldn't believe him. "What?"

"I'm not important to you am I? Whether I'm in your life or not makes absolutely no difference. You're hurt today, but after a good night's sleep you'll be fine won't you?"

The pain in my heart exploded. My purse swung into the air and slammed into his face.

"Fuck!" he roared at the blinding pain.

I watched him reel, his frame cowering at the hit and his plain, disgusting face contorted in pain. The realization this average trash was who I had given my time to and was even willing to spend the rest of my life with made me sick to my stomach.

"Fuck you," I swore with a conviction that made my entire body tremble. "What hurts is that I gave myself to you. That I gave you the fucking time of day. You need a break? I'm the problem? Jesus. Do you even know what you deserve? You fucking loser!"

"Do *you* know what you deserve?" he yelled back at me. "You were only somewhat excited during the first few months of us dating. Afterwards you just lost..." he struggled for the words. "Lost *it*! There was no passion, no... no affection. Dating a dead fish would have been more exciting. There's no freaking fire inside of you. You're just frozen. Fucking frozen. How the hell am I supposed to... spend my life with that?"

I was dumb founded. "What? I slept with you almost every night."

"And it was like you were doing me a favor. Every single time."

A bitter laugh rolled out of me. "Wow."

I inhaled deeply and then released it.

"Alright," I conceded. "Let's say I am the problem. I'm the problem because I somehow talked myself into giving you a chance when I knew right from the start you were not good enough for me."

"And there it is," he said.

"Yup," I agreed. "So thank you for waking me up. Have a great, mediocre life."

I started to walk away but he stopped me with a laugh. "What, you think you're going to find someone better? There's no one for you. And it's not because you're so great. It's because you're dead. You're dead inside Adele and you have nothing to give anyone. No love, no warmth... you're just...," his shoulders lifted. "Dead. So you have a great life too, alone."

He stormed off, and I couldn't move. It felt as though if I took another step forward I would crumble to the pavement.

So I just stood there. Until I could breathe again. Until I stopped trembling. And until I could think.

Then I turned around, straightened my shoulders, and walked.

CHRISTIAN

The constant ringing distracted me.

At first I didn't care to find out where it was coming from since it was accompanied by the humdrum of the bar, but it had now become such a distinct interruption to the ambience I couldn't ignore it anymore. I looked up and soon found the culprit. It was coming from the phone atop the bar's counter, and before the phone was a woman with a slouched back and a tumbler of liquor in her hand. She stared at the phone until it disconnected and then she looked away, uncaring. She then drained the tumbler faster than even I would have. Then she called for yet another refill.

The bartender came to pick up her emptied glass and then her phone began to ring again. "It's a bit grating isn't it," Matthew Steans, the Marketing VP said. He was a tall man with small eyes and a balding head.

"It is," I responded and he lifted a hand. The bar's manager soon came running and as Matthew addressed him I returned my gaze to the woman.

She seemed so dejected... and I was all too aware of the degree of misery that could put someone in such a state.

She seemed like she had been brought down to her knees and I wondered what the culprit was. Was it a lost job, a failed relationship... some sort of discovered illness?

I was quite occupied contemplating all this, so it took me a few seconds to realize she had inclined her head, seemingly now too heavy for her neck to keep upright on account of her stupor, and was staring directly at me.

Her gaze burned, and it made me unable to look away.

She eventually did, which slightly curved the corners of my lips.

But then her gaze returned back to mine.

Her eyes were narrowed and glazed, as though she wasn't even seeing me properly through the dimness of the bar and the considerable distance between us. She however continued the dance.

She would look at me, stare for a bit and then turn away until eventually I had to completely move my attention away from her.

"It'll be handled sir," I heard the manager assure Matthew, and turned to walk away.

"See something you like?" the second man in our company, Gared Jones, our account director asked, and gave me a slippery smile. I had only been acquainted with both men since that afternoon after my introduction at the company. Since I was also new to the vibrant city of Los Angeles, they had thereafter been tasked with introducing its equally exciting nightlife to me and showing me a good time.

My personality wasn't quite complementary to Gared's, as every word out of his mouth seemed to rub me the wrong way. It also didn't help that his hair was filled with so much gel it was distracting, and his features of hollow eyes, a strong nose and thin lips were as sharp as knives.

"Nope," I replied. "I don't."

"But she does," he chuckled, his tumbler of whiskey to his lips. I couldn't help glancing her way again to see she indeed had her gaze on mine. And this time around, she didn't look away.

She rose to her feet.

It was more like a wobble, and would have been amusing if for some reason my breath hadn't caught in my throat. I was absolutely sure she was heading for me and I had absolutely no idea why.

Her gaze was fixed to mine like a predator to its prey or perhaps I was the predator and she was the prey. I couldn't tell.

She staggered, barely managing to hold herself steady until she reached the lounge area where we were seated. The other men had gone quiet from their chatter and amusement, but I wouldn't have been able to hear them either way.

My attention was completely fixed on her.

I had already noted from afar she was incredibly attractive. I was however reluctant to stretch my assessment out to her as beautiful given her current discombobulated state, but there was no denying there was something electric about her that charged me.

Was it the dress she had on? I wondered. It hung from her neck with altered straps before wrapping around her chest, and the color was a velvety olive green. The deep warmth of the material complemented the sheen of her skin, and clung to the dips and curves of her body like a glove.

The fabric stopped just above her knee. What was visible below her skirt was toned, alabaster limbs that made me ache to touch her. She had on blood red sandals that were strapped around her calves, and they were a perfect match to the lipstick on her heart shaped lips.

She stopped with a jolt, and although barely able to remain still, lifted her arm and pointed a limp finger at me.

"You're an asshole aren't you?"

The men around me began to laugh, but at the seriousness of my gaze they immediately abandoned the response.

All my attention was on her as I responded. "What makes you think that?"

She released a deep breath, her gaze fluttering as she struggled for composure.

"You're the most handsome guy in here... so, s-so of course you're ah... a dick."

"I'll call the manager to take care of her Mr. Hall," Matthew said, but I held a hand up to stop him. I wanted to hear everything she had to say.

"You think I'm handsome?"

"Of course," she said and ran her unstable gaze around the dimly lit bar. "I've been watching y-" she wobbled and almost fell onto me. My hand shot out to catch her but she quickly stabled herself and pushed her hair out of her eyes.

"You," she said. "Do you ever lower your standards?"

I was getting much more excited than I could remember being in a long time, on account of the somewhat scintillating conversation with this drunk woman.

"Never," I replied, and a hard emotion shone in her eyes. It appeared to be fury.

"Not ever?" she asked.

She shook her head in abject self-pity. "Well, fuck me," she laughed and the sound was so sad it squeezed my heart. "I lowered my standards for..." she slurred but managed to compose herself. "For a piece of shit and got dumped. Never again."

Ah... so this was the reason for her current state. I'd been there, done that, and learned my lesson but I couldn't very well share my empathy with her given the audience around.

She staggered towards me and my gaze couldn't help but go to her constantly twisting ankles. I had no doubt before tonight ended, they were going to be severely sprained. She placed a hand on the edge of the sofa and leaned forward till she was just a little distance away. By this time the entire bar had seemed to disappear. I was lost in the deep green of her beautiful eyes, so when the manager suddenly appeared out of nowhere and gripped her arm I almost roared. "Leave her alone!"

He wasn't sure he had heard me right, until he saw the clouds that had gathered in my eyes. He quickly let go and stepped away.

She smiled at me. "Sleep with me," she breathed. "For one night. For tonight. I'm beautiful aren't I? I deserve the damn best."

She suddenly straightened and flipped her hair off one shoulder. "I do." she took a deep breath and huffed. "I'm done... so done... with dogs. I'm done... w-with lowering my..."

Then she fell. Arms flailing and frame twisting, she headed for the floor but I grabbed her before she could hurt herself. She went limp.

"Wow!" I heard one of the other men comment as the other chuckled. "Hey, are you the manager? Is this the kind of behavior you permit in your bar? Doesn't this count as harassment?"

Panicked, the suited man stepped forward to take her off my hands, but my gaze stopped him from advancing. I rose to my feet till she was somewhat stable but I could tell now she was barely grasping onto the strands of consciousness.

"Christian, hand her over to him before she throws up on you," Matthew said. "He'll handle things from here."

I watched her closed eyelids and her restless breathing, the smell of her intoxication swirling with the fruity scent of her skin.

I wanted to look into her eyes one last time, but I knew I had reached the appropriate boundary with her given she was a complete stranger. So I reluctantly gave her to the manager, straightened my suit, and sat back down.

"Be gentle with her," I warned, my voice unconsciously harsh, when his hostile grasp of her arms made her wince.

"Of course, Sir," he replied with a smile that was far from genuine.

My eyes followed him as he took her away, and gave quick instructions in Russian to a staff member at the bar to bring her belongings. He settled her on one of the lounge seats by a corner, and left her to continue on with her slumber.

I dragged my gaze away from her, and continued on with my meeting.

CHRISTIAN

W hen it was time to leave, I lifted my gaze and saw she was still abandoned and asleep on the sofa in the corner.

The other men left before I did, but at my still persisting interest in her wellbeing, had not failed to offer their word of admonition. "Be careful with her Hall. She could be trouble."

I was very aware of this, but at the sight of half of her beautiful body dangling off the sofa, of her legs slightly parted and her long hair trailing the floor, I couldn't help but inquire about the manager's plan to help her.

He hurried up to me and promptly responded to my questions.

"We can't get any access whatsoever to her phone, and no calls have come in thus far. We'll just have to wait till one does or she sobers up, and then we can send her on her way."

I sighed, and gave him a nod.

Then I turned away and exited the bar. My driver Gary was waiting for me at the entrance, so I immediately got into the SUV, but I couldn't bear for him to pull away.

"Gary," I called, and the uniformed driver glanced at me through the rearview mirror. "Go in and ask for the manager. There is a drunk girl deposited in the corner. Tell him to hand over her belongings and bring her along with you. I'll get her back to her place safely."

He seemed a bit perplexed at the information but nevertheless, got down to do as I had asked.

What I want to do with her, I had absolutely no idea but leaving her in such a public way was no doubt sure to leave what was left to the rest of her dignity to shreds when she fully recovered. Eight years ago I was in the exact same predicament. A failed relationship, a failed business and my soul gutted. A word of encouragement to me even then would have meant the world not to speak of some sort of support and so I wanted to be one or the other for her.

Plus the very thought of driving away and not allowing her to remain in my world for just a while longer, made my stomach churn with despondency.

Soon, Gary and the manager arrived with the sleeping girl and she was placed beside me in the back of the SUV.

The manager came to my side to address me.

"What are your intentions with her sir? I still believe she would be better off here."

"I'll handle it," I replied. "But rest assured you won't have any problems."

Before he could continue his complaint I rolled up the glass and we were on our way.

"Where to sir," Gary asked as we pulled into the Main Street, I thought on this question for a little while. Heading into a hotel with a drunk and unconscious girl wasn't going to keep any suspicions at perhaps what I intended to do with her at bay, so at the end of the day my best bet was the one and only place I could comfortably take her to - my home.

ADELE

The first thing that assaulted me was a splitting headache.

My eyes barely come open before I shut them back with a wince. As I waited for the pain to subside, fragments of the last time I had been conscious began to come to mind.

At the very vivid memory of the brown eyed stranger... my proposition to him... and then my *glorious* fall... I shot up.

It was a dream. Right? It had to be. Right?

I looked around me and realized I was on a bed, and not in the middle of a street somewhere. I felt relief, but then came the billion dollar question of how I had gotten here, and whose bed was I on?

I stared at the luxurious cotton sheets and then panned my gaze around the room. It looked like a hotel, with its opulent furnishings and meticulous neutral color scheme, but somehow it didn't feel like one.

With my heart in my throat, I scrambled out of the bed and had to stop for a moment at the headache that still hadn't subsided. I held my head in consolation, and it was then I saw the note and pills by the bedside table.

"Here's some pain relievers," it read. *"Afterwards feel free to come downstairs for something to eat."*

The script was elegant and careful, and it brought to mind the stranger I had approached and subsequently fallen onto.

Perhaps… this was his house?

The pace of my heart picked up as I gazed down to assess my body. It hadn't even occurred to me that I could have been assaulted. However, just as earlier noted, there was nothing about me that was out of place. Except the ghastly hangover of course.

I groaned into my hands and felt such immense disappointment in my entire existence.

I then looked around the lavish room once again and after studying the pain reliever, washed it down with the accompanying bottle of water.

My phone was also on the nightstand, as well as my pearled clutch so I immediately grabbed them both, and hurried out of the room. My exit led me into a dimly lit corridor that looked and had the mystique and grandeur of an actual gallery. Oriental and abstract paintings lined the walls, and it was quite the shame I couldn't stop to admire any of it. I soon arrived at the top of the stairs, and there, I stopped.

The apartment was designed in the structure of a loft, so from where I stood, I could appreciate the expansive living room area below and the gigantic windows that spanned the full height of both floors.

This made me realize whoever owned the house would be able to clearly see me or at least sense my movement as I descended since there were basically no walls.

So I composed myself and began to descend, grateful I had been saved by someone who seemed to have their life together.

It was quite obvious now they had pitied my messy state and had been kind enough to take my drunken butt home so I could sleep off my stupor and recover. My depression intensified at the reminder once again I had allowed myself to get so wasted, without a single thought for who was going to take care of me when the intoxication took over.

As I neared the base, a delicious scent wafted over, and as much as it tempted me to linger, my true wish was to escape without having to face whoever had rescued me, especially if it was *him*. I didn't think that what was left of my already shredded self-esteem could take such a battering.

So I began to tip toe away, and soon successfully arrived in the magnificent foyer, undetected. It was as I reached the door however, I realized my shoes were nowhere to be found.

With a sunken heart, I stopped and straightened.

Was I once again about to be humiliated?

All I was asking was to be gifted the mercy of a non-confrontation, and yet I was going to be denied even this favor. I had to be one of the unluckiest people alive. I glanced at the massive door and considered just leaving anyway, but I didn't know what further audience awaited me beyond the doors. And the thought of how much hurt my feet would incur from hopping around the world bare footed wasn't exactly delighting.

So I turned around, and followed the waft of the meal as it led me towards the kitchen.

I indeed met a man seated at the island.

His back was to me as he perched on the stool, his attention on the document he was flipping through.

The kitchen was just as luxurious as the rest of the house, with its fascinating aluminum cabinets, glass countertops and wooden accents.

And so was the man.

He had on a pair of charcoal slacks, and a white, collared shirt stretched across his broad shoulders. He seemed quite tall from what I could see, and his hair was an alluring mass of dark, soft waves. I felt a bit of fear at finally seeing him, now entertaining the possibility that perhaps he would demand some sort of payment for helping me out, or worse even take advantage of me. Perhaps I had only been left alone thus far *because* I was drunk.

I decided then whatever pain awaited my feet without my shoes beyond his doors, was the lesser evil so I turned around before he could notice me and began to tip toe away.

His voice, though quiet, was strong as it boomed across the space. "I made you chicken soup," he said. "Have some before you leave."

I froze on the spot, with eyes so startled they were nearly popping out of my sockets. I turned around then, sheepish and embarrassed.

The first words out of my mouth sounded strangled, so I cleared my throat and tried again. "Thank you... for um... last night. I'll leave now."

He turned around then to face me.

"Do you remember everything that happened?"

I was about to respond when my eyes settled on his face.

Whatever I had intended to say immediately disappeared from my brain, as I was gifted with the sight of possibly the most attractive man I had ever seen.

I stared dumbfounded at him, and only when he cocked his head at the blankness in my gaze and my silence, did I recover. With a shake of my head, I straightened and waited for my wits to return to me but it was as though my entire being had shut down.

I eventually managed to work up a dumb smile.

His eyes narrowed at me and then he rose to his feet. "I'll get you some soup. Take a seat."

He headed over to the stove and at the seemingly harmless invitation, I didn't want to insult him further by refusing.

"I uh... I'm sorry about last night," I said as I took my seat about two stools away from the one he had been seated on. "I think I lost my mind."

My laugh was awkward and my eyes shifty, and in the presence of probably the most beautiful man I would ever lay eyes on, it was quite heartbreaking to see I was a hot mess. My head lowered in abject dejection.

"Here," he said and I raised my gaze.

He was heading over and it took everything inside of me not to jump off the stool to scurry away.

He placed the steaming white bowl in front of me, filled with an appetizing looking broth, chunks of chicken and an assortment of finely chopped vegetables. I supposed I stared down at it for too long because he eventually had to tap his hand on the surface of the glass counter to get my attention.

"I'm sorry," I apologized again, "C-can I... do you have a spare toothbrush or something? I don't think I can eat this otherwise."

"I do," he said. "Just go past the dining room, after the foyer. Then head down the hallway you'll see. The last room on the right will be the restroom."

"Thank you," I responded and almost sprinted from the room.

CHRISTIAN

I watched her go, almost stumbling over her feet and couldn't help my amusement. I imagined she was quite confused at waking up in a stranger's house and no doubt felt immense shame. Then there was the agony from her hangover, which I didn't think was mild.

I'd been alerted the moment she had descended the stairs, and then attempted to depart unnoticed. And I was also aware she had returned solely because of her shoes which were in my custody.

I had intentionally kept them with me, somehow predicting this would be her behavior and I was glad for the foresight. I was going to return them, but at least wanted the opportunity to have a conversation with her before she disappeared.

It was the least she could do after the care I had thus far expended towards her. I resumed reading my document, and soon enough heard her return. I didn't need to turn backwards to realize she was watching me so I just waited for her to speak.

"Did you incur any heavy expenses yesterday on my behalf?" she asked. "Or any expenses at all? I'm more than willing to reimburse you for it."

I turned to her, and saw some color had returned to her cheeks. Her temple was now damp with some strands of her dark blonde hair sticking to the edges and the side of her neck, so I imagined she had also taken the liberty to wash her face. Her dark eye makeup was slightly smudged, and the previous patches of red lipstick on her face were now completely wiped off.

"The only expense so far is the room, and of course this soup."

"I'll pay for it all," she said.

"Relax," I told her. "I'm not going to charge you. It's been a while since I cooked but I came in here and whipped this up for you. So at least eat some of it before you leave."

"Thank you," she mumbled under her breath and returned to the stool.

We both remained quiet, the only sounds around us the ones we both couldn't help - her soft eating sounds and the clinks of her cutlery against the ceramic bowl, the shuffling of the papers I was perusing, and the click of my pen as I picked it up to scribble notes across the pages.

"I'm done," she got off the stool. "It was great. Thank you." I looked to see her empty bowl and was certain she had forced herself to eat it all.

I allowed her to head over to the sink, mesmerized at the soft sway of her hips as she walked. She washed the bowl and then set it on the rack to dry off.

She paused for a moment, and then turned around to face me. She however didn't quite meet my gaze, but instead fixed it on something past my shoulder.

"You have my shoes?" she asked, and I nodded.

"I'll go get them for you."

A few minutes later, I returned with the red, heeled sandals and met her waiting by the island. Her purse was slung over her shoulder and her hands linked together in front of her, nearly wringing the pale skin off. I walked up to her and for the first time, we fully stood in each other's presence.

I studied her carefully, pleased about the opportunity which had been significantly harder due to the dimness of the previous night.

She was several inches shorter than I was, barely reaching my shoulder, and the olive green color of her dress was even more striking against her alabaster skin in broad daylight. She was also just as beautiful as I had judged, with full cheeks, a smattering of light freckles across her narrow nose, and soft, wispy curls at the nape of her neck.

I held the shoes up and she accepted them from the opposite end, unwilling to allow the slightest bit of contact between us. I decided then there would be no beating around the bush. I knew exactly what I wanted from her and had absolutely no qualms whatsoever about asking for it.

"Are you disappointed?" I asked.

Her gaze found a reason to meet mine. "About what?"

"Yesterday... you said I was incredibly handsome. In short, you said I was the most handsome man in the entire bar, and then you started taking your clothes off. Something about never lowering your standards again. And pleaded with me to fuck you."

Her expression contorted into one of pain. "Why are you reminding me of that?" she groaned into the hand that was now covering her face. "I was hoping you'd let it slide so I could save face."

"Well, I would have but I honestly want to know if the offer you made to sleep with me still stands?"

She seemed stumped for a moment, but then her shoulders relaxed as she studied me. "Is that what you want?" she asked and I couldn't help my grin at the resignation in her tone.

"It is, but if the offer is no longer available then a kiss will do."

Her gaze on me remained steady, her eyes searching mine, but for what exactly, I was uncertain. I had no complaints though about watching her so I waited patiently for her response, although a bit more nervous than I would have liked.

I saw the moment something clicked in her gaze, and then she let go of everything she had been holding.

Her purse fell to the ground with a clack, and so did the shoes I had just returned.

"Sure," she said, determination in her tone as she stepped towards me, and it made me wonder as to exactly what extent of my request her agreement was for.

My hands were in my pockets, and I kept them there as she wrapped her hands around my biceps for some balance, and lifted herself on the tips of her toes. She placed a soft, almost innocent kiss on my lips, and the effect on my libido was immediate.

The zap of current to my groin made my breath catch, and it was only when she slanted her head to part my lips for deeper access did it release with a shudder.

My eyes slid closed, and her tongue slinked into my mouth.

In the minutes that followed, I completely lost myself, in the svelte of her tongue as it danced with mine, and in the heat that flooded my stomach at her clean and thrilling taste.

It was only when she broke the kiss I was able to fully process all that had just happened. My eyes remained shut as I reveled in the steady buzz of my blood, its heady response to her hold on my arms, and her voluptuous body still pressed against mine.

"Thank you for last night," her soft voice finally broke through my mental haze, and my eyes flipped open.

"I want to fuck you," I said. "What will it take?"

The emotion that flashed across her face then startled me. It was stark and abashed, and I instantly knew I had offended her. I waited however to hear what she would say.

"I'm not a prostitute," she said, and lowered her body to grab her things.

"I never assumed you were," I said. "I just want to know what it will take to have you. A few dates? Some acceptable time in courtship? I want you."

She paused, and held my gaze. "So you simply want to have sex with me?"

"Yes."

For a moment she seemed speechless. "I'm... I know I offered myself to you yesterday but I was in a very bad place emotionally. It's no longer the case this morning so I'm less inclined to be as crazy. I'm really sorry if my behavior fed these expectations."

"It wasn't just your behavior," I replied. "You're attractive, immensely so and although that's not why I helped you out, I realize now it wasn't a bad idea either."

"So why did you help me out?" she asked.

I shifted my weight from one leg to the other. "You might not remember this, but you mentioned something that alluded to the reason behind your state last night. Something about a break up?"

She lowered her head as a dull pink flush suddenly appeared across her cheeks.

"I've been there too." I said softly.

She stared at me curiously.

"Dumped by a girlfriend for not being 'good enough.' It can eat away at your self-esteem. Still I only partially blame her though. At the time things were quite difficult. I was struggling with a failed business venture and drowning in debt. So I'm no stranger to drinking myself into a stupor in order to numb the pain."

She watched me for what seemed like forever, and then she undid the knot of her dress from behind her neck.

The ties of fabric fell down her chest, her gaze was sharp and clear. They were also ablaze with the exact intensity of passion that was currently ripping through my body. It had been so long since I had felt this turned on by just the mere presence of a woman. She turned around, took a few steps backwards, and pressed her body into mine.

"I'll take one for the road," she said, and my cock swelled in size.

"I'll make it a good one." I promised, and gripped the curves of her hips.

My hand sunk into her soft flesh through the material, and then slid up to trace the outline of her beautiful body. I buried my face in her neck as my hands arrived at her breasts and cupped the full, luscious mounds. A small gasp escaped her lips, and when my lips parted to press a sensual kiss against her warm skin, she ground her ass against my groin.

She felt so right against me, and soon, I could no longer delay my contact with her skin. I pulled the zipper of her dress down her back, and peeled the material away till it pooled at her feet. She stepped out of it, and then turned around to face me with a lacy dark bra on, and a matching thong. I brushed her hair away from her eyes, and then she slanted her head to once again crush her lips to mine.

I burned with yearning for her, her kisses more than enough to make my head spin. I sucked softly on her lips, traced a caress along her jawline, and then returned to get yet another full dose of her taste. I was insatiable and lost myself, until her soft groan returned some element of my awareness to me.

I pulled away, and stared into her eyes with wonder. I couldn't remember the last time a kiss had made me feel this way, completely overwhelmed and quite literally shaken. My heart was thundering in my chest, my breathing ragged and my core painfully tense with the anguish of arousal.

Her hands went to my shirt, and I watched, mesmerized, as she began to undo the buttons. I just wanted to watch her... to take my time in enjoying every single moment of this experience. I'd imagined we would go fast and hard, with nothing in mind but the thoughtless, frantic race to a momentary release but this... this was not that. And with her, it was just the way I wanted it.

She slid my shirt off my shoulders, delicately, as though she was unwrapping a gift, however it didn't entirely seem as though she was receiving one. Because although she was aroused, there was still a glint of sorrow in her eyes she perhaps wasn't even aware of.

I tore the material off my body, lifted her off the ground and deposited her on the island.

I was determined to make her completely forget even though it was momentary... to only have me in mind, and not her troubles or sorrow.

My kiss became hard and fast and with a whimper, she settled into the frantic frequency.

Then I broke away and began to move down her torso, loving the way she writhed as my lips marked her flesh.

When I grabbed the string of lace at her hips her hand shot out in a reflexive alarm and locked around my wrist.

I immediately understood.

She was still so raw and vulnerable, and would no doubt need a bit more time to completely let herself relax with me.

Realizing she was stopping me, she started to move her hand away but I straightened and returned to kissing her, abandoning that path for the time being. I bit softly on her plush lower lips, brushed the tip of my tongue across the pulse in her neck and planted kisses across her collar bone.

Her breathing was in short gasps, and the heat radiated off her and into me like the low but definite impact of a campfire. In no time, her bra was unhooked behind her and her beautiful breasts were set free.

Her head fell backwards as I massaged the beautiful mounds. A hard suck on one nipple and then a little tug on the other, and she was writhing again.

My heart was racing out of control, and soon it became altogether difficult to contain the torrent of delicious ecstasy that was ripping through me. I needed her in my mouth, so with my hands moving to her thighs, I jerked her legs apart and gave the hoarse command. "Move backwards."

For a split second she hesitated, but then at the hungry look in my eyes, she moved a few inches backwards and hooked one leg over my shoulder. I guided the other leg to take the same pose, and after making sure she was appropriately balanced, buried my face between her legs.

The sheer scrap of lace restricted my complete access which was quite an aggravating barrier but I welcomed the prelude, the tease was to the both of us.

Her broken breathing thrilled me, as well as the restless and unconscious dig of her hands and nails into my arms as I devoured her through the lace.

"Fuck," she cursed as she rocked her hips into my mouth, till I could no longer stand the barrier. Mindless with desire, I ripped the material away and returned my gaze to her sex. It was soaking wet and flushed and it made my senses rage with hunger.

I locked my grip around her thighs, and without any preamble, gave her a hard lick, from the pulsing base of her opening to the engorged bud higher above.

It sent a violent shudder through her, or perhaps that was my own body's response. I could no longer tell.

She tasted heavenly, and it made my limbs go weak. The air was heavy with the unbridled sounds of our harsh breathing and soft moans as I speared my tongue into her opening, and the delicious heat welcomed me. She cried out as her back arched, and nearly tugged the hair off my scalp.

Her wild reactions spurred me on, so my mouth moved to her clit while I coaxed a finger into her. Another finger soon joined the assault, so with a swing of my arm around her waist and my body slightly positioned to the side, I drove my finger in and out of her until her hips bucked.

"Fuck!" she cried out, her body overwhelmed by the pleasure and almost desperate to get away.

My arm kept her in place as I oscillated between frantic pumps that had strangled moans erupting from her lips, and hard, deep sucks to her clit.

When she came, it was with a scream that had her tumbling out of my hold. I let go, mindful of hurting her due to just how restless she was.

She couldn't remain still.

Her hand slammed over her sex to ease the delicious ache as she flattened across the counter, writhing and bucking as she tried to ride the wave of the orgasm. I was mesmerized as I watched her return to some semblance of calm. I wondered if I had the patience to carry her all the way up the stairs to my bedroom. All I wanted was to bury myself in her warmth right there and then, and the mere minute or so it would take for us to change our venue seemed like too much to ask.

However, at the realization she was still sore, I realized the momentary pause would indeed pay off. So I hooked one arm underneath her thighs, and the other around her back to lift her off the counter.

She buried her face in my neck until I got to the door of my bedroom.

"Turn the handle," I said softly and she did as I said, her gaze still somewhat hazy and her movements unsteady. Soon, I laid her across my bed and watched as she curled her naked frame into a ball.

Her golden hair cascaded all around her, and her flawless skin was comparable to glistening ceramic upon my plain navy sheets.

"You doing okay?" I asked, as my hand began to unfasten my belt. She nodded without looking at me, and I proceeded with taking off the rest of my clothes.

When I was ready, I got on the bed and crawled over her, wondering how I was going to get her to uncurl herself. But the moment she sensed me, she immediately straightened. She flattened herself against the bed and gazed up at me.

Something exciting shone in her eyes as it perused mine, and I wondered what she saw. Then her hand lifted to the side of my face, and the delicacy of her touch made me melt. Shutting my eyes, I leaned into the caress as my heart thundered in my chest.

"You're beautiful," she said, and I couldn't help but laugh. Many flattering words had indeed been attributed to me in the past, but I didn't think beautiful was among them.

"And so are you," I replied, and leaned down to kiss her.

I started slowly, taking her upper lip in mine and then following with an intense suck on the bottom lip. She moaned at the smacking sound that followed, and then wrapped her arms around me to hold my body even closer to hers.

She slid her tongue into my mouth, and my brain once again stuttered to a halt.

Kissing her wrought an ethereal melody inside of me that I wanted to go on forever.

Adele

Her name echoed like a prayer through my head. It was all I knew of her so far, but at the intimacy and depth of this kiss, it felt like I had known her forever.

Her hips stirred against mine and I knew what she was in search of, so I guided my rock hard cock to slink between her damp folds.

She released a shameless moan into my mouth as she began to writhe her hips, and the carnal massage sucked all the strength out of my body.

I collapsed onto her, and she laughed out in mockery. I was painfully aroused, and urgently needed to find my release within her but at the same time, the thought struck me. I also would have been perfectly happy to just remain like this with her.

The thought woke me up.

This was just sex, with perhaps the most gorgeous stranger I had ever laid my eyes on, and I was going to enjoy every bit of it. So I returned the strength to my arms, and lifted myself to a sitting position.

With my hands around her ass, I hoisted her hips forward till it was perfectly aligned with mine. Then I grabbed the length of my cock, and stroked her flushed, pink flesh with the thick head.

She sunk her head into the mattress at the sensation, while my heart leapt into my throat at the anticipation.

I slid into her, carefully, and that first, greedy grip, shook me to my core.

Her walls deliciously sucked me in, while her hands fisted in her hair.

"You alright?" I rasped out, my voice barely recognizable to me.

"I'm fine," she breathed.

Her hands curved around my ass and it greatly amused me. I didn't need any further coaxing to proceed but at the same time, I didn't just want to plunge into her. So I took my time in sinking deeper, my eyes shut as I relished the hypnotic pleasure of the total welcome of her sex.

A tortured groan eased out from the back of my throat at the clench of her walls around me, and for a few seconds I didn't move, content to commit every tingle of this feeling to memory.

Until her restless fingers began to snake their way into my hair.

Amused yet again, I adjusted my position till I was comfortably settled inside her. Then I pulled out till the head of my cock reached her entrance. It occurred to me then I hadn't even bothered with protection, and for a brief moment this caused me concern. But it was already too late. And moreover, this was a new house and a new life in a new town and I hadn't exactly included a box of condoms in my list of essential requests to the interior designer.

I'll pull out, I swore to myself, and returned my attention to fucking her.

I slid back into her, this time with a little more urgency but I knew it wasn't quite the hard slam that she wanted.

I took my time, and repeated the motion and then I began to feel her relax.

My next move had my hands around her waist to hold her in place, and she perhaps saw it coming, but when my cock thrust into her, with the force and intensity that she craved, her back nearly flew off the bed.

"Holy fuck," she gasped and I understood I had hit a particularly delicious spot inside of her.

Her hands gripped my biceps as her eyes shot open, wild with hunger "Do that again," she gasped. "Please."

I repeated the thrust as requested, and a long, shuddering moan sang from her lips. Her eyes rolled into the back of her head as I continued with my now hurried drives, and she thanked me for it with a heart melting kiss.

Despite the initially cooled state of the room, our exertions had charged the air around us with enough heat to eject sweat all across our bodies. We were sticky and flushed, our most intimate parts deliciously joined as one as I fucked us both of our minds.

I inclined her body to just the right angle, and from then onwards it was a rapid and almost crazed race to both of our releases. It occurred to me to pull out when we reached the edge, so as not to take any dumb risks and to safely release outside of her body, but she wouldn't let me go. Her arms and legs were curled around with a desperation I understood, and I knew it was already too late to hang onto reason.

I crumbled as I finally earned my release, shooting a powerful stream of my seed into her.

She came as well, her strained cries and thrashing resounding across the room. I collapsed and buried my face in her neck to muffle my own struggle for breath.

I continued to drive into her, fucking her through the orgasm in order to prolong it as long as possible until neither of us could take anymore.

I was no longer cognizant of where I was, the only thing I could hear and feel, her scent and warmth, and labored efforts to return her breathing to normal.

All I wanted was to rest, and to bask in her presence, so I pulled her with me till both our heads were settled against my pillow. Then I shut my eyes.

At some point however, I felt her begin to struggle out of my hold and although it registered it was probably appropriate to let her go, I crushed her to my body, the curve of hers settling perfectly into mine, and all I remembered thinking was just how absolutely perfect it felt to have her there.

ADELE

Monday morning found me clocking into work as usual.

However nothing was the same. My life had taken a much more different turn from what I had expected from the weekend, and the abruptness of it all was still quite difficult to process.

My heart ached, and although it was not the state I'd expected to still be in given the consolation I had received from my rendezvous on Saturday morning, I had still awoken this morning with the disconcerting feeling of my feet being off the ground.

I leaned against the steeled wall of the elevator as I rode up to my floor, and once again felt the urge to cry bubble up within me.

It irritated me as I was hoping this time around, the mourning period would be skipped but alas, my body demanded to take the time it wanted to process the loss of the man that just last week I had convinced myself I would be alright with committing my life to. It would forever baffle me though, how someone could mean so much to you in one moment and in the next, you wanted them to not even exist.

I soon arrived at my cubicle and after the basic greetings to the colleagues around me, I began to settle in for the day. Until what, or rather *who,* I had truly been dreading all weekend suddenly appeared.

"Adele!"

Her call was sharp and sudden, and it made my heart jump. I had just lowered my head under the table to retrieve my smoothie from my purse so in my haste to rise, my head slightly banged against the wooden surface.

I soon appeared with a frown on my face to meet the apologetic look on hers, and placed the bottle on my desk.

"Why haven't you answered any of your calls?" she complained. "I've been waiting to hear the good news. Where's your ring?"

I released a deep breath and rose to my feet.

"Keep your voice down," I said, and brought the smoothie along with me as I walked.

When I arrived at the kitchen however, I pushed it aside for some coffee and focused my attention on the mug of steaming Americano as she processed my narration of the weekend.

"What does he mean by you didn't show enough passion?"

I opened my hand to express my equal cluelessness, and kept my focus on my beverage. I truly didn't want to dwell on this any longer and she soon decided to respect my nonchalance.

She came forward and pulled me into a hug which I reluctantly accepted.

"I want to curse him out with you, but I know it's still all too fresh so I'll wait till you're ready. Knowing you though, that should be in about four days."

I was silent and contemplative about this, and without even realizing it the truth came out. "It might take longer. I cared about him."

She nodded in understanding, and gave me a sad smile which although I didn't really want, I still appreciated. And then her gloominess disappeared.

Her face lit up in excitement as she moved on to the next topic of discussion. "The new CEO started today and those that have gotten a glimpse of him have been spreading the word."

"What word?" I asked as I finished with my coffee, and started on my peanut butter and strawberry banana smoothie.

"About how fucking attractive he is. And young. We were expecting a geezer like McClaren but they went out of their way for this new choice."

I couldn't care less about how our CEO looked but her mention of it did take my mind to the stranger that had nearly blown my back out on Saturday. Now, he was who I was hoping I'd somehow run into again although it was highly unlikely. Without my little rendezvous with him, I would probably have been so much more depressed than I currently was so from time to time, the ethereal time I'd had with him slamming his cock into me came to mind.

That had been the most mind blowing sex I'd had in forever and it made me wonder why I had been so fixated on disappearing before he could wake up to still find me in his home.

Perhaps it was because I didn't want to be rejected again by yet another man because to have been thrown out of his house for overstaying my welcome would have been beyond devastating.

"What are you smiling about?" Melinda's inquiry came, and my attention returned back to the office kitchen we were currently whiling away our morning in.

I wanted to tell her about the stranger but it was still all too soon for me. "Nothing," I said and her face fell. I quickly diverted the conversation to the highlights and layers she had gotten in her thick, shoulder length, auburn hair.

"I was expecting you to get a blunt cut," I said and she sighed.

"I know. I was going to but then James talked me out of it and put in highlights instead. I'll probably get tired of this too and just chop the length off myself."

I smiled. "I don't understand why you can't stand your hair ever growing past your shoulders."

"It's too much of a hassle," she replied. "Maybe next time I'll..."

Her words trailed off as a quite notorious colleague came into the space. She was also in the active pool of secretaries as we were, but associated more with other employees of higher rankings than she did with us. Therefore, she didn't see the need to pay us any attention. She was also adorned with the prestige for being the niece to the head of Human Resources, so she truly was too high up in the sky for the rest of us to associate with. Or at least that was what she acted like.

I couldn't have cared less, but Melinda took her highbrow attitude personally, every single time. Although she never outrightly provoked her for the sake of her job, she didn't fail to mock her in her absence.

"Miss-you-know-who has her cloak on today. You know what that means."

I almost snorted out the smoothie through my nostrils. "What?"

"Didn't you notice her outfit?" Melinda sniped as she retrieved a bran bar from the cupboard. "She's ready to claim her rightful place."

I chuckled. She had indeed been wearing a gorgeous, electric blue cloak blazer but coupled with the nickname Melinda had given her, I couldn't help but picture Voldemort.

"Let's get back to work," I said as I drained my cup and headed over to the sink to wash it.

"No!" Melinda protested. "We need to make some sort of stance or something."

"About what?" I asked, wondering why she was so agitated.

"About the new CEO's secretary position. You know Nancy is going to give it to her because they're related."

"So?"

She stared at me, perplexed. "How can you be so nonchalant about everything?"

Alarm bells went off in my head as her comment came

dangerously close to the complaint that Andrew had voiced about me. However I refused to cower.

"And how can you be so worked up about everything? She obviously has an advantage that neither of us or the other secretaries have so why bother making a fuss over it?"

"You don't want to get ahead here? You want to remain in the secretaries' pool forever?"

"So what do you want us to do, start a riot?"

"Well yes! But not now though," she said. "The moment she is selected as the CEO's secretary, I'm going to post a complaint on the company's forum."

I blinked. I had been half-heartedly taunting her but I could now see she was obviously serious about this.

"I'm going to work," I told her. "And you should too. The CEO's not the only executive in this company so if you don't become his secretary then there are others you can be assigned to. You're only angry about this because you heard he's attractive, otherwise you wouldn't have cared less."

"Well, you-know-who's also vying for the position for that same reason too so why can't we?"

"I'm sick of men right now so I don't want to talk about this."

"Fine," she groaned, and we both returned to our cubicles. I was empathetic that the unfairness we weren't all given equal chances to qualify for the position was more than enough to upset her, and I also probably would have been just as irritated but I had enough to be sad about and didn't want to pile up yet another reason to pity myself.

CHRISTIAN

On my first day, I quickly came to realize the golden rule needed to be established for the agency - the thirty minute meeting limit.

Since my day had begun, I had been sucked in from one briefing to the next across the departments, only for the same information I had read in various documents over the weekend to be reiterated to me. None of the meetings needed to have been scheduled, so by the end of my third one for the day which was right before lunch, I wasn't in the best of moods.

Afterwards, there was the courtesy salutations with the heads of the departments, so I was held for an extra twenty minutes past the already exhausted hour and a half.

I was listening to the Account Director as he shared the updates from the agency's latest project with an eyewear company when she passed by the glass walled conference room.

My heart gave an immediate jolt the moment her side view registered, but then before I could turn my complete attention to the passing figure, she was already walking out of sight.

I stared, wide-eyed and struck until she disappeared around the corner, her blonde hair swishing against her back.

Perhaps I was mistaken, but the curve of that body had been much too familiar to ignore.

Or was I just losing my mind?

It had been two days since I had last seen her, and yet for some reason, I still hadn't been able to get her out of my mind. I had woken up with an almost panic that she wouldn't be there, and true enough that had been the case. I recalled vaguely pulling her back to me in the midst of our sleepy haze, and after the most intense fucking session I'd had in years.

She had been voracious and vehement, and I couldn't believe the moron that had broken up with her had labeled her as dispassionate. He was the one that didn't know what he was doing... that didn't know how to draw out the fire from a woman like her.

I'd wallowed in her scent after her departure, and at varying times since then flashbacks of me ramming into her would suddenly hit me. Each time it caused an intense bout of ecstasy to rip through my body, and it always left me breathless.

I knew nothing about her beyond her name which I had gotten from her bank card, and had intended to keep it that way but now I was wondering if perhaps, I hadn't made the wrong decision.

"Mr. Hall? Mr. Hall?"

My attention was dragged back to the shorter man before me, and I smiled politely. "My apologies. Please continue."

She was gone, forever, unless I returned back to that bar and told the manager to keep an eye out for her in case she ever returned.

But then again, wouldn't that be mitigating the whole point of a one night stand? Did I want a relationship with her or did I just want to fuck her again? I decided then any intentional contact was just me courting trouble. After the week had gone by I was certain she would become nothing more than a distant memory.

Afterwards, I returned to my office and quickly settled in. I had a stack of approvals and transfers to get through and thought of getting lunch beforehand. A secretary would be great for assistance on this but one had not yet been assigned to me. I picked up the phone to contact the HR director, Nancy Reyes, but just then there was a knock on my door.

"Come in," I answered, and a plump woman with a blunt bangs haircut and a tight smile walked in. She seemed pretty stuffy and although she looked familiar, I couldn't quite place her.

"Good morning, sir. I'm Nancy Reyes," she said, and my lips parted to form an 'ah.'

"I was just about to call you regarding the matter of a secretary."

"My apologies for being late on that, sir. We had to thoroughly review a few candidates from the pool."

"So do you have someone for me now?"

"I do," she replied and placed a folder on my desk. I reached for it and flipped it open.

"Grace Warren. She's been at the top of the pool in efficiency and initiative for the last two years, so we've come to the conclusion that she would best suit your needs."

The candidate seemed alright and qualified, so I nodded and shut the folder. "Thank you. When will she be resuming?'

"She is outside right now sir, waiting to be introduced to you."

"'Alright, send her in," I said, but then something occurred to me.

"Wait, I have a question. Do you by any chance have an Adele Walters in the company's employ?"

"Adele?" she looked away in thought.

"As a matter of fact we do. She is even one of the candidates we reviewed for the position of your secretary. She is in the pool."

My heart skipped a beat.

"She's in the pool?"

"Yes sir," she responded.

"Do you have her file here with you?"

"No sir, but I can send it to you."

"Can you do it right now? While you're here?"

She seemed taken aback, as though she wasn't quite sure if I was serious but when I leaned into the chair and folded my arms across my chest to wait, she moved into action.

"S-sure. Of course."

She raised her phone to her ear, and made a quick call. A few minutes later, I received the email. I opened up her profile and lo and behold, it was the spitfire blonde that had collapsed on me on Friday night. I couldn't believe it, so for the first few minutes, all I could do was stare.

"Sir?" Nancy called. "Is everything alright?"

"I want her," I said.

"What?" Her shock was apparent but she quickly fixed her tone. "'I mean, you um..."

I made myself clear. "I want her as my secretary."

She was dumbfounded.

"Is there a problem?" I asked.

"Uh... n-no sir it's just that, we screened these individuals thoroughly and she wasn't the best candidate. You need someone that'll be able to keep up and handle the challenges that'll come with being your secretary."

"She'll figure it out," I replied and shut the email. I returned the folder back to her, and continued on with my day.

ADELE

"**H**ow did you do it?"

I lifted my gaze from the correspondence I was sorting out for the media department, to meet 'miss-you-know-who' before me. Her eyes were moist with tears, but at the same time ablaze with fury. I looked around to see the attention of the other colleagues in the adjoining cubicles had also been drawn, especially at the hostility in her tone. For a second, I was sure she wasn't even addressing me as there had never been a need for us to speak to each other.

"Excuse me?" I asked.

Her eyes narrowed as she studied me, as though trying to figure something out.

"How did you get the position as the CEO's secretary? Are you related to him?"

I could feel even more ears perk up from across the space, and even saw Melinda rise to her feet.

I was confused. "What? And no, I'm not related to him. What do you mean by 'I got the position as his secretary?'"

She scoffed. "Are you actually clueless as to what's happening or are you just pretending?"

Up till that moment, I had been doing my best to be cordial to her but her statement immediately put me on the defensive.

"Don't talk to me like that," I shot back. "I have answered your questions and if you don't want to answer mine, then walk away."

"Wow," she laughed dryly. "Who knew you were so sharp underneath all that silence? I guess it's been an act all along. Well congratulations on your new position, however you got it. Nancy wants to see you."

I watched her storm away, her heels clicking on the hardwood floor, and her cloak swishing furiously behind her. I rose to my feet, completely perplexed, slipped into my shoes, and headed down to HR.

The last time I had been here had been on the day of my employment, more than two years prior, and it was my preference not to return but I guess this was one of those times when coming here was good news. I however still couldn't understand why I was chosen as the CEO's secretary instead of 'miss-you-know-who.'

Perhaps there was a mistake somewhere, and Nancy was calling me in to rectify it. I hated my emotions were being toyed with, as this was one of those few days where I wanted to be numb and left alone.

"Have a seat," she said, her tone neither harsh nor polite as opposed to her niece who had let me know exactly what she thought about the current mishap.

"Congratulations," she said to me, her extremely clear skin and bulging forehead glistening in the day's light. She gestured to the chair before her desk and I took a seat. She remained professional as she orientated me about my duties to the new CEO, and handed over all the necessary correspondence I would need to begin.

"Please head over to your new station on the seventy-sixth floor, so you can acquaint yourself with him and begin."

I accepted then this was real, and wasn't some sort of mistake so in a daze, I gathered the folders, and rose to my feet. I had just reached the door when she spoke again.

"Do you have some sort of personal relationship with the CEO?"

By this point, I had learned from 'miss-you-know-who' not to answer the question too directly if I wanted to get answers.

"He was the one that made a request for me?" I asked, "By name?"

She frowned slightly at my response with a question, but still answered. "He did, and that is why I am asking you right now what your relationship with him is?"

I answered honestly. "There is none. I haven't even seen him. I don't even know what his name is."

"Christian Hall?" she supplied, and I was left even more of a blank. I lowered my gaze to think and was very certain I didn't currently know a Christian Hall in my life.

I sent her an apologetic smile. "You might not believe this but that name doesn't sound familiar. I don't know a Christian Hall."

She seemed pissed off then, convinced just like everyone else that I was putting on an act. She slammed the folder on her desk shut, and turned towards her desktop. "Sure. Whatever. Maybe seeing him will spark your memory. Good day."

"Thank you," I responded and shut the door behind me. As I returned back to my floor to gather my things, I thought even harder. Was I missing something? How had he known my name, and/or me? And was whatever knowledge he possessed enough to have so boldly passed over 'miss-you-know-who' in order to appoint me directly? I was worried because there was no doubt this was going to shine more attention than I wanted on me. Throughout the company's almost one hundred employees, my name would most definitely be mentioned over and over within the coming weeks. I sighed deeply, and returned to my cubicle to turn in my final deliverables and to pack my things.

Melinda hurried over the moment she spotted me, just like I'd expected. She dragged me with her to the kitchen, and even though I didn't want to listen to any questions it was better than doing it in front of everyone.

"You know the CEO?"

I had a sinking feeling I was going to be continuously trying to respond to this sole question in the coming weeks and perhaps even months.

"I don't. And I have no idea why he gave me this position."

She paused as she studied me, as though trying to determine whether I was lying to her or not.

"Really? You don't believe me either?"

She hurried to her defense. "It's not that I don't believe you, it's just... it's really weird. How could he have known your name, and specifically requested for you if he's never met you before?"

"Well, maybe he has the list of all the employees and saw my resume? I mean, it's not as though I'm unqualified for the position."

"Or," her eyes widened. "Maybe he's some sort of pervert that's into blondes."

I shook my head to clear it. "What?"

"You never know," she shrugged. I rolled my eyes at her, and turned around to take my leave. But then something occurred to me so I turned back to face her. "You know who else is also blonde? Stephanie and Martin. So why is it easier for you to believe that he might have picked me because my hair is blonde than because of my resume? You're ridiculous."

Without waiting for her response, I turned and returned to my cubicle.

Half an hour later however, it was no longer mine as I packed my things in a box, said goodbye to the colleagues around me who watched with curiosity, and headed up to the new life that awaited me on the seventy-sixth floor.

I had never been up here before, as I had mainly served the lower managers who didn't have their own secretaries, so this was indeed going to be quite the change for me.

My heart was thundering in my chest, and my nerves taut with anxiety as I wondered just what kind of psycho I was going to have to deal with this time around.

I thought hard on how and for what reason I could have possibly been singled out, and still came up with nothing by the time I arrived.

His floor was magnificent and tranquil, decorated with lavish marble and glistening with steel and polished wood fittings.

His reception was massive, furnished with a lounge that looked like something out of a magazine, and a huge flat screen television. And then in the corner, just by the door to his office, was the huge wooden desk that was going to become mine. I placed my box next to the desktop, and then turned around to take in my new space.

Then my gaze turned towards his door, and I shuddered at just who or what would be awaiting me on the other side. Was this going to make my already difficult life even more agonizing, or was it going to make things just a little bit easier?

I earnestly prayed the latter would be the case, because right now, I truly needed the relief professionally so I could recover personally, and heal my bruised heart.

CHRISTIAN

I t was almost the end of the lunch hour when the knock sounded on my door.

I didn't want to respond to it, wary of how whoever was visiting would distract me from my almost completed study of the profiles of the agency's biggest clients. I had to make a phone call to their respective CEO's in the latter part of the day so I needed to be ready. Therefore, any break in the streak of concentration I was currently on would thoroughly affect my progress.

So I ignored it, hoping whoever it was would take the hint, and walk away.

But then the knock came again, and again... quiet and unhurried and it made me groan.

I glared at the door as the knock came yet again. I was almost preparing an irritated response when something occurred to me.

The secretary I had requested for... Adele.

Perhaps she was the one on the other side of the door.

My heart leapt into my throat, making it even more difficult to push the much needed words out of my mouth.

"Come in," I eventually bellowed, and my whole world seemed to still.

The door was pushed open and indeed, Adele Walters stood before me.

I couldn't believe it.

She on the other hand took her time in gearing up to face me.

She turned to shut the door, and her head remained lowered for a few seconds before she finally began to walk towards me.

"Good morn-" she froze.

I almost smiled in response, but kept myself in check. Or at least somewhat in check. I was certain I looked calm on the surface, but I was aware the pen I was holding was flapping anxiously between my thumb and my forefinger. I couldn't stop it.

"How are you?" I asked.

"... Um," she cleared her throat. "I-I'm doing great. S-sir."

I smiled. "You don't have to call me, sir. Christian is just fine."

She stared at me as though horns had sprouted out of my head, and it made me doubt she had even heard my previous sentence.

I waited, and soon enough she was able to gather her wits. One hand fisted by her side as she tucked her hair behind one ear.

She was stunning. Gloriously so. During the previous weekend, her makeup had been smudged with small, dark blotches around her eyes. But her wide eyed gaze, and adorable freckles had made it impossible not to be attracted to her. And then there was her body, curved and encased in that skin tight, olive dress that had kept my libido raging.

Anyway, today she looked different. Vastly different from the drunk and wobbly and teary eyed woman I had met over the weekend.

Right now, she looked powerful and sophisticated, and if not for her obvious surprise at seeing me here, it would have been near impossible to detect an emotion on her face.

She had on a striped, pale blue suit, with matching tailored pants, and a pair of white heeled shoes. Her plump lips, which I could never forget the memory of sucking and nibbling on, were painted in a striking red shade that made me ache to once again have her pressed against me. Her hands lifted to fiddle with the delicate string of pearls across her neck.

"I was assigned by HR to be your secretary."

I gave a nod in response, and her gaze narrowed.

"Pardon me, but did you have anything to do with that?"

I put the pen down, and leaned more comfortably into the chair. "I did."

She went silent.

"Is there a problem?" I asked.

"Um... several," she muttered with a pained smile, but I heard her loud and clearly. "The entire office seems to think I was assigned this position because I have a personal relationship with you, which I *don't*. I mean up till now I didn't even know you worked here."

She was completely perplexed, and at her unfocused gaze and slightly shaking head it was apparent she didn't know how to begin untying the knots surrounding this coincidence. I stepped in.

"Well you're right. Up till now I didn't work here. I spotted you on the operations floor when I was there for a meeting with the team heads. I wasn't certain you were the one so when Nancy came to inform me I would be getting a new secretary, I asked about you, and she confirmed you work here."

Her mouth fell open in comprehension. "Ah," she said. "I understand."

She shifted her weight from one leg to the other, and it made me wonder why she was still standing so far away from my desk. I chose not to address it and leaned forward to interlock my hands atop the desk.

"Can I uh... can I reject this position and return to my old one? It was already assigned to the HR's ni- I mean a different woman, so this sudden and specific change puts me in kind of awkward position."

My smile was quiet. "I think *my* position gives me the ability to choose who I want as my secretary."

She seemed a bit taken aback by my statement. "I understand, but we... we can't so easily work together either, so why don't we just um... keep our distance, so things remain as simple as possible?"

"Adele, we fucked over the weekend. We didn't kill someone and bury the corpse. Things *are* simple. Just focus on your job and I will focus on mine."

"Then why did you choose me?" she griped. "This *will* make things complicated."

"How so?" I asked, and her lips snapped shut. She looked away briefly to think.

"Sir," she said. "We've slept together, so there is no doubt this history will cause a lot of distractions between us. This is why."

"I won't be distracted," I said, and she stopped talking altogether.

At first her gaze was blank, but then slowly it hardened. I wasn't certain but it seemed as though that particular sentence had offended her.

She released an indignant breath. "Alright, sir."

With that I reached for my wallet, and pulled out a card. "Your first assignment."

I held it to her and she finally, finally closed the distance and came over to my desk. "I missed lunch," I said. "Could you get me something quick to eat close by? It doesn't have to be fancy. I just need something to keep me working.

"Will a sandwich do?" she asked, but I didn't respond because she still hadn't taken the card from me. No doubt she was doing all she could to avoid any sort of physical contact between us. At my annoyed gaze and still outstretched arm, she reached for the card by its very tip.

"A sandwich is fine," I replied.

"Do you have any preferences sir?"

That 'sir' irked me but I didn't see the need to repeat myself again in correcting her usage of it rather than my first name.

"Anything is fine as long as it's not too spicy."

"Yes sir," she nodded, and turned around to take her leave.

ADELE

I *won't be distracted! I won't be distracted?*

I got into the elevator and leaned against the steel car to cool myself down. This was the last thing I should have been currently irritated about, but I couldn't help it. Before this glorious statement, I had been ready to proclaim our glorious, mind blowing chemistry as enough of a reason to keep us both as far from each other as possible. But then his response had simply been a convicted, 'I won't be distracted.'

I wanted to punch him in the face.

And then punch life in the face for playing yet another cruel joke on me.

Fucking him had been the best sensual experience of my adult life, and going by the intensity of his moans, and his immediate collapse with me in his arms upon his release, I could have sworn he'd felt the exact same way. However his nonchalance this afternoon relayed a different message, perhaps I was the only one deluded.

Why then did he still appoint me as his secretary? This was what I couldn't wrap my head around.

If the attraction was not so deep to him, and he wanted things to as he said 'remain simple', then why was he appointing me? This would require us to be in close proximity with each other, and it either worked or I lost my job. Because any change in positions from here on out would read like a demotion on my record.

Once again, life was smacking me in the face and I couldn't help but wonder why.

Was this astounding Adele season? How could I have just gone through a break up, and then have the man I had used to numb me from that pain appear as my boss just mere hours later?

I scoffed in amazement.

My initial plan had been to head down to my previous floor to get the contact information of the Deli we were most fond of, so I could make an order for him. However, I wasn't quite ready to face any of the curious or condemning stares of the other employees, and I most definitely didn't want to be subjected to Melinda's chatter.

So I decided to walk to the deli myself.

It was about ten minutes away from our office building in downtown Los Angeles so I slowed my pace, and tried to enjoy the stroll over.

It was a breezy Monday afternoon, and while the reprieve from the office was appreciated, the honking cars and throng of other lunch goers I had to share the sidewalk with didn't do much to calm my discombobulated state.

Soon I arrived at the deli and got in line, courtesy of the lunch hour demand. As I waited, I thought back to the chicken soup he had made for me the previous day, and thus decided on a simple chicken sandwich for him.

At the reminder of how kind he had been to me, my irritation at his sudden appearance in my life lessened. He had extended a helping hand to me, who had been a complete dead ass drunk stranger, and had brought me to safety. He had then taken the effort to give me medicine, and a decent meal so I could recover properly.

Then of course, there was nearly blowing my back out from pounding me into his mattress.

I sighed, my heart slightly warming.

At every point in time of our encounter, from Saturday morning till now, he had been courteous and compassionate, and had even immediately promoted me to the highest secretarial position in the company.

There truly wasn't much to be upset with him about, but I couldn't help but remain wary until his true intentions behind keeping me close to him was revealed.

"Can I buy it for you?"

I looked up at the sudden voice, and was surprised to see it was our delivery guy. Melinda had once mentioned his name to me but currently I couldn't recall it.

"Hey," I greeted with a smile. He was dressed in the delivery uniform of a black, short sleeved shirt with an orange collar, and the deli's logo stamped on his breast pocket. Wexlar's Deli, it boldly read. And then in each hand, he held a plastic bag of orders.

"Hi," he replied softly. "You're here today."

Something about him made me breathe just a bit more easily. There was an innocence to his close set eyes and dark, shaggy hair that appealed to me. His cheeks were gaunt, his lips thin and his gaze, timid. But then he seemed... simple, as though he was content to just watch life unfold around him.

"I am," I replied.

"Can I pay for what you will order?" he asked, and I was a bit surprised by this request. Perhaps he wasn't so simple after all.

"No, no," I smiled. "Thank you but no. It's for my boss so he's paying for it."

"Don't you want anything?" he asked.

"No, I don't," I said as I shook my head. "I don't have much of an appetite today. Thank you so much for offering."

He was at least a foot taller than I was, but looked significantly younger so I almost couldn't resist reaching up to ruffle his hair affectionately.

"I want to repay you," he said. "For helping me."

Once again I was startled by his words, but then I sifted through my experiences with him and recalled a particularly sour incident.

One of the previous year's interns had gotten her order from their deli delivered a little later than she would have liked. She had been quite upset about that, but had become even more aggravated when she found the bag her order was packaged in, slightly damp from the downpour outside. She had blown up at him in the kitchen, and the poor soul had just stared quietly at her.

I'd been with Melinda then, seated and enjoying a cup of coffee, and she had complained and complained. Eventually I got up and offered to pay for the sandwich instead, so he could get back to his job.

I was sure her frustration stemmed from something else, but yet she had mercilessly lashed out at him for something so small. Ashamed at my intervention, she had snatched the order from him, glared at me and walked out. Come to think of it, I hadn't seen her much after that. I supposed she had been transferred to a different floor or perhaps fired? I didn't have a clue.

Since then however, I had sent a smile every time I had seen him, but at first he had been too shy to respond, immediately turning his face away. But then he had gradually warmed up to it, and responded with a very small lift of the corners of his lips. Then later on, a small nod.

I couldn't help myself now from reaching out to pat the side of his arm. "There's no need for that," I said. "It was nothing at all."

His gaze on me was steady. "Okay," he said and just as abruptly as he had appeared, he walked away.

I watched his tall, lanky frame as he went along and smiled again, slightly amused. Soon it was my turn to place my order and afterwards, I returned back to the current place of my torment.

A knock on my new boss's door upon my return had me once again dismayed at the reality of his presence in my life.

It still felt as though my legs were off the ground, and I was floating or perhaps it was the world that was floating around me.

I opened his door at his response, and went in.

He was sifting through a couple of files on his desk, no doubt courtesy of his new position and the various aspects of the company's administration that he had to get familiar with. After I placed the take out bag on his desk, he lifted his head.

I stopped.

Because every time our gazes met something bolted through me. It felt like a mix of attraction, a distressing arousal, unbelief at his presence, and a dreadfully and equally thrilling anticipation. But as to what I was looking forward to, I couldn't decipher, or perhaps I just didn't want to. At least not yet.

"I got you a chicken sandwich," I felt compelled to say.

"Thank you," he replied with a glance at the bag.

"I'll check on the supplies that are available to us so that I'll serve it better next time. The credit card and receipt are both in the bag."

"You didn't get anything for yourself?" he asked.

"I've already eaten," I lied.

"Alright," he said

I continued on my way to the door, but then my emotions intensified their churning in the pit of my stomach. My hand paused on the steel handle and before I could talk myself out of it, I turned around.

I met him watching me, with a gaze so intense it seemed as though his eyes were ablaze.

The question flowed from my lips.

"Why did you request for me?" I asked. "Based on our history, the right move after discovering I work here would have been to put as much distance as possible between us, right? But instead you've brought me even closer. Why?"

He smiled as though he was in on a secret I could not possibly understand.

It made me frown.

CHRISTIAN

W hat were my intentions?

I didn't have a clue. But what I did know was the last thing I wanted was to put any sort of distance whatsoever between us.

I wanted to see her, and watch her, and talk to her. She was probably imagining my intention was to find another opportunity to get into her pants, and although I wasn't opposed to us fucking between lunch breaks, that fantasy wasn't quite at the forefront of my mind. It was, however, quite the feat to see her and not recall what it felt like to be inside her. I thought about how tight her cunt had been, and how it had milked my cock, driving me to the edge of my sanity.

Fuck, I cursed under my breath.

"You might find this difficult to believe, but I don't have any ulterior motives beyond wanting at least one familiar face around here."

Her frown deepened. "I'm not exactly familiar with you," she pointed out.

"You're familiar enough," I replied and returned my attention to the files in hand. That ended the conversation, so she pulled the door open and stepped out.

I ate the lunch she had gotten me, but couldn't help pondering on her question about my intentions. The thought gnawed at me throughout the rest of the day, so I eventually decided it was a good opportunity to meet up with Stacy.

I set the appointment with my spirited cousin for eight pm at some high end restaurant of her choosing. About half an hour before then, I rose from my desk.

With my jacket draped across my arm, I exited my office and was surprised to see her still at her desk. She rose to her feet at my appearance, and it immediately occurred to me she was no longer wearing her jacket.

Concealed underneath the earlier ensemble was a sleeveless blouse, which I couldn't help but notice, showed a very flattering swell of her cleavage.

"You're still here?" I asked, however my gaze remained on her breasts as the memory of what they had looked and felt like in my hands resurfaced. I recalled intensely sucking on her nipples, and how the pale, pink buds had puckered and hardened at my attention.

The bolt of arousal to my groin was instantaneous, and damn near painful, causing a sudden catch to my breath.

"Yes sir," she answered, but by then I had forgotten what I had even asked about.

She went on. "This appointment was kind of sudden so I have quite a lot to get acquainted with."

"What about dinner?" I asked.

"I'm..." she began, but then looked away in thought. I could see then she hadn't even thought about it.

"I'll get something soon, or head home."

I didn't want to fuss over her so I gave a small nod in response, and went on my way.

Just as I got into my car however, I called the marketing Vice President, Marcus Allen.

"How's your first official day going so far?" his voice boomed through the receiver.

"It's been decent," I replied.

"Are you still at the office? I'm about to head out now. Do you want to grab some dinner together? There's this great Thai place over at Century City that I think you'd absolutely love."

"Actually, that's why I'm calling you. I wanted to ask if you knew the phone number for a good restaurant around here. Something quick and close by?"

"Oh," he sounded disappointed. "You're still working then? Sure, I'll ask my secretary. He should know something. I just leave all the food ordering to him. He knows all the great places around."

He didn't give me a chance to respond as to whether I was still in the office or not so before that could become an issue, I brought the call to an end.

"Thank you." I said. "Let's visit that Thai place some other time."

"Definitely. I'll hold you to that."

I started on my drive, and a few minutes later received the call from his secretary. Upon accepting the call, a peppy male voice boomed through the vehicle's speakers.

"Good evening sir. I'm Daniel Mace, and my boss said you want to have food delivered at the office?"

"I do," was my response.

"I'll be glad to handle this for you. Is there something in particular that you have the appetite for?"

At this question I was stumped, as I didn't exactly know what she would be okay with eating. "Something... light?" I said, and of course he was equally as clueless.

"Uh... light. Right."

I thought back to the soup I made her. "Something with chicken will do."

"So... uh... stir fry? Noodles? Rice?"

I arrived at the restaurant, and pulled up to the valet parking service in front.

"Both will do," I replied.

"Okay sir. You want it delivered to your office right?"

"I do. My secretary will receive it."

"Alright. I'll handle this right away sir."

"Thank you."

I ended the call and handed my keys over to the valet. In the dimly lit restaurant, I met Stacy already seated. She gave an excited squeal the moment she saw me, and clapped lightly at my approach. The reception brought a smile to my face, and it only widened when she jumped up and threw her arms around me.

I endured her crushing hug till she deemed it fit to pull away, and only then was I able to get a good look at her.

Her grin was blinding, and her soft, hazel eyes watery, and filled with emotion.

"You changed your hair color again," I noted, as I brushed her pink bangs out of her eyes. "It was green the last time I saw you."

"Exactly," she reiterated sarcastically. "The last time you saw me, which was almost a year ago."

"You text me every week," I pointed out. "Several times."

"It's not the same thing as seeing you," she complained.

"Alright, I'm sorry," I apologized, and placed a peck on her cheek which she accepted wholeheartedly.

She finally unhooked her arms from around me, so we both took our seats. "I really don't think it's been a year though."

"It has Chris," she groaned, and I laughed softly, reminiscent of the similar way her mother and mine also addressed me. "We last saw each other at Aunt Freda's birthday party in New York."

I nodded in agreement. "You're right."

"Anyway, I'm so happy you moved here. I'm going to be stuck to you like glue."

"I'm wide open," I said.

"Well then, I'm going to be spending this coming weekend at your place. Your mom said it has a pool overlooking downtown."

"Yeah," I replied. "It does."

"I'm so excited," she squealed and I laughed again. The waiter came to our table so we placed our orders, and started a conversation about the final year at U.C.L.A. she was currently undergoing. Then we chatted about possible job positions afterwards and soon enough I was able to bring up my matter with Adele.

"I slept with someone," I said, and she stopped chewing.

So I lifted my glass of wine to my lips and waited for her to overcome her surprise at the sudden statement.

She snorted in amusement, so I shook my head and continued on with my braised lamb.

"Why are you telling me that?" she cried, and then her gaze widened.

"Oh my God. It wasn't your first time was it?"

My own gaze narrowed at the joke and the mischievous glint in her eyes. "You text me at least twice a month with some dilemma about one boy or the other, and I've always given you sound advice. So pay attention."

"Of course," she beamed. "I've asked you several times if you were seeing anyone but you've never given me a straightforward answer."

"Well that's because I wasn't seeing anyone."

"So you're seeing someone now?"

"No. We just slept together once."

"So why are you mentioning it?"

"Because I can't seem to figure out what I want more, to sleep with her again or to find a way to get her out of my system."

"Ah, so she got to you," she smiled. "How did that happen?"

"Apart from the obvious," I replied. "I thought I'd never see her again so I guess that would have solved it. But then today I got to work and there she was."

Stacy's mouth fell open. "She's one of your employees?"

"I made her my secretary."

"Fuck!" she cursed and I flinched at the word coming out of her mouth.

"Language," I warned and raised my fork towards her head. She leaned away, bubbling with laughter.

"You're the one discussing such a raunchy topic with me."

"Touché." I sighed and returned to my meal. Perhaps this indeed was too explicit a conversation to be having with my twenty-two year old cousin. However, I didn't have any other females in my life that I was as comfortable with.

"Well, I'm sure you already know this but you definitely can't get her out of your system now. She's physically too close to you. You could fire her, but I don't think you're going to do that."

"Of course not."

"So you're screwed. Literally." she grunted with amusement while I tried to ignore the panic stirring in the pit of my stomach at how complicated things were beginning to sound.

"What is her take on this?" she asked.

"She wants us to maintain a strictly professional relationship."

"Ah, I get it now. She's brought up the walls and you're not sure whether you want to leave it as is or bring them down."

That was basically it, but I stayed silent and allowed it to convey my agreement. I picked up our exquisite Bordeaux, and refilled her glass.

She clapped her hands together in excitement. "Well you're in luck because I have the perfect remedy for that, but you might not want to hear it."

My attention immediately perked up, but I tried my best not to show it. "Let's hear it."

She leaned in as though she wanted to tell me a secret, and beckoned me closer with her hand. I rolled my eyes and ignored her.

"Come close," she complained.

I shook my head and ignored her antics.

"Fine," she leaned back into her chair. "The only way to break that barrier is... to do absolutely nothing."

I paused with a piece of lamb halfway to my lips. "What?"

"She has to be the one to come to you."

I sent the fork to my mouth and thought on her suggestion. I was quiet for a while and knew she was waiting for my response.

"And what if she doesn't?"

"Well, that should put her out of your mind. If you make the first move right now, it might become too overwhelming for her to process as things are still quite fresh. Or she can use your advances against you and things could trickle down to sexual harassment real fast. You've already made her your secretary and slept with her. So all you can do is hope that your charms are strong enough to make her lose her mind, and come to you on her own."

Her statement did sound reasonable to me, so I nodded in agreement. "Alright," I said, and she smiled.

"Don't worry though. I don't think there's a woman alive who can resist you. I'm related to you and sometimes I even find myself drooling."

I shook my head and we moved on to a different topic of conversation.

ADELE

I found myself nearly running towards the closing elevator.

"Hold it please," I called out as softly as possible, so as not to sound out like a megaphone across the quiet, marble lobby.

A hand shot out to stop the steel doors from closing, and I soon arrived, my face full of gratitude. The smile was instantly wiped off however, when I saw who was waiting inside.

He watched me.... boldly and outrightly as I stared at him in surprise.

It was barely seven thirty in the morning! I had chosen to clock in this early to catch up on organizing his schedule and appointments before he even came in.

However, here he was.

"Good morning," I greeted and without waiting for an answer, got in. I wouldn't have been able to tell if he responded anyway, because my heart was now beating so loudly in my chest that I couldn't hear anything else. I focused on controlling my breathing, immensely aware of his presence at the back of the elevator.

The car rode up and the silence was haunting. I prayed then for it to come to a stop so that other people could get in with us, but it didn't happen.

The awkwardness at remaining completely silent became too painful to bear, so I racked my brain for something to say. It was then I remembered the surprise dinner he had ordered for me the previous evening, so I brought it up.

"Thank you," I said, glancing backwards but not turning to meet his gaze fully or to face him. All I could see was his somewhat blurred figure in the corner. "For the meal last night. I didn't expect it."

He didn't respond, and I was starting to think that he didn't hear me when the elevator dinged open.

"You're welcome," he said, just as a group of people flocked into the car. Only a few faces seemed familiar so I deduced that they were staff from the companies located on the other floors.

They continued to fill the space so I retreated backwards to avoid being crushed by the sudden crowd. I held my breath, very aware now that I had been driven so close to Christian that I was nearly pressed up against him. I tried my best to stick as close as possible to the woman beside me in order to avoid touching him, but I knew deep in my heart that I was just pretending. Of course retreating had been necessitated by the sudden influx but automatically moving to his side was as a result of the mysterious and deliberate draw that I felt towards him.

Soon, the circumstance won and my body stood close to his. I felt the warmth from his presence, and didn't dare breathe. The elevator was packed and quiet and I was almost certain that the rapid thumping of my heart could be heard across the cramped space.

The elevator kept ascending, stopping on the different floors so that some people could get out and others could embark.

His scent, I realized then, was quite familiar- a pleasing mix of vanilla and coffee. It swirled around, and enticed me until I couldn't fight the draw anymore. I allowed the movements of the people in the car to push me even further backwards till my back lightly pressed against his torso.

The ding of the elevators sounded once again on the thirtieth floor, and more people got in. The adjustments sent me staggering backwards and before I could stabilize myself, his arm slid around my waist. The steel band held me to him though I was able to regain my balance.

The elevator continued its climb and the torment of my ass against his groin was all I could think about. I held onto his arm, hoping to subtly push it away but he didn't budge. I couldn't breathe and wished he would let me go but he didn't, and instead curved me into his frame under the guise of an innocent shield.

"I'm alright," I wanted to say but my mouth wouldn't work, so I waited until the elevator began to empty out. His forehead lowered and I froze, as it came to rest on the back of my head.

This was inappropriate.

We were supposed to be keeping a solely professional relationship so we could work as harmoniously together as was possible, but at this point in time, it was incredibly difficult to maintain this stance.

His breathing burned deliciously against my skin, so I slightly tilted my head so his face could rest in the sensitive nook. He pressed a soft kiss on the overheated flesh, and my knees weakened.

Molten lust pooled between my thighs.

Then his hands tightened around my hips, and with my eyes on the people with their backs to us, he ground my ass against his swollen cock.

I grabbed onto his wrist for balance, uncertain at this point whether I was still standing by my own strength, or courtesy of the support of his frame.

The next ding of the elevator sounded across the space, and his face lifted from my neck. The batch of people that had entered all exited at once, and we were left alone.

I wanted to kiss him as badly as I needed to take my next breath, but instead I heeded the warning of my sole remaining brain cell, and moved away. However before I could go too far he caught my hand and spun me to him. In the next moment, my back was pressed to the steel wall, and his tongue was in my mouth.

My blood began to boil, with excitement and fear, of just how scandalous and unnerving this was. He wasn't gentle, his hands intrusive and restless as they fondled my breasts and ass.

His tongue was demanding, the kiss ravenous as his tall frame twisted in order to devour as much of me as he could in the little time that we had. Although my eyes were clenched shut, my vision still spun at the overwhelming flood of ecstasy that coursed through my body, leaving me whimpering and trembling.

My arms went around his neck as my head slanted to kiss him even more deeply, reveling in his taste that was of unattainable dreams and a passion that was just as painful as it was sweet.

My coherence faltered, and I felt myself begin to fall. One arm tightened around him while the other lowered to desperately grip the front of his dress shirt. Our harsh breathing and guttural moans bounced off the steel walls and it felt as though the entire world was watching us.

Suddenly, there was yet another ding of the elevator and a jolting alarm struck me. I pushed away from him as though I had been burned, and turned around to face the wall.

My nerves were taut with the fear we had been caught, so I refused to turn around. He walked away and the elevator doors slid shut. I didn't care where it was going and didn't bother to check until once again, it dinged to a stop. I turned and realized that my purse was on the floor. While the new riders embarked, I retrieved it and kept my gaze glued to the floor. Until we reached the sixty-fifth floor. I immediately jumped and fought my way through the throng of people to get out.

All that rang in my mind was that I needed to see Melinda.

It was however, only after I walked into the operations floor to see the cubicles were still empty, that I realized it was still too early for most people, especially Melinda to have clocked into work. I no longer had a desk of my own here so I dropped my purse on Melinda's and headed straight to the bathroom.

I just wanted to hide, so I locked myself in one of the stalls, sat down on the commode and leaned against the tank with a heavy sigh.

CHRISTIAN

I appeared calm as I strolled towards my office.

When I arrived at the reception and passed her desk, my gaze lingered on the empty seat, all too aware of why she wasn't yet in it. It should have been amusing, but humor was the last thing I currently felt.

I was so excruciatingly aroused that it bordered on painful, the message very clear the only thing that could sate me was a release. However, my very vivid recollection of just how that release had felt when it'd been drawn out by her cunt, made me curse under my breath, but given the current circumstance, that happening was a long shot.

So I headed straight to the bathroom and slammed the door closed. My cock was released from my pants and it was as hard as stone.

I had a very hectic day before me to tackle, so a hard on that I knew wouldn't go away on its own, especially given it's instigator was just a few feet away, was not part of the problems I wanted to deal with for the day.

So I gripped the thick column in my hand, and began to milk it. My motions were rapid and brutal, the delicate flesh and bulging veins glistening with the dampness of my discharge.

Her beautiful face and sensual body formed an ethereal picture in my mind, the echoes of her soft moans and whimpers ringing throughout my head. Goosebumps broke out across my skin as my hand pumped faster, my cock hardened and swelled and the ecstasy that coursed through my veins as I was taken deeper and deeper into its throes nearly made my knees buckle.

My hand slammed against the tiled wall before me as I was finally gifted with my release. It wreaked through my dick with a powerful force, and splattered in creamy bursts in and around the toilet bowl.

The groan that tore out of me was guttural and unbridled, radiating from the storm of emotions in my chest. My frame collapsed with a grunt, my veined arm against the wall the only thing keeping me standing as I recovered from the burst.

This buzz of pleasure was nothing close to what it had felt like to come inside of her, but it was more than enough to heighten my desire and resolve to have her. My intention thus far and just as Stacy had advised, was for me to be courteous, to allow her to be the one to make the decision on where she wanted things between us to go. I had agreed but after this morning, it was apparent that I severely needed to work on my patience.

Grabbing a handful of tissues I wiped myself and the stained surfaces clean, and tucked my dick back into my pants.

It was going to be quite the feat to work with her so close by, and it made me start to consider that making her my secretary was indeed a downright crazy and reckless move.

ADELE

"What are you doing here?"

I turned around from the cup of steaming coffee that I had just raised to my lips.

Melinda was watching me with a bit of surprise and pleasure in her gaze. I returned the smile, glad to see a familiar face.

"Did you lose your way?" she came into the kitchen. "Or did you forget that you're now the CEO's executive secretary?"

I sighed, not quite sure of how to answer that question so I turned away from her and took another sip of the Americano.

With a watchful gaze on me, she came over to also pour herself a cup from the freshly made pot while I headed to one of the chairs and sat down.

She turned around. "What's going on? Is there something wrong with him?"

This was a question that I could answer. "I wish there was," I replied. "I really do."

She smiled, and it lightened the weight on my heart. So I forced myself to spit it out. We were both on the clock anyway and needed to return to our desks pretty soon. I shared mine and Christian's history with her, and her mouth hung open.

"What?" she screeched.

"Yup," I said. "That's why he asked for me."

I expected her to be in abject shock, therefore I couldn't understand the barely contained smile that lit her face up like a light bulb.

"Is this that entertaining to you?" I asked.

"This is beyond entertainment," she replied. "This is the stuff the best office fantasies are made of. You met a random guy at the bar and not only did he help you, he screwed your brains out and then turned out to be your boss. Then he promoted you and started your day off with a passionate assault in the elevator! What the hell is your life? I'm so fucking jealous."

I frowned at her. "This reaction is not going to help me at all."

"You don't need any damn help. What are you complaining about?"

My gaze at her was incredulous. "What do you mean 'what am I complaining about?' All of this tangles and complicates our professional relationship, and it puts my position here in jeopardy should things go awry. What is there not to complain about?"

Her voice was quiet. "What if it doesn't?"

"What if it doesn't?"

"What if things don't go awry, and instead, it all works out perfectly in the end?"

My lips parted to give some snarky comment about how life was a bitch that was constantly looking to stab you in the back, but before the words even came out I lost the strength. Or perhaps I stopped because I didn't really believe that either, because the truth was despite how messed up things seemed to be, once in a while it always turned out in your favor.

"Adele," she said. "Right now the most powerful man in this company, who is also the hottest in this building and quite possibly the entire state has the hots for you. Relish it, revel in it and enjoy the hell out of yourself. And when and if it does come to an end, then you'll have it at worst, as a fun memory to treasure. And if somehow it does jeopardize your position here so be it. You've never really enjoyed being a secretary anyway. Or, you can even sue him for wrongful termination and make a quick million or two as compensation. Again, when and if this happens, my cut is ten percent, for you know, this golden consultation service that I'm giving to you right now. Either way things go, you have very little to lose."

I was dumbfounded as I stared at her, while she raised her mug to her face and hid her smile behind it. So I gave up on responding altogether and focused on my own beverage.

A few seconds later she called again. "'Adele."

I rolled my eyes. "Don't say anymore."

"This is the last thing, and I have to say this. You need to stop overthinking things. I know you're still reeling from that piece of shit... and you deserve the time away from complications to heal. But I don't want you to completely shut yourself off, and possibly miss out on what could turn out to be something amazing."

"That was what I thought about Andrew in the beginning. Remember?"

"So now you're never going to trust anyone else again?"

"Melinda, why are we talking about this?" I groaned. "This is not the matter at hand. He is not asking me to trust him or to have a relationship with him. All I'm saying is that our... relations or whatever, will complicate things and I don't know how to extricate myself from it."

She straightened, her gaze obstinate. "I don't want you to extricate yourself. I want you to play things by ear. Don't try to steer them into going the direction you *think* you want and just go with the flow."

I rose to my feet then, exasperated. "You still don't understand me. I don't want anything to flow."

"So you didn't enjoy the kiss in the elevator this morning then?"

I stopped at her question. The kitchen became too quiet as my mind automatically returned to the scene and brought to mind the very vivid recollection of just how affected I had been by it. A flush began to burn across my cheeks so before she could catch it, I turned to the faucet to rinse my cup. I, of course, spent more time at the task than what was needed, but when I turned around to face her, she was still watching me!

My hands lifted and fell in exasperation. "Am I wrong now? For trying to be professional, and to keep the needed boundaries?"

"You're not," she said. "So if what you want is to keep a serious distance between the both of you, then tell him that. And the next time he comes onto you, don't kiss him back."

"I'm leaving," I said.

"You want him," she called after me. "Keeping the needed boundaries is just the excuse you're giving to yourself on why you shouldn't allow anything to happen between the two of you but you know that's not your real motive."

I stopped and turned to her. "So what is my real motive then, miss know-it-all?"

Her smile was kind. "You're still hurting from losing Andrew. After all, it was just a weekend ago. Last week your life was completely different from what it is right now, and it's painful and heartbreaking, I know. But tell the CEO about this, so he can understand and keep his distance until you're ready. But don't push him away. He just might be the calm that was sent to soothe after your storm."

My brows furrowed in dry amusement at the phrase. "Doesn't the calm come before the storm?"

"It also comes after. No storms rage forever."

I continued on my way but she stopped me again. "If you don't agree with what I'm saying then pass him to me."

"What?"

"Rather me than that swine and you know she's going to swoop right in if you give up that position. Rather your friend than her right?"

I couldn't refute the logic. "Right," I said with a tight lipped smile and she waved me a hearty goodbye. The time available to me to hide was up, so I grabbed my purse from her desk and headed towards the elevator. It soon dinged open and the sound made my heart jump. It made me wonder then if I would always connect these dings to the memory of the thrill and fear of getting caught earlier from our rendezvous in the elevator. The doors slid open, and a handful of people got off. I got in without meeting anyone's gaze, and only when I turned around to press the button for the seventy-sixth floor did I realize there was someone familiar and unpleasant still in the car with me.

I turned to glance at the tall, dark haired beauty, and immediately returned my gaze back to the buttons. It was miss-you-know-who.

"It must be nice..." she began, and I sighed. My prayer had been that she would resist the urge to engage in any communication with me, but alas it didn't seem like it would be the case.

"...successfully lobbying your way to the seventy-sixth floor, while the rest of us have to claw our way up solely on merit."

I turned to her, completely astounded. There were some people in life who allowed their bitterness to turn to delusion, and as I watched her I realized she was one of those.

"Weren't you going to do the same?" I asked. "Use your aunt's authority to get there yourself?"

Her face darkened menacingly. "I wasn't chosen because the head of HR is my aunt. I was chosen because my skills are incomparable to yours."

"Sure," I scoffed. "Keep telling yourself that as though it's possible you will ever get anywhere in this company without your aunt manipulating the system for you. Keep deluding yourself that you have what it takes."

My words were curt and sharp, and I regretted nothing. I thought she would respond with an equally malicious remark but as the elevator came to a stop, her heels clicked angrily on the floor as she stormed out.

She did however stop to address me. "It's only a matter of time," she said. "Just watch. You'll be dragged out of there soon enough."

With that she turned around, and went on her way. I felt a bit embarrassed as there were a few other employees present and listening. The elevator doors slid shut and I tried my best to console myself with the fact that I wasn't familiar with these people. So what did it matter to them, if they found the time to chat and spread this tidbit of office gossip. I resolved therefore to solely focus on the day that was ahead of me, despite its already immensely unsteady start.

CHRISTIAN

J ust as I expected, she maintained her distance from me all through the morning.

I tried my hardest to focus, but having the instigator of my arousal just a few feet away from me, and with just a door separating us, was a notched up level of temptation and distraction that I had not yet garnered the experience to deal with. About an hour before lunch time however, the intercom phone began to ring. I looked away from my computer, excitement tingling through my body at the flashing red light. I picked up the phone and stilled myself to listen to her voice.

"Yeah?"

"Sir, Mr. Sims is here for his appointment with you."

"Send him in," I replied.

"Alright. Would you like something to drink sir? He has asked for some oolong tea."

"No, thank you," I replied and she ended the call.

Soon, there was a strong rap on the door, and one of the advertising managers at the fourth largest advertising agency in the state, Hawthorne, walked in. Marcus Sims, a six foot five once New Yorker, who had been a close acquaintance since we had met about seven years ago at our positions as interns for Blue Moon Media.

"Randolph!" he called out my infamous and for the most part, hidden middle name and it made me appreciate just how effective of a distraction he was going to be.

"Don't call me that," I scowled as I rose to my feet. He ignored the hand I held out and instead rounded my table. Soon I was encased in a bear hug, and although we were the same height and of similar build, his boisterous tone and presence still made me feel a tad bit smaller in size.

"You're finally in the land of milk and honey," he said and I shook my head as we pulled away from each other.

"Milk and honey?" I arched an eyebrow at him. "If this is the land of milk and honey, what then will you call New York?"

He pulled out a chair before me, a wide smile on his face. "The land of rats and legal criminals."

Every word was the truth, so I nodded in agreement and took my seat. "Well, you at least haven't had to deal with the rats for five years now so you should be bursting with joy for that."

"I was, until I heard that you became the CEO of Firstborn. I had to run out of New York given these cardinal sins while you on the other hand were offered your ticket out on a plate of gold! CEO of freaking Firstborn? You're number two in the entire state and then some. My jaw dropped when I heard, and it's remained like that ever since."

I laughed at his mumbled speech as he indeed left his jaw open.

"Well, we'll be number one soon enough."

"I believe you. You're a beast, man. You brought Accenture out of bankruptcy! How the hell did they agree to let you go?"

"Who knows?" I said and he gave me a knowing look.

"Randaaaaayyyyy," he taunted and the smile disappeared from my face much to his amusement. "You're still as tight-lipped as ever. I'll always respect you for that."

"Thank you," I replied.

"Well, I'm hoping you won't be tight fisted though. I'm looking to move up the ladder at Hawthorne and I'm going to need a hoist from you for that."

"Of course. Anything I can do to help."

He pulled a folder from his briefcase and handed it over to me.

"Sun Oil," he replied. "They're releasing their updated avocado oil brand in a few months and need a full campaign behind it. Our department is working on the design and marketing side but I convinced them not to bother outsourcing the video campaign because I know the CEO of Firstborn. The moment they heard this they signed the deal. Apparently they applied to your agency and got rejected because you all don't currently have any openings for their stipulated time frame."

I gawked at him. "And so you thought accepting this with my name would magically create the opening?"

"Of course, you're my brother. Family always makes a way for family."

"Exactly," I replied and snatched the folder from him. "Family always makes a way for family, not stand in the way of family. I just got this position and yet here you are forcing me to step on the toes of overworked managers just to get it done for you?"

"It's a big campaign Randy. Not the biggest you've ever seen but it means a lot to us underdogs. I couldn't let it go."

I sighed and focused on quickly reading through the brief. Just then there was a knock on the door.

"Come in," I replied.

"Mr. Sims," she announced and he turned to face her.

"Thank you."

"Would you like to have it in the lounge or at the table?"

I stepped in. "Let's have it in the lounge. Too many documents here."

"Alright," he agreed and we rose to our feet.

The lounge was a small sitting area, west of the office. Gleaming black leather chairs surrounded a glass coffee table and overlooked the downtown skyline.

We both took our seats across from each other and Adele served the golden steaming beverage.

"I know you said you didn't want anything to drink Mr. Hall, but I took the liberty of making enough just in case you changed your mind. If you also would like something else I.. ow!"

The back of her hand had touched the body of the glass teapot.

"Are you alright?" Marcus asked just as I felt my heart squeeze in my chest.

"I'm fine," she smiled and handled the pot more carefully. She poured the tea but it was impossible to notice that she was not fine. The scalded skin had instantly begun to turn red.

"Do you have any balm to put on it?" I asked.

"It's alright sir," she said as she placed the tea down. "I'll handle it later. Do you want me to get you something to-"

"Handle it now," I couldn't help but snap. "Doesn't it hurt?"

Aggravated, I flung the folder on the table and got to my feet. I walked back to my desk and retrieved my credit card from my wallet. "Go get yourself an ointment to treat it right now. I recommend Acinat…"

I returned to meet her watching me with a complicated gaze on her face. It was partly embarrassment and partly apologetic.

"There's no need I'll just…"

"Take it!"

She stopped and a second long silence passed between us. "I'll purchase it on my own, sir," she said. "Thank you."

With that, she turned and exited the office.

I stood there for a few more moments to settle my temper before returning back to Marcus.

"That was interesting to watch." he said in amusement as he lifted the teacup to his lips.

"What are you talking about?" I scowled as I returned to my seat and picked up the folder.

"It was just a light scald but you acted as though she had slit her wrist."

That made me stop. When I looked at him though and his excited expression I decided I wasn't going to take him seriously.

"Let's get back to work."

"No, let's talk about your personal life. I need an update."

"You might as well stick out your pinky as you sip that tea," I said and without hesitation, his short, stubby finger struck out.

I couldn't help but laugh out as I returned to my chair.

"You're mental Marcus."

"My wife says the same thing every day."

"She's right," I said. "How is Anne by the way?"

"Exhausted," he replied. "Three kids and a busy husband is constantly knocking the wind out of her."

"You sound guilty," I noted.

"Of course I am, l but what can I do? I've been in the same managerial position for three years now. I have to put in the extra hours and genius to get up the ladder so that I can provide more for them." I narrowed my eyes at him. "Is this another ploy to get me to take on this project?"

"It is," he replied boldly. I shook my head in amusement.

Being a straight shooter had always been my favorite quality about him and I was incredibly glad that he had stuck with the trait.

"Anyway, back to the blonde. She's just your secretary?"

"Drop it, Marcus," I said calmly as I flipped the page. "Or I'm dropping this file."

"Yes, sir," he replied while I, on the other hand, tried my best to push her out of my mind.

ADELE

I didn't know how to feel.

On one hand his concern for me had been heartwarming, but on the other it had been embarrassing, and this had made the entire incident quite uncomfortable. I would have much preferred for the scalding to go unnoticed, so that no attention whatsoever would be brought to my carelessness but instead he had made quite a big deal out of it.

My sigh was heavy as I collapsed into my chair, wondering what his guest's perception of the whole incident would probably be. A newly arrived message on my phone, however, soon captured my attention.

"Lunch?" Melinda wrote, and I glanced at the time on my phone to see that it was indeed well past noon. I thought about it for a moment and then sent my response.

"Not today. Boss is still in a meeting."

She sent a laughing emoji. *"You call him boss?"*

"What else am I supposed to call him?"

"His name??????"

"Too personal," I replied.

"Uh huh... still keeping yourself on the other side of the wall huh? Have you both talked about the kiss in the elevator?"

"There's nothing to talk about, and please don't bring it up."

"Well, keep me updated because you're the only one that doesn't want to bring the matter up. He's going to mention it soon and as soon as he does, I want to know what his take on it is."

I dropped the phone and was about to rest my head on the desk, when the door to his office suddenly opened. His exit was accompanied by his friend's boisterous laughter, and a smile across his face as he walked out behind him.

That smile was electric.

It enlivened his usually stoic expression, and presented him as a dream. I almost couldn't look away.

"Goodbye, sir," I rose to my feet.

"Goodbye, Miss-"

"Adele Walters."

"Alright," he said. "Hopefully I'll be coming around again for some good news." he turned to Christian, and gave him a look and that made my stomach tumble in a bad way.

What did that mean? What did he mean? My expression turned sour as I turned to Christian, to see he was indeed watching me. His friend exited the reception and we were left alone. I wanted to ask him about it immediately, but in the end decided to take a little time to think it through. He was still above all else my boss and the CEO, so speaking to him in my current state of indignation would be a very bad choice.

So I pulled my gaze from his, and took my seat.

"Did you get a balm for the burn?" he asked.

I decided then this would be the perfect time to voice my concerns.

"Not yet."

"Why?"

I rose back to my feet. "Sir, I need to speak to you. Um, I understand that our relationship is a bit... i-it's a bit complicated but you cannot allow that to influence the way you speak to me. Especially in front of other people."

He folded his arms across his chest and leaned against his door's frame.

"What's wrong with how I treat you, or speak to you in front of other people?"

Although his tone was serious, it still felt like he was mocking me.

"You know what I mean," my voice trembled.

"No, I do not."

I couldn't stop myself from glaring at him. "Insisting that I get treated immediately even after I have said that I will?"

"Isn't that a perfectly normal human reaction? Anyone else with empathy would have done the same thing. Aren't you thinking much more into this than is warranted?"

His argument stopped me, but I pressed on.

"No, I'm not."

"You are," he said and turned around to leave.

"Then what about your guest?" I called after him.

"What about him?" he turned back to face me.

I didn't want to bring this up and tried convincing myself to let it go, but I couldn't help it. It was going to haunt me otherwise.

"What did he mean when he said: *'Hopefully I'll be coming around again for some good news?'*"

His brows arched and it gave me the distinct feeling that I was the one now crossing the line.

"Am I now obligated to discuss the details of my meetings with you?"

I didn't have a response to that and decided to shut my mouth so that it wouldn't further dig me into a hole. But it didn't mean I was going to be intimidated into letting this go.

So I kept my gaze on him and even lifted my eyebrows to very clearly express my annoyance.

The corners of his lips tilted as he gave his response. "Alright," he said. "Mr. Sims brought along a proposal for a new campaign collaboration with Sun Oil. I'm reluctant to accept it but he has pleaded with me to consider it carefully. Would you like to know more?"

Shame drenched me like a bucket of ice cold water over my head.

I kept staring at him as my brain went into overdrive to figure out how I was going to correct my error, since it was now very clear that I was the problem.

"Um," I lowered my gaze from his. "No sir."

Without another word, he turned around to leave and it felt like the door was slammed shut behind him.

ADELE

I needed to get him some lunch.

However, all I wanted currently was to keep my head buried in the sand. I stared at the phone, wondering how I was going to get the guts to call him, when his door suddenly opened again. I jumped to my feet, and in the process knocked over the mug on my desk. Thankfully it was empty so I quickly caught it before it could fall to the floor. When I straightened afterwards, the last thing I wanted was to look him in the eye.

"I'm heading down to see Allen" he said as he slid his arm into his suit jacket. "I'll be back soon."

My mouth moved before my brain could intercept. "What about lunch, sir?"

"Get me the same sandwich from last time. It will do."

"Alright," I replied just as he walked through the door. I plopped down into my seat, relieved, and called the deli to place our order. About half an hour later, there was a quiet knock on the door.

"Come in," I answered and it was our usual delivery guy, the one I had bumped into at the deli a few days earlier.

He pushed the door open and stood by it reminding me once more of how painfully shy he was.

"Hi," I got up, a wide smile across my face. "Come on in. "

Only then did he move, while I circled the table to meet him half-way.

He placed the paper bags on the desk, and I inspected it to ensure that the chicken sandwich and rice bowl was all intact. My stomach rumbled in anticipation. "Oh thank you," I said. "Did you bring the hot sauce?"

"I did," he replied. "It's by the side."

I checked to see that it was indeed there, and could have given him a hug.

"Thank you," I sang again. "This will make my day a thousand times better, you have no idea."

I returned to my seat, however he didn't leave. He looked around the magnificent office.

"You moved," he noted.

"I did," I said as I retrieved my rice bowl. "I now work directly for the CEO."

He nodded, and then kept looking around. I figured he needed some sort of a break so I let him take his time, and took the first spoonful of rice into my mouth. The flavors of barbecued meat, cream, and the hot sauce all hit my senses with the impact of an emotional song. The world stilled, my eyes fluttered shut and I felt incomparable bliss.

For a few seconds, I even forgot that he was there until I opened my eyes to see him watching me intently. It was a bit embarrassing so I sat up and licked my lips. "I'm sorry," I blushed. "But your deli's fried rice is one of the best things in this world."

"It's spicy," he said, and I nodded vigorously. "Exactly! That's one of the reasons why it's amazing. You don't like it?'

"It's okay," he smiled and I returned one in agreement.

"Do you like it here?" he asked, looking around once again.

There was no reason not to be honest. "Not really," I replied.

"Why?" he asked, and since I didn't expect him to pursue the matter I had to think up a response.

"It's too quiet? And..." I was aching to bad mouth Christian so I heartily gave into it. "My new boss is a bit of a tool."

A deep frown came across his face, and it took me aback. "A tool? Was he disrespectful to you?"

His startling concern made me feel a bit guilty. This was the second time he had shown his heartfelt annoyance towards my complaints, and yet I didn't even know his name. I resolved then to ask Melinda for it. Asking him personally now would no doubt be a bit uncomfortable, and embarrassing for me for not bothering to find out earlier. Especially since he had been singularly delivering food to us at the office for the better part of two years.

"No, no." I replied. "He's just..."

What? Overbearing? Sexy? Kind? What truly was the complaint I had against Christian, beyond my conclusion that we had been too intimate with each other to be able to professionally work together?

"Don't mind me," I said.

"Maybe you could get another job?" he suggested in his thin voice. "One with a better boss."

I was beginning to see now that he took everything that I said quite seriously.

"Um, perhaps but getting another job is not easy at all. All the interviews and the screening having to start all over again? It's too stressful."

"You could get a job at the deli," he said, "We have an opening right now so I could speak to our manager for you? It won't be stressful."

This, I definitely did not know how to respond to.

"What's the opening for?"

"Barista," he responded in a heartbeat.

I truly now wanted to just eat my meal in peace. "I don't know anything about coffee," I said.

"It's easy to learn," he said. "I'll teach you."

"I'll consider it," I said with a smile, hoping this would bring the chatter to an end.

"Okay," he said and turned to take his leave. "I'll speak to my manager."

My hand shot out automatically to stop him, and just then the door to the reception was swung open.

We both turned to see it was Christian so I quickly spoke to the delivery guy in a hushed tone.

"There's no need to do that," I leaned in. "I like it here."

"But you said you didn't," he pressed and my head nearly fell off my neck in exasperation.

I turned to see Christian glaring at us, and I wondered why till I noticed that his gaze was particularly focused on the hand that I had closed around the delivery guy's wrist.

I immediately let him go.

"I was kidding," I said with a painfully wide smile that I hoped would be enough of a plea to get him to leave.

Christian began to move then so I straightened and sent him a smile too. The delivery guy took his leave, but I didn't miss the hostile gaze that Christian sent his way. Both men soon thankfully left me to myself, one to his office and the other back to his job.

I immediately sent Melinda a message before I forgot.

"What's the delivery guy's name?"

"What delivery guy?" her response immediately came in.

"The young one from the deli."

"Ah Tim."

"Thanks.".

"Why do you ask?"

"No reason." I replied, and put the phone aside so that I could enjoy the rest of my lunch. But then I remembered I had to deliver Christian's own to him.

With a groan at how I couldn't get a break, I dragged myself to my feet, got rid of the paper bag and dutifully laid the sandwich out on a plate and tray for him.

Then I headed over to his door and placed a knock on it.

"Come in," I heard his call.

I went in, and didn't see him at his desk so I turned towards the lounge area to find him staring down at the skyline below.

He had his hands in his pockets, which stretched the material of his trouser tight across his ass. The brief view of the perfect cheeks just before he turned around brought to mind the reminder of my hands digging into them as he had fucked me senseless. My pelvis was immediately struck with desire, and the intense sensation reflected across my face.

"Are you alright?" he asked, and I looked up to see that he had turned around.

"I am," I replied with a smile. "I have your lunch. Do you want to have it here or at your desk?"

"Here is fine," he replied and took his seat.

I placed the tray before him and he said his thanks. Just before I took my leave however, he spoke. "Do you have any plans tonight?"

I was a bit perplexed at why he was asking me this question, but nevertheless I responded truthfully. "No sir, I do not."

"Then let's have dinner together."

He said it so casually as he unwrapped the paper around his sandwich.

"Sir?"

He looked up then. "We need to talk," was all he said and who was I to refuse?

"Yes sir," I replied and exited the office.

CHRISTIAN

She refused my offer for a ride, and insisted she would head to the restaurant on her own.

So I left ahead of her, and went on my way.

Something had occurred to me earlier on, in the midst of my irritation with her at insisting on an insurmountable wall between us but yet smiling so cheerfully at the delivery guy.

I had walked in, and my heart had stopped.

Since I'd met her, I hadn't seen such a smile on her face when it came to me, so it had especially irritated me that the case was apparently different with him.

It had crowned her with a halo, and embittered me with jealousy.

Until something had occurred to me, she had just gotten out of a relationship.

I didn't know how serious it had been, but it most definitely had to have been something special for her to react so tragically at its termination.

So I came to realize just how self-centered I was being. Granted, our first time together could have been somewhat beneficial in helping get her mind off the breakup, but then forcefully appointing her as my secretary and insisting on a more intimate relationship between us was sure to have been terribly overwhelming.

So tonight, I was going to speak as honestly as possible with her so the air between us could become clear. I was ready to realign the boundaries of our working relationship and quite possibly even relieve her of the position if it wasn't what she wanted. A few months of paid leave would no doubt give her the chance to rest, and allow her to be able to return to the company unscathed by rumors of incompetency.

In no time I arrived at the downtown restaurant and was shown to the table that Stacy had reserved for us.

After my invitation to Adele, I had immediately called her to recommend somewhere that would be relaxing enough for the both of us to have a conversation in.

She had suggested this place, with its gardens and natural ambience.

"She'll love it," Stacy had assured me and I believed her.

I ordered a bottle of Sauvignon and settled in to await her.

Soon she arrived, and I raised my gaze to watch the gorgeous woman as she approached. Her blonde hair was blowing away from her neck to the rhythm of her strut, and her sinfully sexy body was encased in a white, calf length dress.

"Good evening sir," she greeted me and I almost smiled to myself. She had no doubt resolved on her way here to do whatever she could to maintain this outing as a strictly official one.

"Good evening," I replied and raised my hand to call the waiter over as she settled in.

"What would you like to drink?" I asked, and she shook her head.

"Nothing," she replied. "You said you wanted to speak to me?"

"At least get a glass of water," I complained. "I've already called him over."

She agreed and placed her order as requested.

It was only then that I took the liberty of thoroughly watching her, and it was enough for me to notice the irritation and sadness across her face. I also noted, much to my relief she now had a band aid across the back of her hand. At least that matter I didn't have to address.

"What's wrong?" I asked and she lifted her gaze to mine. In those clear, blue pupils was a blazing fire of annoyance.

"Why did you bring me here? Sir." she asked and the bite in her tone was impossible not to feel.

I went straight to the point.

"You just ended your previous relationship," I said. "I apologize for being inconsiderate of that. It only came to my mind today and I realized that manipulating your access to the position, and not keeping the needed boundaries between us could have indeed been quite upsetting.

She regarded me, her gaze softening, and then relaxed into the chair.

"I'm grateful for this position," she replied. "It has bumped up my salary almost twenty percent more than my peers so I have nothing to complain about."

I knew she wanted to say more, but she hesitated. So I nudged her on.

"Except?"

She smiled shyly and picked up her glass of water. Then she took a small drink from it before setting it down again.

"Except that, I'm really not certain of how to relate with you. Perhaps we could agree now that our history from that weekend should be completely erased?"

My gaze on her was steady and calm, and I could tell it made her slightly nervous as her nails were scraping softly against the table cloth.

"Is that what you want?" I asked.

"It would be best wouldn't it?" she replied.

I was about to fully agree, but I stood my ground and included the needed parenthesis. "It would be the best for you, not me, but I'm willing to accept these terms."

"Thank you, sir," she muttered and drained her glass.

"Are you ready to order?" I asked.

"Um, I am, but there is one more thing."

"What is it?" I asked as she looked around the restaurant with a pained expression on her face. This expression made my chest contract in a bitter sweet way because although it showed her displeasure, it also made her look extremely adorable; the wrinkle of her button nose and the slight pout of her plump and pale pink lips. I couldn't believe I had just agreed to keep my distance from her.

I poured myself a glass of the wine I had ordered as she spoke.

"This is quite possibly the worst choice for a restaurant that you could have made."

I stopped with the bottle still in the air.

"Why?" I asked.

"This is where I got dumped two weeks ago," she said. "And at that table over there,"

She pointed to a secluded corner, the space surrounded by plants and flowers and I gently set the bottle down.

"I apologize," I said and she laughed softly.

"It's alright. You couldn't have known."

"My cousin recommended this place to me. She said that it would be calm and relaxing."

"It is," she replied and nodded when I pointed at the bottle to ask if she also wanted to share the wine with me.

"Or at least it was until the whole breakup debacle."

The gushing sound of the wine hitting glass permeated our space.

"He's a fucking moron," I said as I set the bottle down. She lifted her wine glass to the air and slightly raised it to me in a salute. "Amen to that."

I smiled and we both took a drink.

"This is amazing," she said as the glass left her lips. "It's fruity but still quite dry."

"It's my favorite Sauvignon," I said. "I first had it a couple of years ago on a business trip to London, and it's remained near the top of my list since then.

"I love it," she said and grabbed the menu. "I wonder how much it costs?"

I patiently waited for her to find where it was listed, and just as I expected her eyes widened at the price tag attached to it.

She instantly shut the menu and I couldn't help but laugh.

Then she leaned in. "Is it this pricey because of the restaurant, or is this close to how much it actually costs?"

"It's similar," I replied.

"So it's about four hundred dollars? For a bottle?"

I nodded and she gazed at the bottle with disdain.

"I'm definitely keeping my job as your secretary because I need this at least once a year. The waiter came over then so we both placed our orders, for me a simple beef steak while she opted for duck confit ravioli.

After he left, we both became silent but I soon decided there was no reason to be. "Can I ask about how you came to be a secretary? Too personal?"

"Oh no," she replied, her eyes glistening. "You're my boss so of course you should know this much about me."

"It was never really my plan," she said. "I majored in accounting at college, so my expectation was that I would go on to become an accountant but after working at a firm for about two years, I decided I was most definitely not cut out for that line of work."

"How come?" I asked.

"Too slow," she replied. "Too structured... too dull. I suspected it would be the case in college but I didn't have any other options then so I just stuck with what would help me take care of my student loans. So after I cleared a significant part of it I quit. I've always been very creatively inclined so I figured marketing and advertising would be an interesting experience. However when I applied for the entry level positions I wasn't accepted since I'd never really been active creatively and was just switching industries based on a hunch. Then a friend recommended at the time perhaps a temporary secretarial position would be acceptable. So I applied and got the job."

"You've been working at the company for two years?" I asked.

"Yes sir."

"Any attempts so far to join the creative teams then?"

She wanted to speak but hesitated. "Would it be appropriate to share this with you? Won't it introduce some element of bias?"

"Our relationship is now strictly professional, remember? Don't worry, I'll be sure to keep any of my favors from reaching you."

"Yikes," she said and I chuckled.

"Anyway to answer your question, I have from time to time peeked in on their projects, but I haven't actually taken any concrete steps to participate. I've been too busy being a secretary I guess."

"Are you particularly close with any members from the marketing or design teams?"

"Just marketing team two. I'm quite friendly with their project manager, Audrey. We connected during last year's year end party when she had a little wardrobe malfunction. I had a couple of safety pins on me so I was called in to save the day."

I nodded at the story and took another drink of my wine.

"What about you?" she asked. "Is it too rude to ask about how you got into the industry?"

I smiled as I set the glass down. "Shouldn't you already know most professional details about me? You are my secretary after all."

"I'm aware of the general details. Business school at Columbia, career start at Accenture and then worked your way up to CEO of their North America division. Then suddenly you gave that up and moved down here."

"That's the story," I said.

"Was there a particular reason you quit? You don't have to answer if it's too personal."

"I'm aware," I replied. "And it's not too personal. My mom was diagnosed with stage two breast cancer a few months ago. She's doing fine now and undergoing chemo. I want to be here for her, and for my other family as well. Most of my aunts and cousins live here in L.A. while there is no one but me in New York so I saw this as a chance to slow down."

She smiled. "I understand. My parents are in Minnesota, and I really wish I could live closer to them but I cannot stand it there."

"Too suburban for you?"

"Yeah," she replied. "I'm not quite drawn to the bustle of New York but lakes and a slow pace is not quite what I crave either. L.A. gives me a balance of the two.

"I know what you mean," I replied. "For the longest time I couldn't stand L.A. but I guess the years have caught up with me and it's time to actually slow down."

"What years?" she scoffed. "You're only thirty-one."

I shrugged and began to unfold my napkin. Just then the waiter arrived and the appetizing plates were laid across our table, looking delectable under the candle light.

"Bon appétit," I said to her and she sent back the greeting. Then we both picked up our forks and dug in.

ADELE

"You turned him down?"

I adjusted the volume of my car's speakers as I engaged in the call with Melinda. "Well, there wasn't exactly an offer on the table."

"So you shut him out?"

I sighed. "Things have been resolved, and I like the consensus that we've come to."

"You're going to regret this," she said, and my chest constricted.

"Don't say that. That's unfair."

"I know, I'm sorry," she quickly apologized. "You're on your way home now?"

"Yeah, but I wanted to speak to you about Audrey. Do you think asking her to speak to her team leader about including me in any of their current projects would be inappropriate?"

"Hmm, that I don't have an answer to."

"Right? Doesn't it sound like I'm looking to take someone's job away?"

She laughed. "Not necessarily. You're friendly with her right? So you could just say you're looking to expand your horizon. To test the waters to see if perhaps you would enjoy the creative side of the company more."

"You think?"

"Yeah, I mean, that's not a bad thing. Plus, if she objects to it then you could just participate in the company's bi-annual competitions? Any member of staff can apply to those. That was how the current project manager in marketing team four got promoted from being just an intern."

"You're right," I agreed with her.

"You looking to pursue this path?"

"I am," I replied. "I mean, I have been considering it for more than a year now. So why not go for it?"

"Did the CEO say something? Is that what's prompting you to act?"

"Not really," I replied. "He just asked me if I've ever considered moving in that direction and I realized I never have. I was more or less occupied with my life outside the office, but now that's no more, I better start thinking of advancing professionally at least."

"You have advanced," she reminded me. "You're the CEO's personal secretary."

"Well, no one seemed to believe I earned that," I said. "Plus, I don't necessarily want to be a secretary forever. I want a job that creatively challenges me."

"Alright, sounds good. Go for it then. I think you should try speaking to her on Monday. Let's see what she says."

"I will."

There was a momentary silence.

"You really turned the CEO down?"

"There was no offer on the table," I frowned once again.

"If there had been one," she asked. "Would you have accepted it?"

I paused to ponder on a response, however no definite answer came my way. I told the truth.

"I don't know. Perhaps not."

"Alright," she said. "Well now that you've thrown him back in the water, I'm going to take my shot the next time I catch him in an elevator."

Her voice turned sultry. "I'll press my back oh so gently against him, and apologize, because you know, it's not my fault. The elevator's just too crowded."

"Be careful not to get fired for sexual harassment," I warned her, and she seemed to choke on whatever she was drinking. "I'm not going to plead for pardon on your behalf."

"Don't bother talking me out of this," she laughed. "I want to retire and be cared for so I'm going to give this my best shot."

"Good luck," I responded, amused.

"You said my halter neck dress was what caught his eye? Should I wear it to work? Maybe once he sees it he'll shift his attraction for you to me?"

I was bemused by her line of reasoning.

"Um... that's not appropriate office attire."

"Tell that to mini-skirt Jane on our floor. That girl's skirts are so short we can almost see the underside of her ass."

"She's short, so it's not as provocative. Your legs go on for miles."

"The olive dress isn't short,"

"It does reveal side cleavage, and your shoulders."

"So I'll wear a jacket."

"Alright," I conceded, just as I pulled into my apartment complex.

"Any other 'tips' I should know about?"

"Like what?" I shut my engine off.

"You know, his preferences. Sexual preferences."

"Okay I'm ending this call."

"Adele!"

"You're on your own," I stated and disconnected the line. Then I grabbed my purse and headed back to my apartment. It had been a long and dreary day but all in all it had come to quite a pleasant end.

I thought of Christian, and of how decent our time together had been over dinner. Once in a while I had forgotten myself and gotten lost in his searing gaze, but a mental slap had always done the trick and snapped me out of my haze. Then our legs had touched quite often and mostly accidentally under the table. In order not to make things awkward, I had allowed it until breathing became a difficulty. The warmth from his skin flowing into mine from below, and the impact of his smile above to the pacing of my heart was way too much appeal for any one male or female to handle at a time.

With a sigh, I inserted my key and unlocked the door. However I felt something on the floor and set my hand on the wall to feel for the foyer light.

I switched it on and there it was.

A plain white envelope that had been slipped underneath my door.

Is it mail? I wondered, as I lowered to retrieve it.

I turned it over however and saw it couldn't be as there was no address. This had been personally delivered. I took it with me into the apartment and after setting my purse down on the sofa, proceeded to open the envelope. Inside of it were a bunch of pictures.

My curiosity was piqued so I pulled them out.

I went through them, one after the other and as I did, all the life slowly drained out of me.

ADELE

The photos flew from my hands as I spun on my heels, and *bolted* for the door. I slammed into it so hard that it took more than a moment for me to catch my breath. With shaky hands and my eyes burning with tears, I pulled the latch into place and turned the key several times until it was securely locked.

The fear that had struck my heart from the moment I had sighted those pictures was now beginning to spread to every nook and cranny of my body. It turned me numb until I could barely hold myself up, but I was too scared to lean against the door. So I crawled away from it to the wall by the side, and with my arms folded around my knees tried to rock myself calm. However it was to no avail, as the images, clear and vivid, fled through my memory.

I was being watched. Perhaps even at this very moment.

The realization once again hammered into me, and my eyes shot open in horror. I jumped to my feet and drew all of the curtains solidly shut. I was too scared to go into my bedroom. Or my bathroom for that matter. The images once again came to mind and the tears poured down my cheeks.

I couldn't remain here, but then again I was too scared to go outside.

I eventually decided anywhere was better than here so with my heart in my throat, I grabbed my purse and keys. In no time, I was out of the apartment and in my car.

I didn't look back, and didn't slow down until I was well on the highway and far away from the apartment. I was choking on sobs, my throat constricting and my breathing out of control. The only thing I could think of then was to call Melinda. I placed the call and soon the ringing tone filled the car. I thought about what explanation I was going to give of what was happening, I realized it wasn't exactly something that was so easy to voice.

Perhaps later on the time would come, but currently, I didn't know how I would be able to give the report that someone had somehow broken into my home, and installed some sort of surveillance on me. And that in the mail, I had received photographs of my naked body. In my bedroom as I laid undressed on my bed, and as I walked around unaware I was being watched. In my bathroom as I had showered within the frosted glass and as I had stood by the sink drying my hair. My breasts bared and my ass on full display. The photos had been crisp and close, showing there was for certain some sort of surveillance equipment inside my home and it shook me to think about just how long it had been there.

"Hello?" the line connected, and Melinda's soft voice came through.

I jolted in response, my attention returning to the present. "M-Melinda?"

"Adele, hey. What's up?"

"Uh..." I breathed. "C-can I come over? Just for a little bit."

I heard her muffled giggle then. "Um.." she began but was once again interrupted.

"I-is it urgent? Do you need something?"

"Do you have company?" I asked.

"Stop," I heard her say in a hushed voice. When she returned to me her tone was somewhat back to normal.

"I do, but what do you need?"

"It's fine," I shook my head. "Forget I called."

"Are you sure?" she asked. "It's quite late."

"It's fine. Everything's fine. See you tomorrow."

I ended the call before the matter could be dragged on any further. My intention had been to perhaps find a place to go to but now it seemed that road was blocked. I thought of going to a hotel, but then my gaze couldn't look away from my rearview and side mirrors. What if I was being followed? Was the security in a hotel enough to guarantee I would be alright and not attacked?

My chest burned once again and a hot stream flowed down my cheeks as I sped through the night, checking after every couple of breaths to see if I was being followed. The problem was it was too dark to see and too easy to miss a tail if there was indeed one.

This devastated me even further. After nearly being hit by a couple of cars on account of my emotional distress and distraction, I decided to get off the road before I killed someone or vice versa.

And the only place I could think of that had some degree of security that was decent enough was the office. There was also the police station but I didn't want to rush things. I wanted the chance to properly think things through.

When I arrived the building was nearly emptied, and the lights dimmed. I rode up to my floor and the moment I got into the receptionist's office, locked the door solidly behind me. There was no way that whoever was on my tail would so easily be able to bypass the ground floor security to attack me.

I headed straight to my desk, but the thought of settling into the chair nearly crippled me with frustration. So instead I went into Christian's office, and headed straight for one of the more comfortable leather chairs in his lounge.

I allowed my purse to fall down to the ground and curled like a ball into it. Spinning the chair around, I stared at the magnificent L.A. skyline with its sprawling buildings. The scene beyond seemed ethereal... the world magical and then there was me whose life had just become a nightmare.

I needed to sleep... to forget, but I didn't know if I would ever be able to close my eyes again. I looked around at the dim office, my eyes going to the chair where Christian usually spent his days.

What would he think about this if he knew, I wondered?

Or perhaps... another fear struck me. He was the one behind this.

What about Melinda then? What if *she* was the one behind it?

The very thought taunted me with the verdict that I was losing my mind, but what if it was the truth? After all, from all of those in my personal and professional circles she was the only one that had been to my home... several times.

But what then would be her motive for the harassment?

My mind of course sought deep and far and immediately halted on her comments earlier in the evening of doing all that she could to earn Christian's affection. Getting me out of the way would usher the ploy into existence would it not?

I buried my head between my knees, but not before I struck the side of it.

I truly was losing it to be able to even conjure up such a ridiculous thought, but then again, being surveilled in my own house and having extremely vivid and naked pictures of myself published was even more crazy wasn't it?

And yet, that was now my current reality.

I released a deep sigh. Would this be my life from now on? To suspect everyone around me? How could this matter be promptly dealt with?

My best bet was still the police, but I didn't want whoever was behind this to grow furious and aggravate the situation. I wanted to at least hear what they wanted from me first.

It felt like I was standing on a landmine, too afraid to lift my leg because even more scary than the fact that I had been recorded nude, was the possibility and perhaps reality that those images or perhaps even videos were already circulating the internet.

Panicked, I grabbed my purse, and poured out all of the contents on the ground in my haste and frustration.

I soon found my phone, and immediately input my name into google. I found nothing beyond the basic information of my social media accounts, so with a trembling heart I scoured the porn sites and typed out phrases that could be connected to me.

G*irl in her bedroom naked*

Girl showering

Girl lying on her bed naked

Girl touching herself

Girl with a vibrator.

Blondie making herself cum

Blondie dancing in the bathroom

Blondie taking a shit.

Blondie live web cam?

I scoured through the site, seeing other blondes exposed and for the very first time began to wonder just how many of these women had this content recorded and published without their consent.

After searching for a while, nothing came up but I didn't feel a single iota of relief.

Beyond the pictures sent, I wondered just how many others they possessed? And if they did, the last thing I wanted was to provoke them into releasing them.

CHRISTIAN

Ve were readjusting my schedule for the week when I noticed the stain.

It was on the right corner of her dress shirt, and was a small, faded hue of red. At first, my concern was that it was blood and she had been hurt, but then I realized it was probably from some other colored liquid.

I looked away, but then it suddenly occurred to me this was the same outfit she had worn the previous day.

The same silk, ivory shirt with the bold print of a red flower draped across the shoulder, the same fitted pencil skirt, and heeled shoes.

In the days I had known her thus far, I had noticed the meticulous care put into her appearance at all times, so it struck me odd that she would ever show up to work less than stellar.

I wanted to ask about it, but I didn't want to make her uncomfortable so I ignored it and returned my gaze to my folder. I also didn't want to bring attention to the fact that for some reason, I had remembered what she had worn to work the previous day when I couldn't even remember what I had for breakfast just that morning.

"Your meeting with Bloomberg on Friday might bleed into the one you requested with the team leaders since you'll have to return from Century City to attend it. Should we adjust the time or reschedule?"

I also couldn't help but note the dullness in her tone, and the dreary look in her eyes. She always looked sharp, her voice alert and her posture trained, but today it was as though she was barely managing to remain awake.

"Sir?" she called, and I realized I had been staring blatantly at her.

"No need to reschedule," I replied. "I'll study their project reports before then so the meeting will be brief. Could you return these approved contracts?"

"I will," she answered. She accepted the folders from me and went on her way.

However something happened. Just before she reached the door, there was a crash from the corner of the office. She gasped so loudly that my attention was immediately drawn to her instead of the picture frame that had fallen to its demise. She had crouched down, her hand over her head, and her entire frame rocking on her heels.

I immediately jumped to my feet.

"Adele!"

She was trembling when I got to her, and only after she had wiped the tears off her face did she find the courage to rise with me.

"Are you alright?"

"I'm sorry," she tried to force a smile but still refused to look at me. She turned towards the wall where the crash had happened.

"It's alright. Are you okay?"

She finally met my gaze and in her eyes, I saw terror.

She stared at me for a few seconds as though she was seeing me for the first time. And then she twisted her body out of my hold.

"I'm fine," she said and took several steps away.

"I'll get this downstairs and... uh," she glanced back at the wall, still visibly shaken. "I'll get that sorted out too."

"Don't worry about it," I said. The last thing I wanted was her hand near the shards of glass. "I'll handle it myself."

With an absentminded nod, she continued on her way and shut the door behind her.

I stared at the closed door and wondered what was wrong? Had something happened at home? She seemed unusually jittery and dazed.

Or perhaps it was just all in my head. I recalled then our agreement just the previous night to maintain a very professional distance, so I shook my head to dispel the worry.

I most definitely didn't want to be the one to yet again breach that boundary.

ADELE

I had never been as guarded as I currently was.

As I strolled through the hallways of my former floor, slipping into the various department offices and delivering approved correspondence, I couldn't help but gaze at everyone and everything with a vicious suspicion that I didn't even know I could generate. Every smile, every nod, every gaze whether intentional or unintentional made the nerves in my stomach clench with fright.

It was no way to live, and with my sorrow nearly choking me I disappeared into the break room for a much needed reprieve.

To my relief it was empty, so I leaned against the wall, hunger, exhaustion and fright all converging to drain me out of the little strength I had left. I gazed at the files in my hand and didn't know how I was going to make it through to the end of the day.

I spotted the bags of instant coffee on the counter, so I placed the documents on one of the chairs and headed over to make myself a cup.

"Hey!" the call suddenly came just as I was pouring some boiled water into my mug.

I spilled it all over as I jumped. It would have been a devastating burn if I had spilled it on myself.

"Are you alright?" Melinda rushed over.

I pulled my hand out of her grasp. "I'm fine," I said curtly, and turned away to retrieve paper towels from the roll at the corner. Plus, I needed a few moments to prepare myself to face her otherwise it was going to be more than obvious that something was haunting me.

I hurriedly wiped the water from the counter, and tried to force a smile to my face as I faced her.

"Hey." she called cautiously, and I cursed under my breath.

I so badly wanted to speak to her about what I was going through.

It was slowly killing me on the inside, but then at this point, everyone was a suspect especially those that had been in my house and right now, she was at the top of the list.

"Hey." I sent back a greeting.

"I spotted you delivering correspondence. I thought I'd say hi."

"Yeah," I replied. "I was going to say hello too before I left. It's been so hectic today. I'm exhausted."

She was amused. "It's ten am."

My head shot up in surprise. With the way things had been going thus far, it had felt as though lunch time would be any minute. And I was looking forward to it so I could steal a quick nap in the bathroom. This time around, I couldn't hold back my frustration so I released a heavy groan. She laughed.

I managed to crank a smile too in the hopes it would dispel our earlier friction.

"You must be really exhausted."

"I am," I replied as I threw the dirty towels away. I refilled my cup and headed over to the sofa as my strength could no longer keep me standing.

"Does this have anything to do with why you called me last night?" she asked.

I found a quick lie. "The AC in my room broke. It got hot so I wanted to crash in your spare bedroom.

"Is that also why you didn't get any sleep?"

"Yeah."

"But you have a ceiling fan don't you? In your bedroom. Didn't that help?"

"It did. That's why I changed my mind about coming over when I heard you had company."

She blushed at that, barely able to meet my gaze.

Then she began to turn her face away to hide the flush on the swell of her cheeks, but I threatened her.

"You better start speaking. I thought you wanted to go after the CEO?"

This was my opportunity to lightly ask what her true intentions were, because when she had voiced them earlier, I hadn't taken it seriously.

Now, a lot had changed.

"Are you kidding?" she said. "I was joking about that. He's yours and I'm not dipping my toe into that pond."

"He's not mine," I protested

"Well, tell me that again in a couple of months after you've both fallen into each

other's arms and pants, again. I'll believe you then."

"I told you we set clear boundaries for our relationship last night."

"Sure, and how's that been working out so far?"

"Well, as you've just pointed out, it's just ten am, but so far I don't have any complaints."

"Alright," she chimed and I rose to leave.

Any more chatter, and I would completely run out of the energy to hold myself together. Which would then result in me either falling asleep right there on the couch, or suddenly breaking out in tears.

So I took my mug to the counter, poured what was left of the dark liquid into the sink and quickly washed the cup.

"You're leaving already?" she asked, disappointed.

"I've got to deliver the rest of those contracts and get back to my floor."

She sighed. "I've got to get back to work too. How is it though? Truly. On the seventy-sixth floor?"

I shrugged. "Well you know what they say about the top."

"It's lonely?" she asked.

"Quite."

"Well you know how to-" her voice trailed off as a quite unwanted guest came in.

Miss-you-know-who.

I was immediately alarmed at her entrance because she also ranked quite high on my suspicion list. Her gaze went to Melinda, and then to me which was already quite peculiar as previously she never even bothered to spare either of us a look.

And then she addressed me.

"How's it going?" she asked, but before I could respond Melinda stepped in.

"That's none of your business."

She turned to gaze at Melinda as though she was something that she'd just discovered was stuck under her shoe.

"Excuse me, but am I talking to you?" she snipped, and a headache ripped through my skull.

At that moment, I didn't even care anymore if she was the culprit. The possibility of listening to any sort of exchange between them was currently a much more dire fate than being stalked and harassed.

"Excuse me." I picked up my files and left the room.

"Adele!" Melinda called after me but I didn't respond.

Hopefully, without the catalyst present they would realize any petty exchanges between them was unwarranted.

After delivering my correspondence, I hurried back up to my floor and considered requesting for the remainder of the day off. Earlier on, before the work day had even started I had searched through a few of Christian's bathroom supplies, and was incredibly happy to find an unused toothbrush.

The very thought of having to leave the building to even get that basic necessity had filled me with so much dread, that I wondered if I would ever have the guts to leave again.

That position was especially scary because with the corporate culture and magnitude of this agency, a clean mouth wasn't all I needed to look and function to an acceptable degree.

I stood at my desk for a few minutes, deep in thought until I noticed a new stack of correspondence had been delivered to my desk by one of the temps as per usual. So to distract myself, I picked them up and began to sort through them.

I went through the credit card promotional letters, invitation to industry events, but then soon came upon one that wasn't addressed. It had absolutely nothing written on it and in an instant, I was reminded of its similarities with the envelope I had received the previous night.

It had been plain and unaddressed, and just as bulky. Rather than a simple letter or card, it contained photographs. Sweat beaded across my skin as I stared at it.

Everything stilled to where all I could hear was the thundering of my heart in my ears.

If this was what I suspected it was, then I was sure I was going to lose my mind.

CHRISTIAN

I walked out to the reception, and she didn't turn.
She didn't even realize I was standing there.

It was a bit strange, but as I was about to continue on my way, my gaze fell on her hands. It wasn't what she was clutching that caught my attention, but that her hands were trembling and it made me stop.

Alarm immediately zapped through me, which was in correlation with my earlier inkling that all was not well with her.

Then to my horror, tears fell from the corner of her eyes and traced down her cheeks.

"Adele," I called, and she jumped.

She was so frightened she almost fell backwards, the desk behind her the only thing that stopped her retreat and broke her fall.

I was stunned.

With her hand gripping the edge of the table, she righted herself, quickly wiped the tears off her face and then turned to me.

"Are you alright?" I asked.

"I'm fine," she replied, then lowered to gather the photographs that had fallen to the floor. Her movements were lightning quick, and soon she had them all in hand. "I'm just a bit groggy," she said with a laugh as she returned to her seat. "I probably just need some coffee."

"You didn't get enough sleep?" I pressed. "If you need to, you can take the day off."

She shook her head in refusal, and settled into her chair. Prying any further would be akin to breaking the rules of our engagement as laid down the previous evening, so I resumed putting my jacket on.

"I'm heading over to James's office for a quick meeting. Buzz me if anything needs my urgent attention before I return."

"Yes sir," she nodded, her gaze fixated on the screen of her computer.

I left the office, but couldn't shake off my worry at how startled and sad she had looked.

She was deathly pale, as though there was only an inch of life left inside of her and it frustrated me that there was no way to find out about whatever bind she seemed to be in.

Was it financial, or physical? I wondered.

A heavy pressure settled in my chest. Or was it perhaps emotional?

Did it have something to do with the moron that had broken up with her?

Once again, I truly wished we had met prior to her previous relationship, or at least further down the line. Being benched in this way with the permission to only watch, was going to drive me insane.

I arrived for my meeting with the CFO, and after some brief courtesies we immediately got straight to work.

When I returned about an hour later, I met her in the same morose state.

It appeared as though she was working, since she was slightly moving her mouse on the desk. However her stare was blank, and her lids fixated on one spot on the screen. She wasn't even blinking, and it was clear to me she was currently very far away from the building.

"Do you have the Lokai brief?" I asked, and that quickly jolted her attention back.

"Sir?" she asked as she sat up.

"The Lokai brief," I repeated, and she nodded in response.

"I do. I'll bring it in," she said, and I continued on to my office.

A little while later, she came in with her shoulders straightened, and a little more color in her face.

Her lips were now painted a stark red, and her hair was now neatly tied to the back of her head. She looked better, which made me wonder whether perhaps whatever the problem was, wasn't too serious.

She handed the document over, and I relayed my message.

"I'll leave a bit early today. I don't have any scheduled meetings after 3pm right?"

"No sir, you don't."

"Alright, thank you. I'll leave then."

I thought she would look relieved. Because it meant that she would also be able to leave after I did instead of her usual clock out time of six. However, she looked as though absolutely no difference would be made to her well-being. There was no relief in her eyes, or even a glint of light.

My gaze returned to the dull stain on her shirt, and I sighed. I wanted her to open up to me, but she had solidly shut that door so there was currently nothing else that could be done.

I turned my face away and returned to work.

At three, I grabbed my jacket, picked up my remaining work for the day and left my office. I found her at her desk, but this time around she was a bit more active. She was sorting through some files on her desk and that relieved my concerns to an extent.

"I'm heading out," I told her, and she lifted her gaze.

"Yes sir," she said.

"You can leave too. Get some rest."

"I will," she replied and I went on my way.

I had a late lunch date with someone that I was very happy to see. A gorgeous woman with silver gray hair, cut into a bob that bounced around her shoulders. It was held back with a black suede band, and on her lobes were the same simple diamond studs I had gotten her almost five years prior.

"Mom," I called as I walked into the Japanese restaurant. At the call, she looked up from the novel she was perusing, and her face lit up like the sun.

"Christian," she cried, and immediately rose to her feet.

Her arms came around me and I gripped her tightly, feeling all the tension and pressures from the day just wash away. But as I shut my eyes, there was still a pair of haunted, blue eyes that floated in my mind. I hoped she would be better when I saw her the next day, and she would truly take the time today to get some rest.

ADELE

L ater that evening, I sank further into my chair, and focused solely on breathing. I paid attention to my inhale and exhale, hoping for a clear head, and some relief to the pressure in my chest.

The knot in my stomach however, that seemed to be tangling even more with each second that passed, was a lost cause. But for now I was safe, and until the next morning I would remain so.

I ignored the envelope on my table, and picked up the phone to call for some dinner. My ultimate comfort meal, the golden rice from the deli, topped with lemon marinated chicken, salad and hot sauce, was all I craved and wanted to think about. I made the order, but then I also had to think about what I was going to wear the next day since it was now my in-negotiable fate to remain in the office through the night yet again.

I could get away with it once, but wearing the same outfit three days in a row was going to raise a few eyebrows. And then there was also my personal hygiene to consider. I now comprehended how truly special a bath was, and beyond the meal I was expecting, it was all I could think about. Candles lit all around, the scented and soapy water swirling all around my body and soothing me of my troubles and fears. I didn't have a bathtub in my house, and had never truly considered buying one, but I swore there and then, I was going to get one after this ordeal was over.

But then the knots in my stomach tightened again, as I wondered if it would ever be over. If I would survive this and the person who seemed to have made harassing and possibly harming me their sole mission.

With a heavy sigh, I logged into Zara so that I could search for an outfit that would tide me over till the next day. The trouble however was that the quickest delivery option available was an in person pick up from the store.

But then there was no way in hell I was going to leave the safety of the building, so my heart sank even further. Nevertheless, I kept scanning through the items to keep my mind occupied so my current nightmare wouldn't overwhelm me. Therefore it came as quite the shock when a knock sounded on the door.

It was light, but still resounded sharply across the expansive and quiet space.

I was hopeful it was my order so I jumped to my feet, and headed over to open the door.

The delivery guy from the deli stood before me, and once again I couldn't recall his name. Melinda had told me just the previous day but that now seemed like an entire lifetime ago.

I ushered him in with a smile and hurried over to my desk to get my wallet. It was as I was counting out his fee that I realized he could help me out with the other pickup deliveries that I urgently needed.

I studied his quiet, shy gaze that couldn't quite meet mine and hoped he would be able to help.

"What time does your shift usually end?" I asked.

"At about seven," he responded.

"Oh," I smiled and handed the cash over.

He turned around to leave and although I hesitated, I finally found the guts to ask.

"Could you please help me out? I'm kind of in a bind."

He turned back to face me and nodded, and it made my heart do a little jump.

"Could you please help me pick up some things I ordered? The stores are not too far away from here. I am uh... buried in work and don't think I will be able to get to them before they close for the day."

I expected him to refuse, however he only took a few moments to give this some thought before he finally agreed.

"Thank you," I said, my face full of gratitude. "Can I please have your personal phone number?"

He gave it to me and I quickly saved it.

"Here is a little something for your help," I said, and held out a slightly folded hundred dollar bill. He gazed at it for too long, and it made me panic slightly. Perhaps it was not enough given the trouble? But I couldn't necessarily afford anymore. This was already going to make quite the dent in my budget for the month.

I was about to apologize and offer a higher amount, when the corners of his lips lightly lifted. "Thank you," he said and reached out to take it. It was only then I realized I was hoping he would reject it and ask for a lower amount.

"No, thank you," my voice croaked. "I'll send you the details of the delivery soon."

"Alright," he said, and went on his way.

Afterwards, my world felt a little bit settled. Having some face wash, a change of underwear and new clothes made tomorrow look less tragic. But there was still the matter of my homelessness and the possible threat to my life. After I shut down my computer, I grabbed the envelope from where I had hidden it underneath my desk. I turned the lights off so as not to draw any attention to the office from anyone that was still present on our floor.

I went into Christian's office, and cursed under my breath he didn't have a long enough couch. So I settled into the armchair before the window, and switched on the lamp on the stand beside it. I held the envelope in my hands for quite a while before finding the courage to once again pull the pictures out.

They were of me, being watched like prey. Heading into the office and heading out. And then of me in the grocery store around my home and in the adjoining park eating a popsicle.

This had been taken just a weekend ago after I had returned from Christian's home. I had needed the walk to calm my head and heart so I could get through the coming week. Who would have known that just a short time after, the break up would become the least of my problems.

I sighed as I continued to stare at the images in turn. In them I was oblivious and absent, and most of the time I looked unhappy. Seeing myself in this way, I wondered what whoever had taken them had thought. What was their possible motive behind this? To make me even more miserable than I currently was? I felt exhausted and betrayed despite my humble request of the world for some peace and ease.

This wasn't someone I had inadvertently hurt was it? I mean, I had been more or less stuck in this office for most of the last two years and thus far, nothing eventful had happened until I got the position as Christian's executive secretary. Apart from miss-you-know-who who had outrightly expressed her displeasure at me getting the position, no one else had shown any animosity towards me. But then again, the appointment as Christian's secretary had only come recently and the first batch of pictures sent to me were weeks, if not months old.

There was also the fact that both envelopes hadn't come with addresses, so they had to have been personally delivered.

Suddenly, a light bulb went off in my head. I could check the cameras. There were none in the corridor at my apartment complex, but the office was crawling with them. However, for that to happen I would have to get explicit permission from an executive. That would mean I would also have to explain just exactly why I needed to see the surveillance records.

With a loud groan, I buried my head in my hands and choked back tears.

I couldn't go on like this. My best bet was still to go to the police, but I was scared I would probably either be killed on my way there or thereafter for even entertaining the thought. If this person could get such vivid and up close shots of me in my most private space, then where else couldn't I be reached?

Before I could think myself into the grave any further, my phone began to ring and I saw that it was the delivery guy.

I got up and headed over to the door to retrieve the items, and they were handed over to me in a tote bag.

Relief washed through me, and I thanked him profusely.

"You should rest," he said, and I didn't miss the concern in his gaze.

"I will," I replied and with a nod, he took his leave.

I examined the bag in the office, and found the toiletries, outfits and undergarments to be satisfactory.

So I headed over to the bathroom to clean up as best as I could. I brushed my teeth, washed my face and applied the newly purchased lotion. Afterwards I felt a bit more human, especially with the AC blowing some much needed coolness into the room. I wanted to immediately go to sleep so I unbuttoned my shirt and leaned against the headrest of the chair.

It was however not comfortable enough, so I pushed the coffee table aside, and laid on the soft rug beneath.

I used one of the sofa cushions as a pillow and tried my best to get some sleep. However, it eluded me so I laid on my side and stared at the magnificently lit skyline through the small gap underneath the chair.

I didn't know how I was eventually able to fall asleep but when I awoke, it was as though I had only just shut my eyes for a minute. The office felt eerily darker and I was slightly freezing, but that wasn't what had woken me up.

My brain quickly booted and by the time I realized what was wrong, goosebumps had broken out across my flesh.

I was too scared to move, much less breathe at the realization of the disastrous turn that things had just taken for me.

The lights to the office came on, bright and piercing... and my heart shattered.

CHRISTIAN

I couldn't believe what I was seeing.

I stood at the door, and right on my carpet was a woman. With shiny blonde hair spread messily all around her, and her skirt bunched around her thighs. Her feet were bare, and on the table were items of clothing, toiletries and take-out food.

I thought of how to proceed, and considered just leaving but then I caught her stirring.

Then she froze.

There was now no way that either of us could pretend to be unaware of the other's presence. So it was either we addressed the situation at hand in the privacy of the late evening, or things were going to catapult into a different level of awkwardness when we met the following morning.

It was just a few minutes past ten. I had been on my way home from my extended time with my mother when I had realized I had left the proposal for a project I was scheduled to have a conference call about the very next morning, in the office.

So I stopped by to retrieve it, and was met by this scene.

I turned the light on, and waited.

And I was prepared to keep waiting until she turned around and addressed me.

When a few minutes passed however, and she didn't raise her head, I called out to her.

"Adele."

She buried her face in her arms. "Please leave. I beg you. Just for a minute."

Her voice was little more than a whimper, but every single word clearly drifted over. With a sigh, I turned away and shut the door behind me.

I waited for the minute to be up.

And then another passed by. And then a few more, but there was still no sign of her. My mind considered she could have jumped through the window just to avoid the confrontation with me, but the slight jest wasn't even the least bit amusing.

After a good ten minutes had passed and she was still not out, I headed back to the door and was about to push it open when the handle moved from the opposite side. I stepped backwards, and she appeared.

She stood by it, with her head lowered.

Neither of us spoke, but I was certain it was quite apparent she was the one that burden was placed on, and I couldn't wait to hear why she was asleep in my office, instead of heading home.

She raised her head to mine, a tight and almost unnoticeable smile across her lips.

"I'm sorry sir. This looks quite bad doesn't it?"

I didn't respond. Instead I retreated until I reached her table. Then I leaned against it and folded my arms across my chest, making it very clear I was very ready to listen to her explanation and wouldn't dismiss this otherwise.

Her chest rose, and fell. "I have some... leakage at home. They said it would take a couple of days to fix so I have to find a temporary place to stay. I wasn't going to spend the night here but the time just sort of got away from me, so I decided to just rest for a little bit."

Her explanation wasn't making a lot of sense to me, but I ignored the incoherence of the smaller details and addressed the bigger ones.

"Why didn't you stay at a hotel then?"

"I was going to..." she replied. "That's why I said t-that I kind of fell asleep."

She was such a terrible liar. I cocked my head to gaze at the assortment of items on the coffee table, which alluded more to an intentional stay overnight than a simple accident of falling asleep.

"That's not what it looks like."

Her gaze on me was steady, and so was mine on her. And I wasn't going to back down.

"I'm sorry," she said. "Please let this go. I'll leave right now."

Fury burned in the pit of my stomach. I knew we were technically strangers but for God's sake, I had my face between her legs and my tongue inside her. Didn't that count as a level of familiarity enough for her to reach out for help when she clearly needed it? Why the hell was she so stubborn?

I turned around without saying another word, and stormed out of the office.

Then I waited in my car.

It hadn't been my intention, but for some reason when it came to her, I was starting to realize it wasn't quite so easy to walk away.

I saw her exit the building with her things in hand, and then she went over to her car.

I held the faint suspicion she would sleep in her car, so I paid rapt attention. The lights of the vehicle didn't come on for a long time and it tormented me, as I wondered what exactly was making her so desolate.

Was this all due to her breakup?

Had she shared a house with the guy and now he had kicked her out, thus she had nowhere else to go? This seemed like the only plausible explanation for her current homelessness, and it fueled my anger even further.

I couldn't take it anymore.

It didn't matter if she revealed what the problem was to me or not, but there was no way in hell I was going to let her spend the night in her car.

So I got out of mine, and slammed it shut.

I began to march towards her, however she suddenly started the vehicle and the glow of her headlights filled the parking lot. I froze in my steps and watched as she put the car into gear and drove away.

ADELE

I had never in my life felt more ashamed.

He had looked at me with pity in his eyes, and I had shriveled up inside.

Right then, I had felt so ashamed and embarrassed, and for the second time in the same month that kind of battering to my self-esteem was too much to take.

So I switched on my engine, and drove straight to the downtown police station.

I arrived at the brick building, and took a few deep breaths in my car. I no longer cared about what could happen, but the last thing I was going to allow, was for the bastard that was harassing me to continue to get a kick out of humiliating me. I didn't care if I got hurt or even died in the process.

But I wasn't going to willingly submit, and play the victim.

Furious, and much too close to the edge of tears, I shoved open the door to my old Camry and got out. I headed straight into the building and asked around for the person I needed to speak with to report a crime. Soon enough, I was speaking with an officer in a small interrogation room and he was asking for all the details of the harassment. It couldn't otherwise be classified as blackmail since no requests had been made, and this was what terrified me because it insinuated there were more surprises to come.

The officer duly noted this concern and assured me that an investigation would immediately begin. When it was time however to hand the pictures over, I felt reluctant.

Now faced with the stark reality of what was going on, my earlier bravado began to fizzle out.

I first handed over the most recent and decent ones, before reaching for the more explicit stack. However, my hands wouldn't pull it out.

"You said you received some photographs of you in your house?"

"I did," I swallowed.

"Where are they?"

"Uh... in my car. I forgot them. I'll go get them."

"Alright," he said and continued to file the report. I got up and returned to my car and sat in the dark, dreary silence. I was going to hand them over, but I just needed a moment to work up the guts to allow him to see me in such an indecent state.

I pulled them out of my bag, and once again began to flip through them.

My eyes burned with tears, but I didn't want to crumble into a hysterical fit.

Suddenly, there was a tap against my door and everything flew out of my hands.

I ducked my head underneath the stirring wheel, swearing and praying I could disappear. I was trembling so hard it was as though the car was rattling along with me.

The door was jerked open, and I could no longer hold on to my indignation.

The knot of frustration and fear within me tightened even further, and the tears gushed from my eyes. With my hand over my head, I sobbed uncontrollably, waiting for the impending strike or worse, a bullet through my head.

However...

Nothing came.

"Please... please..." I pleaded. "Don't hurt me. I'm sorry. Please."

"Adele."

I heard the call, but I couldn't respond till an arm touched mine. With all the trembling, it took a while for the contact to register, and then even longer to realize I still felt no pain. A flow of calm began to return to me as I realized I wasn't hurt. So perhaps it was the officer instead that had come to get me? But that made no sense.

I cracked one teary eye open, and then slowly lifted my head.

Set against the backdrop of the bleak, starless sky, was the last person I wanted to see. But then as I stared at him, I began to realize in this moment, he was also the only person I wanted to see.

The concern on his face shook me to my core, as what seemed just like the pools in my own eyes gathered in his.

"What's wrong?" he finally croaked out, his voice barely audible "What's happening? Why are you like this?"

His voice was beyond soft and calming and it made me feel like I had dunked my head in water... submerged just enough to escape all the ghosts and terrors, and able to exist in another space even if it was for just a tiny moment.

I scrambled out of the space with a frantic desperation, banging my head and twisting my frame but I didn't care. With my arms stretched out, and a fresh bout of tears running down my cheeks, I clung to him for dear life.

I held him so hard I knew it would hurt, but he didn't seem to care. His arms came around my waist and he hugged me back, encompassing me and accepting me into the safety that he was.

I would never know how long we remained in that position, with his scent of vanilla and coffee surrounding me. I focused on breathing. Slowly and steadily. In and out.

The knot in the pit of my stomach began to unravel, and it gave me the hope that maybe, just maybe things would be okay.

When the true fear appeared that I was crushing him, I started to pull away but realized he was hugging me so hard my feet had almost left the ground.

I didn't want to escape any more, but this time around I returned my feet to the ground with the knowledge he was still supporting my frame, and my hand was still held tightly in his hand. I refused to let go, and he did the same.

CHRISTIAN

W e were seated in my car, the windows rolled up and the doors solidly shut to all outside noise.

Nothing but our quiet breathing, and the cool waft of the conditioned air filled the space.

In my hands were the pictures, and as I went through each of them, a bitterness and fury that I had never felt before rippled through my body. But I remained calm, more for the sake of the girl that was sitting next to me than for anything else.

Afterwards, I slipped the pictures back into the envelope and took a deep breath.

"Who's the officer in charge of taking your statement?" I asked.

She thought about this for a little bit and then spoke softly. "Brady. Or Branson. I was too nervous to pay attention."

"I'll find him," I told her and pushed the door to get out of the car.

However, her hand settled on mine and I stilled.

"I didn't... I don't want him to see me that way," she muttered.

"It's alright," I assured her. "I'll cover it all up with markers or something before handing it over."

She let me go then, but her eyes were still filled with worry.

"Do you want to come with me?" I asked.

She shook her head, as she looked nervously around. "I'll be fine."

That wasn't enough to assure me so I pulled my phone out and called her. She jumped at the sudden ring, and after realizing I was the one calling, turned to me with surprise in her gaze. "Pick up," I told her. "And stay on the line. You can listen in and if you get nervous out here you can alert me immediately."

She nodded so I squeezed her arm reassuringly, and got out of the car.

In the station, I found the officer in charge and discussed the investigation with him. Then after making sure the photographs were decent enough, I handed them over.

"Where is Miss Walters right now?" he asked.

"She's waiting in my car," I replied. "And from now on, until things are resolved, she will be staying with me so you can always contact me whenever you can't get ahold of her."

"And you are?" he asked.

"A close friend," I replied, but that seemed too light for me. "Family," I added, and thereafter took my leave.

Back in the car, I slipped my key into the ignition, and started the engine. And in no time we were on our way.

"You're too quiet," she eventually whispered.

"I'm taking you to my apartment," I said, and through my peripheral vision saw her snap her head towards me. I waited for what she would say, for her to refuse but nothing came.

"The police will immediately start the investigation. I'll go to a hotel soon so I won't inconvenience you for too long."

My plan had been to ignore her statement, but eventually I couldn't stop myself from commenting on it. "If you would feel safe in a hotel then why didn't you go to one all along?"

She went silent, and so did I.

The first thing I did when we arrived was to register her for a key. I notified the concierge at the front desk, and after procuring her details, he assured us of its delivery the following morning.

"Take the day off tomorrow," I told her as we got into the elevator.

She sighed, and tried to lean into me but then stopped herself. I caught the move and slipped my arm around her.

She glanced up at me, and even though I was staring straight ahead, my jaw clenched in a chilling anger at the discoveries of the night.

She leaned her head against my shoulder. "I can't," she replied. "You have back to back meetings between nine and lunch time.

"I'll get a temp from the pool."

"No," she said. "They'll start to entertain ideas about stealing my job and I'm already in hot water with my boss for catching me asleep on his carpet. I haven't made that great of an impression so far."

I understood she was trying to lighten the mood, but when I considered her words, it upset me even further.

"Is that why you kept this from me?" I asked, and turned to her. She lifted her head off my shoulder to stare into my eyes, and just then we arrived on my floor.

The elevator door dinged open and I broke the contact. Staring any longer into those ocean blue pools of hurt and despair was sure to break my heart.

I walked ahead, but waited for her after opening the door to my apartment. Then I slammed it shut and secured it with the bolt. It wasn't needed though because given the sturdiness of the door, only a small bomb would be able to break it open.

I then led the way up the stairs, and she came with me.

"There are three bedrooms," I told her. "Mine is at the end of the corridor, to the right. Do you want us to go through the remaining two so that you can get a feel for the one you'll feel more comfortable in?"

"The beige one," she replied in a small voice. "The b-beige one that I stayed in last time."

I nodded in agreement, and led her to it.

Inside, the beddings were crisp, the room scented, and the lighting warm.

"There's a bathtub," I told her. "Take a long bath and then come downstairs for some dinner.

"I've already had dinner," she said.

"Well, maybe come down for a snack? I want to see you before you go to bed."

Despite vicious heat in my chest at my anger, those words softened something inside me, and perhaps even struck a chord of panic because it was no longer quite so easy to breathe.

I unbuttoned a button at the top of my shirt, and left her to settle in. It was as I was midway down the stairs I realized I hadn't brought her anything to change into, so I returned to my own room to pull out a T-shirt and a pair of cotton pajama pants that I usually wore to bed.

I hoped that she wouldn't mind these as I placed them on her bed, her curtains billowing in the light wind from the balcony beyond. I glanced towards her bathroom door, knowing that she was in there trying to stabilize her life and emotions. I wished I could do more to help her.... for as long as it would take. However, I was still currently shut out, and although it was quite easy to bemoan the barrier, I reasoned that just a little while earlier she had refused to share anything of what was going on with me.

"Little steps," I consoled myself and headed back to the kitchen.

ADELE

J ust a little while earlier, I had been dreaming of a bath.
Of how its warmth and scent would wash away my
worries and the strain in my bones.

And now, I was in one and I was happy.

The massive crystal rock tub was filled to the brim with
warm water, lavender oil, and Epsom Salts and it was the
perfect treatment. I would have gladly stayed longer but it
was already incredibly late, and I had agreed with Christian
that I would come down to see him after I was done.

He had an early and hectic day tomorrow, and needed all the
hours of sleep he could get.

So regretfully, I left the tub and its soothing magic.

When I got to the bedroom, a towel around me and another
drying my hair, I saw the change of clothes he had laid out
for me.

My gaze was steady on the neatly folded stack, as something
warm buzzed through my veins. None of the clothes I noted

appeared new. I tossed the towel aside to pick them up, and when I brought the materials to my nose, I sniffed in his familiar scent of vanilla and coffee.

I was soothed, and touched.

He was by many measures, still a stranger to me, but time and again, he had extended his warmth and assistance, and twice saved me from losing my mind. I didn't know how I was ever going to repay him.

I put the clothes on and although the pants were way too long, the elastic waistband was able to fit snugly around mine given my curves. The shirt however was so broad that my frame disappeared in it, and only the slight swell of my breasts gave a hint as to my body underneath.

It was comfortable, so after carefully folding up the striped, navy blue pants till they weren't dragging on the floor, I exited the room and headed down to the kitchen. There, I watched him seated at the counter with his iPad in front of him. He was gently scrolling through the file that he was reading on it while sipping from a cup of something steamy.

I stood for a few moments to take in the warmth of the space, and his presence within it.

It was indeed beautifully decorated, and spoke of a wealth and elegance that I had only been able to admire from Pinterest boards.

He also seemed to belong here. With his elegant perch on the stool and his dark beautiful hair somehow still arranged in pristine and orderly waves.

He too had changed or perhaps he had just taken off the dress shirt to reveal the white shirt he now had on, which had probably been underneath.

As for pants, he still had on the gray slacks he'd worn during the day.

Although there was no need to, I couldn't help but feel slightly intimidated by his powerful presence, especially given my currently raw and vulnerable state and the fact I had now become the charitable beneficiary of a man I had so boldly drawn a boundary with before.

He seemed to sense my presence then because he stirred, and turned around to gaze at me.

The set of molten brown eyes arrested me on the spot, and I couldn't take a single step forward.

Not till he invited me over.

"I made us some chamomile tea," he said. "It'll relax you and help you sleep."

I nodded because it felt like if I spoke my voice would be too small. I went over to sit about two stools away from his, as he rose to prepare a cup for me. He soon returned with it and after a heartfelt thank you, I lifted the mug to my lips. Its design was very intricate. It was a soft off white, with interesting carvings of flowers and vines etched into its sides. I couldn't help asking him about it.

"My mother hired an interior designer just before I moved in. All I gave was the color scheme hence why the house is more dark and warm, than bright and purple. Purple is my mother's favorite color."

"Ah," I replied with a smile. "She did a great job then. This cup is extremely beautiful."

"I can ask about its origins for you if you would like?"

"I'd appreciate that," I replied and he nodded in agreement.

I kept sipping, aware he was watching me. I didn't want to complain about it after all he had done for me, so I endured the gaze and tried my best to hide my nervousness.

"Did the bath do you any good?" he asked.

"It did," I replied, relieved. "Thank you. So much."

"No need," he said and returned back to what he had been reading. I stole a glance at it and immediately recognized the heading. OASIS International. It was one of the companies he had a meeting scheduled with for the following day.

More than ever, I felt more like a burden than a secretary. I was meant to be making his life easier, but it seemed instead I was just complicating it.

"I need to go back to the station," I told him. "To get my car. I need it tomorrow to get to work and I have some clothes in there as well."

He turned to me, his gaze somewhat stern "I told you not to come in."

"I need to," I pleaded with him. My gaze held his, and I hoped he would see the words that I didn't want to explicitly voice out.

"Please. If not I'll just wallow around and feel worse about myself."

"Why would you feel worse, or even bad at all? None of this is your fault."

I shrugged, and once again raised the cup to my lips. We both knew it was more an excuse to look away from him than anything else.

"Who do you suspect?" he asked, and although I did have someone in mind, I didn't want to voice the suspicion.

"I have no clue."

It took a little while before he spoke again. "Your ex." he said. "Was he bitter? Is he capable of something like this?"

"I don't know," I sighed, which made me feel even more ashamed that he was the man I was going to allow myself to marry. I must have been out of my mind.

"But why would he though? Our breakup wasn't the smoothest, but we didn't part with that much antagonism either. So why would he be harassing me now? And... h-he was the one that wanted to end things with me, so it's not as though I broke his heart and became the motive for him to take this sort of revenge against me. And from the pictures, I can tell this whole surveillance nightmare dates back to about five months ago. We didn't have any problems then and were quite amicable, so why would he do this?"

I turned to Christian, and realized my response had been quite rapid and lengthy.

"I'm sorry-sir," I apologized.

"Don't call me sir," he said, and before any of us could dwell on the topic he moved on.

"Who else do you have in mind?" he asked, but I couldn't very well tell him all of the employees in his company were under my suspicion. So I finished my drink and again, shrugged my shoulders.

"I'll get to the bottom of this," he assured me. "But in the meantime, please make yourself at home here."

"I will," I replied softly, eager for anything to say that would express my deepest and sincerest gratitude to him. "Thank you."

"I'll get Gary to retrieve your car from the station first thing in the morning. He's usually at work by seven so it might take a little while for him to get everything sorted. This means you will be about an hour or two late to work. I'm sure your boss can manage at least that, and I'm hoping you can too."

For the first time in days, a little smile curled across my lips.

"I can." I replied and once again lowered my head.

CHRISTIAN

The next day, I watched Adele's eyelids grow heavy in the middle of our meeting with OASIS International.

We were on the operations floor, and seated amongst five other attendees in one of the conference rooms. She was all the way at the end of the table along with the CFO's secretary as they both took notes of the important meeting. I however couldn't keep my eyes off her.

She struggled and fought her way through it, and my heart ached.

I had hoped she would be able to get some sleep after her bath and with the safety my home provided, but it seemed that wasn't the case.

So when I couldn't take it anymore and noticed she was about to fall off her chair, I rose to my feet.

That immediately brought everyone's attention towards me, and also startled her awake.

"I have an emergency to handle," I quickly announced. "Let's conclude here and pick this up on Friday. My apologies."

I was allowed my exit and called out to her to come with me. She did, and soon we were riding the elevator together on our return back to our office.

"I'm sorry," she apologized in a frail voice, and it tore at my heart to hear her that way.

"You weren't able to sleep last night?"

"I tried to," she replied.

"I told you to take the day off."

I tried to keep the frustration out of my tone, but it no doubt still came clearly across.

"I'll go running today," she said. "It might help wit-"

She stopped mid sentence. I turned to her to see the realization of something that had made her pause.

"What's wrong?" I asked just as we arrived back on our floor.

"I can't go out," she said. "It's too dangerous."

"There's a private gym at the apartment," I told her. "It's on the ground floor, on the same corridor with the bathroom. There's a treadmill there you could use. You can also go for a swim."

She was silent till we reached her desk, but then she croaked out her gratitude once again before I disappeared into my office.

"Thank you," she said and I nodded in acknowledgement. "No need."

I shut the door behind me and checked the time. It was nearing the end of the work day in a couple of hours, so I used that as some motivation to keep me glued to my seat.

I couldn't however resist calling the cops for an update, and the report was the same as earlier. "They would be performing an immediate sweep of her apartment the next day to uncover all of the bugs."

I ended the call and decided not to wait. I was too riled up, too much steam swirling through me and I needed a release. So I rose to my feet.

"I'll be back," I told Adele and left the office.

About twenty five minutes later, I arrived at the building in Crenshaw.

There was the very plausible possibility he would not be around so my intention was to thereafter trace him down to his workplace as some store's manager. Either way, I was not going to let him go scot free without knowing what my fist felt like.

I headed up to the second floor apartment and banged on the door.

There was no response, but when I listened closer, I realized I could hear the faint rhythm of music from inside the apartment.

So I pounded on the door again, this time even more loudly and angrily. It was a wooden door, far from sturdy, so I gave him another minute to respond before I kicked the door down.

The minute passed and I reached the end of my rope.

I took several steps backwards, but just as I was about to swing my leg, I heard his answering shout from within.

"What?!" he roared and pulled it open.

The music appeared with him, grating and irritating, just as he was. He was bare chested, with a pair of shorts that he seemed to have hurriedly put on but didn't even bother to button or zip up properly. I was even more disgusted. My eyes traced up his torso, to the patches of hair across his chest, and then to his massive head.

His bulging eyes had previously flared with annoyance, but when he properly regarded me and the way I was dressed, his gaze became a bit more courteous, no doubt wondering who I was.

I didn't know where to start. All the anger that had been simmering within me from the previous night gathered into a massive ball in the pit of my stomach that threatened to destroy me from the inside.

I took a deep breath to calm myself, bringing my position to mind and the reminder of the possibly disastrous financial and legal consequences that would ensue if I did give in to the gnawing need to break his neck right then. So I took a step backwards, the only precaution I could manage and got straight to the point.

"Are you harassing Adele?"

It took a second for the question to dawn on him, and when it did his eyes slightly widened.

"Adele?" he looked perplexed, his brows furrowing deeply. "Why the hell would I harass her?"

He seemed genuinely shocked by the accusation, which led me to suspect perhaps he wasn't the one behind this. Plus if he was, it would be extremely foolish as he of course would be the very first suspect. But then again, he had clearly broken up with Adele, somehow managing to convince himself he would be better off without her so I couldn't attest to the proper functioning of his brain either.

Just then, there was a call for him from within the apartment, past the piles of clothes and trash on the floor. He turned around just as the woman appeared without a bra and in a red thong.

"I have a fucking guest," he complained, and she gave him a little pout as she pushed her messy bangs out of her face. She perused me, her eyes widening with appreciation, and her lips parting with perhaps... awe?

"Gloria!" he yelled, and she sent him a frown.

Before turning around to leave however, she winked at me, her smile extremely suggestive. I watched her as she then took her leave, barely seeing her but willing to look at anything but the bastard before me.

She soon went out of sight and my gaze was forced to return to him.

He was now agitated, his hand restlessly tousling his hair. I decided then I was done with them both.

"Y-you said she's being harassed. By who? How? And why? What did she do?"

He seemed to genuinely care, and it made me hate him even more.

"It's none of your business," I told him, and turned around.

"Hey!" he caught my arm, and I didn't think twice.

My fist swung into the air and connected solidly with the side of his face. He flew back and crashed to the floor, as though he weighed nothing more than a chair. I stared at his crumpled frame down at the floor as the curses sputtered from his lips.

He had been the one to touch me first. That, I would remember when the suit came.

Bile rose up to my throat at the thought of who he had been to Adele.

"Stay away from her," I warned through gritted teeth, and went on my way.

ADELE

I made it a point to leave before Christian.

For one, I was still reeling with embarrassment at how he had to cut his meeting short earlier just so I could be saved from dozing and falling off my chair.

The very memory of the incident once again knocked the breath out of me. I stopped just as I got to the door of his apartment, and inhaled deeply. I tried my best to imagine the smoky, dark form of the negative emotions of shame that were currently plaguing me, and purposefully drove them out with my subsequent exhale.

They could return the next day for all I cared but tonight, my only goal was getting a good night's sleep. I arrived at his door and as I punched in the key code, wondered about the late working session he was currently having in the office. He had returned from his earlier outing, and without a word marched straight into his office.

Needless to say, my head had lowered even further.

With a sigh, I pushed the door open, and saw the chandelier hanging from the ceiling and into the foyer was shining brightly.

I slightly panicked, wondering if I had forgotten to turn it off upon my departure in the morning since I had left after him.

Or perhaps it was his cleaning lady, Anne.

I turned it off and went in, once again taken aback by just how massive the space was. It was then the scent tickled my nostrils.

It was enticing, and it was food.

Someone was cooking.

I was startled, knowing it definitely couldn't be him since I had left him in the office. So I headed towards the kitchen and suddenly two people jumped out.

"Surprise!" they sang, and my heart nearly jumped out through my throat.

"Oh my God!" I gasped and jumped away, my tone on the verge of a scream. I had retreated as far back as the door before I was able to recover enough to understand what was going on.

Two women stood before me. Or I guess a mature woman and a young girl. One's hair was a shiny silver, while the other was a vivid pink and they were both wearing matching aprons of hemp cloth and white stripes.

They both watched me, surprised, and I did the same until the younger one finally spoke.

"I'm sorry," she said. "We wanted to surprise Christian."

The older woman was less defensive, and instead took offense at my intrusion. "Who are you?" she asked.

I realized then, that although I didn't necessarily know who these women were, they had to be somewhat related to Christian to be able to so easily access his home.

That realization made me nervous so I moved my gaze from them to think up a quick response.

A light bulb soon came on over my head so I straightened my posture. "I'm Adele Walters," I quickly introduced myself. "I'm Mr. Hall's secretary."

"Oh," the younger girl said, her face now beaming with excitement. "Adele. It's very nice to meet you. I'm Stacy, Christian's cousin and this is his mom, Theresa."

It was just as I had suspected. "It's very nice to meet you both," I said, my eyes on Stacy rather than Christian's mother so as to avoid the daggers it felt like her eyes were shooting at me.

"It's very nice to meet you," Stacy said. "I've heard great things about you from Christian."

I started at the comment, and was about to ask about it when his mother spoke again.

"What are you doing here?"

Her tone was crisp and curt, and it was very clear she was far from pleased. "Uh, Mr. Hall told me to bring some files to him," I replied, and her gaze moved down to my empty hands.

"They're in my car," I quickly responded, digging myself into a bigger hole.

She cocked a perfectly groomed eyebrow at me.

"Why are they in your car when you're here to hand them over?" she asked and I was stumped. Stacy however grabbed onto her hand and dragged her along.

"Aunt Theresa," she groaned, and I almost collapsed in relief. After they disappeared, I turned around and immediately headed for the door, resolved to flee.

I was however stopped the moment my hand landed on the door's latch.

"Adele?" a soft voice floated over to me.

I turned around and saw the disappointed look on Stacy's face.

"You're leaving already?"

"Uh, I was about to-"

"You can't leave," she said, and came forward to hook her arm around my elbow. "We just made chili con carne and it's Christian's favorite. Aunt Theresa's recipe is the best in the world so you have to stay for a bit to at least get a taste.

"I'm alright," I started to say but with every passing second, I was pulled farther and farther away from the door. When we arrived in the kitchen, she plopped me onto one of the stools and then headed over to join her aunt at the stove.

"Where is Christian?" his mother suddenly asked.

"Back at the office ma'am," I responded, and she seemed even less impressed with me. I decided then to just head out and find somewhere else to stay because this was the last thing I truly wanted to deal with tonight.

So I rose to my feet, "My apologies but I have to leave now. I'll give Mr. Hall a call to explain things to him. It was a pleasure meeting you both."

My resolve was solid so even when his cousin tried to call me back again, I shook my head and began to head back to the foyer. Thankfully, she remained across the room, a cute pout showing her displeasure but didn't come after me.

I was glad to have escaped, and decided I'd just head over to Melinda's house.

Just as I pulled on the handle however, the door opened from the front, almost knocking me over.

There was somebody on the other side so I stepped back, and lo and behold, Christian appeared.

He looked exhausted.

His hair was lightly tousled, his suit jacket draped across his arm, and the collar and sleeves of his light blue dress shirt, unbuttoned and rolled up his arms respectively.

His searing, brown eyes bored sharply into mine.

"Where are you going?" he asked.

In response, I turned to glance behind me and he raised his head to do the same.

His brows furrowed at the soft voices and the waft from the spicy beef stew, while I on the other hand just stared up at his strikingly handsome face. The warm light of the foyer seemed to set his skin ablaze, and for a few moments, I found it impossible to look away from the exposed olive flesh between his unbuttoned shirt and his strong neck. His

Adam's apple bobbed, making my mouth water till I yearned for the chance to softly kiss the small bulge.

I realized what I really needed, and it wasn't sleep. At least it wasn't only sleep.

All of this stress and anxiety plaguing me over the last several days had bottled up into a ball of frustration that sleep just didn't have the power to dissolve. I needed to be fucked, hard and senseless by him, to ride his cock until it knocked me out of my senses.

Feeling the blush spread across my cheeks, I lowered my gaze from his but then he returned his attention to me.

"Is this why you're leaving?"

I didn't know how to respond to that.

My lips parted but no words came out, but when he grabbed my hand, I sputtered out a response. "I w-want to give you the space to be- Christian."

I gently pulled my hand from his grasp, and he turned a dark gaze to me. It made me go still.

"Come with me. Let's have dinner together."

"They'll ask about why I'm here," I pleaded for his understanding.

"I'll handle it," he said, and I felt my resistance begin to melt. There was something in his gaze that was sure and strong, and I wanted wholeheartedly to lean on it. I didn't want to head out once again on my own, and be forced to wander aimlessly looking for a place to stay. So I nodded and went with him.

"Christian," Stacy beamed the moment she saw him, and then her eyes became even brighter when she saw me by his side.

"Adele, you came back!"

I sent a tight lipped smile to her, and took a seat on one of the stools all the while avoiding his mother's gaze.

"Adele has some personal issues to work out so she'll be staying here for a few days," he said and my head shot up at the announcement. It had been so sudden but in a way, it worked. I watched as he went over to his mother, and pulled her surprised self into his arms for a hug, and it seemed to instantly make her forget about whatever questions, or dare I say complaints that she wanted to make.

"What's for dinner?" he asked, and just like that the attention was off me.

Stacy had momentarily disappeared so I was left alone to watch as he chatted lightly with his mother, and then began to assist her in bringing the stew and rice over to the island. I started to rise to help but he waved his hand and told me to rest instead. His mother glanced at me and although her scrutiny still felt uncomfortable, her expression now was more of curiosity than hostility.

Stacy soon returned, bounding down the stairs. "Christian, do you have any red wine?" she asked with a sheepish smile, and he gave her a peculiar look.

"There's some on the counter right there."

"They're too dry," she said. "Do you have something sweet?"

At his delay, she exploded. "Oh for Pete's sake! I'm not a kid anymore, and I've literally been drinking since I was sixtee-"

The room went quiet, and even I turned to face her.

"I mean-"

She tried to correct the blunder, and I couldn't help my smile.

Suddenly she came over, and hid behind my back.

"I'm telling your mom," Theresa said, and Stacy shook me softly.

"Adele help me," she cried, but I too was at a loss of what to do. Christian, amused at the both of us, shook his head and started to walk out of the kitchen.

"I'll get you something sweet," he said and just like that I was released. She jumped after him and I nearly panicked when I realized I would be left alone with his mother.

They disappeared into a storage room around the corner and the kitchen was left in an eerie silence.

"I'm sorry about my cold reception earlier," his mother suddenly apologized, and my head snapped up. She was taking her seat on the stool across from me, and had a smile on her face.

"No, it's all right," I said. "It wasn't cold."

"Yes it was," she said. "And you my dear, are a terrible liar."

"I'm sorry about that," my gaze lowered, and she laughed softly.

"It's alright. You were startled, and I was defensive. I've been alive for a long time so I have seen one too many secretaries intrude into the lives of my friends and family.

"Oh," I said, unaware of how to respond to that. She went on.

"Christian though seems to truly not mind you being here, so I also have no qualms about it."

I took my hands off the table, and couldn't help wringing them anxiously on my lap, a polite smile across my face.

"And don't worry, I won't pry any further. He would be angry if I did and it would also be disrespectful to you. Have you had chili con carne before?"

"Yes, I have," I replied.

"Well, Stacy wasn't exaggerating if I do say so myself. So you're about to be blown away because my recipe tops everything else that you might have had in the past. My entire family has been raging about this stew for as long as I can remember."

I smiled in response, now much more relaxed and even amused at her boastful confidence in her stew.

"Here," she picked up a spoon and scooped up some of the spicy stew. "Have a taste."

It all happened too fast for me to refuse, so I accepted the spoon from her and slid the tip into my mouth for a small taste.

My mind was more focused on what compliment I was going to give her afterwards, so it was totally unexpected, when the taste of the stew stunned the processing thoughts out of my head.

The combined flavors of her seasoning, the meat and beans together, formed a creamy, deliciously savory explosion in my mouth that shocked me.

I looked down at the spoon in wonder, my eyes slightly widened and she burst out in delighted laughter.

"This is amazing," I said.

"Right?" she replied and I slid the entire spoon into my mouth.

Just then, Christian and Stacy returned.

"What happened?" Stacy asked.

"She tried my stew," Theresa replied, and Stacy beamed.

"It's amazing right," she said.

I nodded. "It really is."

My gaze went to Christian's and even though he still looked exhausted, the shimmer in his eyes flooded my chest with a burning heat. They both came towards me, with Christian taking his seat by my side, while Stacy showed me the bottle of wine she had retrieved.

"Adele, have you had this before? Do you prefer sweet or dry wine?"

I could barely read the cursive script so I just shook my head. "No I haven't, and I enjoy them both. Although because of how spicy the stew is I think the sweet wine would be better."

"Exactly," she grinned and set the bottle on the table. Then she went to Christian, curved her hand around his neck and planted a kiss on his cheek.

I felt envy, at the ease in which she could do such a loving and carefree act.

She then went over to sit by her aunt and we began to eat.

"Do you know how to cook?" Theresa asked.

I nodded in response. "Just a little, the basics. Some rice, eggs, but nothing like this."

"I can teach you," she said and my heart warmed even further. "I'd love that. Thank you Theresa."

"You're welcome," she said and returned her gaze to her son.

"So how's work going Christian?"

"You're not going to offer to teach me how to make this?" he asked, and she gave him a fond, but rebuking look.

"I have offered, and even downright insisted on it several times in the past but you never took me seriously. Now you're interested?"

He shrugged, his grin boyish. "I guess I just needed the right motivation."

At these words, his gaze didn't turn to me but that of the other two women did and needless to say I avoided them all.

Thankfully, Christian proceeded to answer her question about work and began to give a surface report about his progress with settling into the company. I listened quietly, well aware of all of the details.

She didn't pry any further than what he had told her, and it made me wonder about their relationship. They didn't seem exactly close and affectionate, but there was a mutual respect and fondness between them that was just endearing enough.

It brought to mind my own mother and her constant and unrelenting intrusiveness. It was endearing too but with the blatant judgment that would most of the time follow, it had eventually served to drive me further away from her rather than closer.

We continued the rest of the dinner with light conversation and I listened through most of it. Christian did the same, and soon his mother announced her intention to leave.

"These two need to rest," she told Stacy, and rose to her feet.

"Can I at least swim for a little bit," Stacy pouted and Christian nodded.

"You can sweetheart."

"Mom, let's share a drink in the living room before you leave."

"Alright," she said and turned to me. I responded before she could ask.

"I need to rest," I said with a small laugh. "I'm incredibly exhausted so I'll just head upstairs for some sleep."

This earned Christian a scolding look. "Is this your fault?"

"Partly," he answered, with a fond but concerned look at me.

"It's not, Theresa," I countered and rose to take my plate over to the sink.

I helped in rinsing off the dirty dishes and loading the dishwasher, and soon I was back in my room. I collapsed on the bed at the smooth conclusion to the evening that could otherwise have been very stressful for me.

Without wanting to think any further, I forced myself to rise so I could prepare for bed.

I washed my makeup from the day off in the bathroom, brushed my teeth and changed into a silk nightie. It was decent enough, stopping in the middle of my thighs while the chest area was covered in lace that exposed the creamy swell of my breasts. I thought of taking a shower but I already felt somewhat drowsy from the wine and didn't want to exert myself any further than was needed so my brain could shut down easily and allow me to sleep.

I then crawled underneath the covers and pulled the comforter over my head.

CHRISTIAN

I stood outside of her door, wondering if she had been able to catch some sleep. My family had spent a bit more time than I had anticipated, but in order not to let my mom feel any suspicion, I had not bothered in rushing them to leave.

Stacy had enjoyed her swim in the lit pool, while I had chatted lightly with my mother about her treatments over a second bottle of wine, as we watched Stacy through the massive balcony doors.

And then she asked the question I knew she had been itching to all evening.

"Are you interested in her?"

I thought of what answer to give, and when I couldn't make up my mind, resorted to my tried and true response.

"I'm still thinking about it. I'll get back to you after I've made up my mind."

She had nearly growled at me for the somewhat predictable response. After all it was the same one I had given in response to her constant cajoling over the years to consider moving to LA.

Now, as I stood before Adele's door, I was glad it had taken me as long as it did to make the move.

Otherwise, perhaps I would never have met her, and there was currently a part of me that couldn't even bear to entertain that thought. And seemingly at the right time because perhaps any sooner or later and I wouldn't have met her.

I had subtly watched her tonight, quiet and graceful by my side and it had severely impressed me. No one would have been able to tell she was currently being psychologically tormented by some stalker. This brought the reminder once again that the bastard was still loose and was probably not her ex, and it pulled me back to my previously sour mood.

I listened a bit more for any sign of restless movements in her room, and when I didn't hear any, retired to mine. I took a quick shower, needing the soothing warmth to console me after a hard day of putting out fires from seemingly every angle. Then afterwards, I slipped on just a pair of cotton pajama pants, and slid into bed.

I was asleep in seconds.

However, it was only a short while later before my eyes came open again.

I stared at the shadows on the ceiling, only dimly lit by the external lights of the city's skyline coming from beyond my massive windows.

I remained still, wondering what had woken me up and realized it was movement.

I thought of Adele, and got up.

Before walking out of my room to check on her I hesitated, wondering if perhaps I wouldn't be intruding. But then again, I considered she might need my help in finding something but would most definitely be too polite to wake me up.

So I walked out of the room barefooted, and sure enough found the door to her room slightly ajar. A peek inside revealed an empty bed with a slightly disarrayed blanket, and her phone's charging light blinking upon it.

I went past the door, and began to head down the stairs.

I heard her in the kitchen, trying her best to move around as quietly as she could. Eventually I arrived, and it didn't take long to figure out what she was doing.

The water in the electric kettle was bubbling softly in the corner, and on the counter was a mug and spoon. She on the other hand was in a short, pale pink gown which given her struggle to reach the cupboard above, was now riding quite high up her thighs.

The immediate kick to my libido was painful, and I shook my head at the now predictable assault.

Only the warm, overhead light from the range hood was switched on, as she no doubt hadn't wanted to call any attention to her presence.

She eventually retrieved the jar of tea that she was reaching for, and not wanting to startle her into shattering it, I waited until she had settled back on her heels before making my presence known.

"Can I get a cup too?" I asked just as she set the jar down.

She spun around, with a low gasp that sounded across the extremely quiet space.

"Christian," she called in surprise, and I took a seat on one of the stools to watch her.

"You wanted something to drink?" I asked.

"No just... some tea." she said. "You mentioned that chamomile could help me sleep."

"You can't sleep?" I asked and she shook her head. "I keep waking up."

A momentary silence passed between us.

"I'll make you a cup then," she said and went over to retrieve the electric kettle. "I hope I didn't wake you up."

"You didn't," I said automatically, more occupied in listening to the soft tone she was trying to speak in given the time of night. She was usually quite mellow in her tone at the office, but right now it was more sultry and breathy as she tried to maintain an audible whisper.

The intimate tone sent awareness prickling through my skin as I had heard it before. She had called my name with it several times when we had fucked. And back then, she had been barely coherent and completely out of breath. As I watched her now, I wondered if I would ever get the chance to be that intimate with her again.

She glanced back at me as she set the mug down. "I'm sure I did, and I'm sorry. I'm just a bit desperate. The last thing I need tomorrow is to be falling out of a chair during a meeting."

I smiled at the reminder, and of course she watched me to see what my reaction would be. Her eyelids once again lowered in embarrassment.

"I'm so sorry about earlier today, and thank you for saving me. I would have been the talk of the whole company especially as no one thinks I even merited the position in the first place."

I could see now why it would be quite the feat for her to fall asleep. She had so much going on in that brain of hers.

"Relax," I told her. "Just let go of expectations and of what anyone else might be thinking and saying. Just relax. You're already going through enough."

She nodded in response, and then directed all her attention to carefully making the tea. When she was done, she brought the two mugs over and placed one in front of me.

We both drank our tea in silence, but from time to time, my gaze fleeted over to watch her and it was almost impossible not to notice the enticingly exposed swell of her breasts through the lace of the material.

She on the other hand kept her gaze to her cup, trying her best to finish it as quickly as she could so she could no doubt escape. I didn't feel the need to fill the silence with further conversation, so I just simply enjoyed her presence.

The awareness however that the one woman I desired in the world right now was currently in such an intimate setting with me, scantily dressed, and with the golden glow of the hood's light reflecting off her skin, but yet there was very little I could do about any of that. It was pure torture.

"Do you need any additional information for your meeting with CGV tomorrow?" she asked.

My response was automatic. "I don't want to talk about work."

Truly, I couldn't even stand the thought because at that moment all the blood in my brain had rushed straight down to my groin.

I got up from the stool, not caring that I was possibly very visibly hard, and headed over to the sink to rinse my cup.

The plan was to immediately head back to my room for my second cold shower of the night in order to chase the release I most definitely needed to return me to my normal, unruffled state.

Otherwise I would be unable to sleep, and I didn't particularly fancy the idea of nursing a hard on for the remaining part of the night.

"Goodnight," I told her as I walked away. "Don't hesitate to call me if you need anything."

"Thank you," her soft response followed. "Goodnight."

ADELE

I watched him walk away, and couldn't quite look away from his broad shoulders and taut ass.

I sighed, exhaling a shuddering release as I thought unashamedly of the one thing that I needed right now.

This realization had been established earlier and it wasn't this damned tea. I looked at the golden liquid with disdain, and rose to my feet. I needed my hands digging into the flesh of his ass, and my legs wrapped around him as he pounded, preferably mercilessly into me. His cock was what I needed, in my mouth and in my cunt, and at this point in the other available hole between my ass cheeks. My entire body was burning up with anxiety and frustration, and I was sure that before this very long night was over I was going to somehow explode. Now it was whether it happened with a scream and a burst of tears, or with a scream and a burst of his cum shooting into me.

The former option was particularly unpleasant and the latter, a bit of a stretch to attain so I returned to my room and focused on the third and least extreme amongst the earlier two. I laid flat on my bed, peeled my thong from my legs, and raised my knees.

I shut my eyes and with the pad of my middle finger began to stroke the already swollen bud of my sex. I was already thoroughly soaked, my cunt pulsing and hungry for the one thing that it craved, to be coaxed and drilled into an ethereal release.

I knew whatever I would be able to work up now with just my fingers would be far from satisfactory, but it would at least get me somewhere.

So I gathered the slickness from the base and spread it all around the delicate flesh. A finger slipped inside of me and then another and my eyes fluttered shut to bask in the pleasure of my simple thrusts.

They dug in and out of me in regulated rhythms, pausing momentarily to also give my clit the attention that it needed. Soon, I was writhing on the bed, my head gently thrashing from side to side as a trickle of pleasure began to flow from my groin and into my veins.

My breathing grew heavy, and my mind gradually blank until all I could focus on was the chase towards the very much anticipated release.

It seemed to go on for longer than usual, so I slanted my body at just the right angle to draw it out. I took pauses when it was needed, my back arched and my head sunken into the pillows.

One man came to mind and at the reminder of the heights his mouth and hands had taken me to, an intense heat began to burn through me. My left hand slipped through the easy access that the heart shaped cut of my nightie offered, and fondled my swollen breasts. I stroked the hardened tip of my nipples and the added stimulation pulled me closer and closer to the edge.

The speed and brutality of my coaxing continued and the pressure in my core began to build powerfully. I thought of Christian... and of his beautiful brown eyes and his kind smile. His muscled torso and of his deliciously curved ass. And then his cock... I wanted to take it in my mouth, to suck on it until I saw all the blood drain away from his face.

The roar at his climax as he had come inside of me previously rang in my ears, the memory of the deeply animalistic sound pushing me over the edge. I came with a heady rush, the delight washing through my body in gentle but intense waves had me gasping his name.

"Christian," I called over and over, barely able to catch my breath. Just as quickly as they had come however, the waves began to recede and my heaving chest began to calm.

I turned my face and hid it in the pillow, my soaked fingers spreading my release all over my sex and milking what little pleasure that was left out of my clit.

I then brought the fingers to my lips to taste myself and wished over and over again I could have him with me. With this, I had barely managed to float amongst the clouds but with him I would be able to touch the moon.

I returned my hand to my sex, far from satiated and willing to work myself up to yet another release until I was consoled enough to fall asleep.

He's just a room away, my heart whispered to me but my brain wouldn't allow me to act. *He is also your boss*, it reminded me *and right now you are helpless and living under his roof.*

These thoughts promptly sucked away what remaining arousal I felt, so I let my still damp hand fall to my side and opened my eyes to gaze helplessly at the ceiling.

I remained still for the longest time, until I decided to head to the bathroom to wash up.

It was then I heard the small knock on my door.

My heart jumped into my throat.

I stared at the door, wide eyed and alarmed, and then looked away to think of just how loud I'd been. We're the walls thin? Surely I couldn't have been loud enough to have reached him all the way at the end of the corridor.

The soft knock came again, and I scrambled out of bed. Putting my gown back in order, I hurried over and stopped before the door.

"Christian?" I called.

"Yeah," he replied, and I noted the gruffness in his tone.

I pulled the door open and met him leaning against the opposite wall.

"I brought some sleeping medication for you. I was about to head to bed when I realized I had some left. I haven't used them in quite a while but I've checked that they're okay."

"Thank you," I said, but yet neither of us moved to either hand over or accept the medication from the other. I couldn't tear my eyes away from the way he was looking at me, his lids heavy and lips slightly parted.

"I heard you," he said softly, and my heart thundered.

"I heard you call out my name, repeatedly. Why deprive yourself when I'm just a few feet away?"

I didn't know how to respond so all I could do was stare at him. He moved his body from its leisurely lean against the wall, and stretched out to hand the medicine over.

I gazed at his hand, truly wondering if I would internally combust the moment I touched him. I decided then I didn't want or need the pills.

"Fuck me," I lifted my gaze to his. "That's what I want."

Something lit up in his eyes as he watched me, and then he threw the bottle aside. With a shake of his head, he approached my door and I began to retreat backwards.

"Why do you insist on torturing both of us, Adele?" he asked, as his hand curved around the metallic handle of the door. Then he slammed it shut behind him.

I jumped, now barely able to catch my breath. My mouth had gone completely dry so swallowing was now quite the task. He licked his lips and I curved my hands on the edge of my nightie. I pulled the material over my head and threw it aside.

"Fuck me," I breathed once again just as the back of my legs connected with the frame of my bed. I allowed myself to fall onto it, and immediately spread my legs wide and unashamedly.

He came over and kissed me senseless, before turning us both over with his hands on my waist. I thought that he was going to balance me on his groin but then he pulled me up until my ass was directly over his face.

"You've been busy," I heard him say, but my eyes were clenched shut and my mind nearly half gone.

His tongue slid out of his mouth and I felt the heat of his touch before the velvety, smooth pad gave my sex a long, hard lick.

I shuddered violently, my entire pelvic growing numb at the first dose of the delicious agony that was to come.

I positioned my hands on the bed, my knees digging into either side of his head as I received the first instruction from him.

"Ride me," he said. "Take what you need."

My heart almost gave out then. I arched my hips and then rocked myself onto his tongue and lips.

I choked on a moan as my face lifted up to the ceiling. With my hands digging into my hair, I fucked his face with a shamelessness that stunned me. His mouth ravished me greedily, stroking and sucking and licking, and even the unintentional scrapes of his teeth against the sensitive flesh gave me absolutely nothing to complain about.

I relished his feasting, tears stinging my eyes at the delicious ache as it curled through my body, and most of all at the unbelievable decadence of what we were doing.

This was my boss. The man I would show up to work with the very next day and have to call *sir*. His every need was my responsibility, and his word was enough to make or break my career in the company. And yet here I was grinding my ass into his face.

His hands cupped the cheeks, roughly enough for the pain to register and even that I wholly enjoyed. Then he began to feel up my body until his hands reached my breasts and I surrendered the jutted mounds completely to him. I was going to come this way once again, and it would blow my mind. The intimacy was searing, the urgency abysmally carnal, and it was all I could do to keep from crying.

I felt the ratty knot that had previously been lodged in my stomach begin to unravel, no worries or concerns daring to come into this place as I lost myself in his worship.

My climax tore a thready and agonized cry through my lips as I released onto his face with a powerful stream. My hands wrenched the sheets away from the frames until they were nothing more than a tangle of fabric around us. But still, I didn't stop grinding and pumping my cunt onto his mouth.

Eventually, my hips bucked and twitched, forcing me to come to a stop as I cried out at the sheer magic of it all. Afterwards I collapsed onto the bed, completely spent but still brimming with vigor and excitement. That had to be one of the most erotic things I had ever done and the experience filled me with an awe that kept my eyes wide open.

He turned around then, came in between my thighs and began to trail heated, burning kisses up every inch of my flesh. The dip of my navel, the sides of my abdomen, each of my breasts and across the curve of my collarbone. I was intoxicated by his warmth and scent, surrounding me and claiming him in that moment as beyond precious to him. My gaze focused on his head of hair as I sunk my fingers into the mass, needing to hold onto any part of him within reach.

"Christian," I gasped over and over again.

I didn't know what I wanted to say, or what I could say, but I did know I never wanted to not have his name in my mouth.

"How was that?" he asked as he nibbled on the curve of my ears, the flesh of my bottom lip and the tip of my chin.

"Fucking amazing," I sighed, and caught his lips in mine. He submitted to the kiss and my legs wrapped desperately around his body, trapping him in my small arms.

I never wanted to be away from his embrace, every fear and concern I had felt in the previous few days all falling away to dust with the weight of him on me.

I felt the rock hard bulge of his cock against my thighs, and wanted nothing more than to have him inside of me.

"Fuck me," I pleaded, as my hands splayed across his muscled back. I could feel the strength in the movement of his limbs as he lifted himself slightly off me and proceeded to answer my request.

"With pleasure sweetheart," he said, and moved briefly away to sheath himself. Then he returned and angled my opening to the thick, pulsing head of his cock. He slipped in, earning a gasp out of me at the sudden fullness. But then, he pulled back out and proceeded to run the slicked rod up and down the folds of my sex.

"Christian!" I cried out, my body writhing and arching off the bed in a crazed anticipation, eager for him to fill me up till it was all my senses could register.

He heeded my complaint, slid back into me and then held me in place as he gripped the side of my thighs. He slammed into me with one fluid thrust, and I nearly lost my mind.

"Fuck," I cried out, near choking on my own breath as a torrent of pleasure wreaked through my body.

"Oh god," my back collapsed back to the bed, a string of dirty incoherent curses flowing from my lips.

"Christian, again," I panted, and he slid out again before slamming just as forcefully back into me. I completely gave in then, to all he intended to do with my body.

The room was dark but my vision registered sparks and blotches of light, and then brief glimpses of his face and of the emotion that had consumed him.

"You feel so good Adele," he groaned, his voice hoarse and labored as he relentlessly jerked my hips to meet the force of his thrusts. The bed was creaking and slamming into the wall, and even the very ground beneath seemed to be moving as the deeply erotic sounds of flesh loudly smacking against flesh resounded into the night. His rhythm was what completely enthralled me because sometimes it would be slow and drawn out, and at other times it was fast and maddening.

When I climaxed for the third time that night, the head of his cock hitting that almost evasive spot inside of me, it felt as though my soul had left my body. I floated and fell apart in his arms, and at his tortured collapse against me, I knew he was in the same state. He buried his face into my neck to muffle his belly deep groans, but I could feel it in the shudder of his entire body. Our chests were heaving, our bodies sticky and joined as one, and I never wanted to let go.

I tightened my arms around him and began to cry. I tried to quiet my sobs but it was to no avail because a few moments later he began to kiss the tears off my faces

"I'm sorry," I breathed, but I felt the shake of his head.

"No sweetheart," he said. "Let it out. Let it all out."

So I sobbed into his neck and he rocked me, the blissful aftermath of our orgasms wrapping us both in a cloud of intimacy that I had never felt before. Eventually, all the emotion was wrung out of me and he curled my body into his, tightly imprisoning me in his arms and ensuring I basked in the heat and safety of his presence.

"How do you feel?" I thought I heard him ask, but I was too spent to even give a response. I let my subconscious slip away from me and fell into the deepest and most restful sleep I had encountered in months.

ADELE

The next morning, I left the apartment before Christian.

Although when I found myself tiptoeing down the staircase and then dashing for the front door, it became clear I was trying to escape more than anything else.

My face was flushed when I finally arrived at my car. I jumped in and immediately slid the lock in place.

Then I released a deep breath, and just stared.

And then the quiet question came.

Why are you running?

I broke out in a low, muffled laughter which was aggravated when I spotted my pink cheeks and wide-eyed gaze in the rearview mirror.

Shaking my head at how silly I was, I put the car in gear and reversed out of the parking lot.

It had been barely an hour earlier that I had gotten out of bed.

At first I had been alarmed, until I realized we were actually in my bed, and I was still encased in his arms. He was the one that should have left before the sun rose, so I wasn't in the wrong for overstaying my welcome.

Then I relaxed, a smile tugging at the corners of my lips at the soothing cocoon his warmth had wrapped me in.

I understood then why I had slept so well.

Well at least part of why I had slept so well. There was the euphoria of his arms holding me to his body, the gentle rise and fall of his chest mirroring mine, and then there were the three orgasms he had wrung out of me the previous night.

Those had efficiently drained away all the stress, fear and anxiety that had plagued me over the past few days.

I was grateful to him, but as I realized after emerging from the shower and meeting my bed empty, the rumpled sheets were the only evidence he had been there, I wasn't quite ready to face him again.

So I'd run.

And it was as amusing as it was frustrating.

I arrived at the office in time to prepare for the day and got straight to work. The usual agitation at my still existing predicament of being stalked reared its ugly head, and tried to pull me back into its clutches of despair and fear. I pushed the still very vivid memories of my night with him to the forefront of my mind however, and thus was able to keep it from overwhelming me like it had previously.

The sudden flashbacks of him slamming into me, were more than enough to momentarily numb my body and mind of everything beyond the buzz of pleasure that was coursing through my veins.

My breath caught as arousal pooled between my thighs, then my gaze went to his door, hoping he would soon arrive.

At nine, as was usual, the door to the office was pushed open and my eyes almost refused to move from my computer screen.

My lips parted to send a greeting before I found the courage to turn to him, but the 'good morning' died on my lips when I saw the look he had in his eyes.

It was a cold regard that almost made it seem as though the previous night had only happened in my head. It was the usual stoic expression he wore, but today it felt particularly unpleasant especially since I had seen him smile, laugh and moan deeply into my ears barely hours earlier.

"Did you get breakfast?" he asked, and my mood sprung back to life.

"No sir, not yet." I replied, and he frowned.

"There's cereal at home, and eggs and bread even."

My gaze lowered. "I didn't find the time."

"Try to grab something quick next time," he said and pushed the door to his office open. He hadn't stopped for a moment and had just strolled past as he spoke, his shirt a crisp white, and his jacket slung over his arm.

I collapsed back into my seat, and only realized then that I had been slightly standing. It was quite the apt representation of the dynamics of our current relationship, so the question plagued me as the morning continued; what was now too formal between us, and yet what was too informal? It was a delicate balance, and I consoled myself with the thought that time would find a way to sort it out for us.

Two hours later, I was taking the minutes of an important meeting with him on the operations floor when the attending client suddenly blew up.

"We're running out of time," he groaned menacingly and the conference room of a dozen attendees stilled.

We all gave him the attention he sought and he went on. "This is the third pitch I'm attending in six weeks, and yet nothing concrete has been produced. The Knox line launches in less than three months and yet there is no marketing, or even a plan for an ad campaign to back it up. What then am I paying you thousands of dollars for?"

He directed this question at the leader of the team, Andrew Thompson who was more familiar with him.

Christian simply watched, his gaze moving calmly and steadily from client to team leader and it made me wonder about just what exactly was going through his mind. He seemed almost bored, but I sensed it was very unlikely because more often than not it was near impossible to ever accurately guess what he was thinking.

His face maintained that steady, stoic expression, like the heavy gush of water down the side of a cliff. Mesmerizing, but also fear inducing.

Andrew, flustered at being barraged with criticism, not only in front of his boss but his team as well, he hurried to defend himself but before he could even let out a stuttering sentence the client cut him off and went on. "You assured me your pitch today was going to be the perfect fit, but what is this?"

"It's what we can achieve given the stipulated budget" the project manager, a curly haired woman said but then the client roared at her. "Eighty thousand dollars is not enough to get me something more decent than using memes?"

The room shook with the boom of his voice, and that was when Christian stepped in.

"It's not," he replied and the entire room went silent.

His voice was colder than that of the client's, and even more fear inducing because this time around every single eye turned to him.

"What you're expecting is we'll be able to make endorsements happen with celebrities that won't even answer the phone for anything less than three times that amount."

"The first pitch they presented was painstakingly crafted to maximize every cent of the available budget. It focused on collaborating with the most engaging influencers, whom we have tried and tested with other product launches and confirmed that they are worth every cent with the results they produced. But you turned that down. And your judgment was solely based on the unimpressive numbers of some of their following, which as we explained to you is not that important because engagement is what produces a positive ROI, not follower count. You rejected that so they collaborated with the ad department to craft empathetic concepts for the campaign videos, targeted to the various demographics of your customers and you rejected that too, refusing to understand why one singular video would be unable to perform as well as several. Now they have-"

"Mr. Hall," the client interrupted. "I don't need a narration of my disappointing experience thus far with your agency. All I need is-"

Christian rose to his feet, startling everyone in the room. However his gaze and tone remained as steady as ever.

"No, what I need is for you to make up your mind on if you're going to let us do our job and trust we'll deliver the results possible within your stipulated budget or, if you're going to keep sending the team around in circles that satisfies no one."

"Mr. Harlton, we're going to present one more pitch to you, and if by then it's still not satisfactory enough then please, feel free to take your account elsewhere. They have other clients to attend to and I cannot tolerate the crushing of their morale any longer."

With that, he grabbed his phone from the desk and stormed out of the room.

For the first few seconds, no one moved, or dare I say even breathed.

The client's scowling and bearded face underneath the cowboy hat he wore, reddened profusely before he too rose to his feet and walked out of the room.

The moment he did, everyone else heaved a sigh of relief. I realized too that my boss had left so I was no longer supposed to be there either, but I had just gotten too wrapped up in the drama of it all.

I hurried to my feet, and grabbed the iPad I had brought with me, sorry that I wouldn't be able to hear the conclusion of the meeting. I soon returned to my office and settled back into my seat.

I stared at his door, wondering if he had returned or if perhaps he had stopped by another department. Just then a message came in and I looked down at my phone to see that it was from Melinda.

"Let's have lunch together today. The deli?"

My stomach immediately tightened with anxiety at the reminder I still had more severe problems of my own to handle. I didn't however want to give yet another excuse for not wanting to leave the office building so with a sigh, I sent back my response.

"Sure."

ADELE

"Don't you look rested," Melinda's greeting fleeted over as I approached the table she had selected for us at the deli.

I was twenty minutes late, and it was intentional. I felt apologetic towards her, but the less time we had to chatter beyond the safety of the office, the more I could maintain my peace of mind. The last thing I needed was another batch of pictures delivered, proving to me they were also aware of just how I liked my favorite rice from the deli which was currently the plate awaiting me. The tomatoes had been removed, the lettuce kept to a minimum, and double the usual amount of hot sauce.

"Thank you," I told her as I sat down, and immediately dug in.

"So," she began, her eyes sparkling. "I heard the CEO told off Harlton this morning."

I smiled despite myself. "Word's already gotten around?"

"Of course. The entire floor's been talking about it, and of course all the women are swooning. Especially Nanny McPhee."

I almost snorted out some rice through my nostrils. "What the hell? Who's Nanny McPhee?"

"Melissa Mayor. Senior copywriter."

"Oh,' I said, the image of the rotund woman with the dark suits and moles coming to mind. "Isn't she married? And how do you come up with these nicknames?"

"She is, but what does that matter? All the women in the office will pee their pants if the CEO so much as smiles at them. The word around the floor is that most of them have gone blank when he's asked direct questions."

I would have believed she was exaggerating if I didn't know the man to the degree I did, so I nodded in understanding, also a victim of his electric appeal.

"And it's not just the women. Jeremy had a hard on in the break room when Alexa was giving us the details and of course, David pointed it out. He groaned and blamed it all on the CEO. I nearly died laughing."

"Um..." I was taken aback. "Isn't that inappropriate?"

"It is, but it was just a few of the interns and the other more idle staff. Plus the floor's gotten significantly cooler since you left."

"Lucky me," I said dryly, and she gave me a giddy smile.

"So, tell me. Is he that fierce on the seventy-sixth floor? I'd thought he would be quite chill, especially because he's so young and seems so calm but now everyone's starting to realize why Mr. Abbott chose him as his successor."

I didn't have much to say about how stern he was at work, but I did however know about just how fierce he had been with me the previous night. I was hit with another mind numbing flashback of us entangled in each other's arms, and my thighs clenched desperately together underneath the table. I poured myself a glass of water, and then looked away to re-stabilize my breathing.

When I returned to my meal without responding, she became offended.

"Adele, you've become so tight-lipped these days. What the hell's going on with you?"

"Nothing," I replied.

"Then why won't you respond to me about the CEO?"

"I'm eating," I complained too. "You know this is my favorite meal. I want to enjoy it."

"Have you slept together again?" she asked, and my spoon missed its way to my mouth.

She laughed out at my reaction, while I gave her a dry look.

"C'mon," she nudged me with an arm. "Have you? Tell me!"

My gaze temporarily wandered away from her, and I spotted a pair of eerie gray eyes.

He was at one of the corner tables, just down the row from ours and sipping on a cup of coffee. His jean clad legs were crossed loosely, his dark shirt raggedy, and his hair quite shaggy. With a deliberate look at me, he set the cup of coffee down and then with a dark smile, returned his gaze back to the screen of his phone.

My heart seized with fear.

"Adele?" Melinda called but I didn't respond. I didn't want to remain there for a second longer, but I couldn't quite find the courage to rise to my feet. I placed my hand on my phone, aching to call Christian over but I knew the very thought didn't make sense. However, currently absolutely nothing did.

What if this man was the one behind the threats?

"Adele!" Melinda called sharply, and my gaze snapped back to hers.

"Yeah?"

"What's wrong?"

My voice was small. "W-what do you mean?"

"Well you look like you've just seen a ghost. For a second I thought... well, I didn't see hi-" she stopped mid-sentence and turned sheepish. Then she immediately lowered her gaze from mine. I recognized the look on her face, and it was immense guilt.

"Were you just about to mention Andrew's name?"

I waited for her to deny it but instead her sigh was heavy.

"He called me this morning, and said he had been trying to reach you but couldn't."

"Of course," I replied. "I blocked him."

"Well, he pleaded with me and said he only needed a minute or two with you. That he had something very important to discuss with you."

I glared at her. "And?"

"I told him to meet us here."

Several moments of silence passed, before I could get past my anger enough to move. My aluminum chair scraped across the tiled floor as I grabbed my phone and rose to my feet.

"Adele!"

I turned around and stormed away.

"Adele!" she called after me but I ignored her.

What I wanted was to disappear, far away from this place before any of them got to me. So I hurried towards the entrance, bumping into tables and people. Perhaps it was the fear I would be attacked, or perhaps it was the fear I would see Andrew and be sick to my stomach all over again.

It didn't matter because I didn't stop.

I burst out of the deli's doors, and kept marching onward.

"Adele!" I heard the sudden call, and despite the buzz of the afternoon street I immediately recognized it.

It was too late! I was too late.

I no longer wanted to run so I reduced my pace to a stroll, and adopted a casual gait for my return back to the office.

A few seconds later, I felt a hand solidly close around my wrist.

"Adele!"

Bile instantly rose from the depth of my gut as I shook the hand away as though it was a snake that had just touched me.

"Don't fucking touch me!" I yelled, and the world seemed to come to a standstill.

Multiple eyes turned to us, and I could see it made him immensely uncomfortable.

"Adele," he lowered his tone. "Let's talk. Please. Just for a moment."

I glared at him, wishing at this moment that he would just disappear. This all too vivid reminder of his existence was scorching me from the inside, making the simple act of breathing almost unbearable for me.

Without a word, I turned and continued on my way.

"Who was that guy?" he called after me. "Were you the one that fucking sent him to punch me in the face?"

My brows furrowed at the statement, but still I didn't stop. However I couldn't help but wonder about who he was referring to. And then my heart slammed into my chest because the only person that instantly came to mind was Christian.

He had punched him in the face? When?

"Adele," he called out again, making me realize that although he kept his distance, he was still trailing me.

"Adele!" he called again, and my eyes scanned around, searching for something I could hit him with. Even his very voice agitated me blind.

"He said you're being harassed," Andrew relayed. "What's that about? What's going on?"

"Adele! Ade- *Ow!*" his sharp cry of pain suddenly shot a bolt of fear through my heart.

I turned around to see him bent over, his hand covering what appeared to now be a bleeding nose.

"The *fuck!*" he cried out, and it made me jump. Especially when I noticed before him and with a heaving chest was the delivery guy, Tim. He had seemingly come out of nowhere.

Before I could pull him away from Andrew's wrath, his hand struck out in retaliation and the delivery boy went down. He was struck down to the pavement without making a single sound, while Andrew turned livid.

"What is wrong with the men around you?" he roared. "Why do they keep fucking punching me in the face?"

I ignored him, now beyond concerned as I hurried over to the boy and lowered to assist him in getting up.

Tim," I called, relief washing through me that I remembered his name. "I'm so sorry. You didn't have to do that."

He complied as I pulled him up with me and soon we were both on our feet. He however pulled away from me, his hands closing around my wrists to take my grip off his arms. His head was lowered and turned away but I could very clearly see the reddened bruise now forming on the side of his face.

I turned to Andrew, fuming.

"If you don't leave right now I'm going to call the cops."

His hand was still over his nose, but some blood was already slipping through his fingers.

He spat out some inaudible curses, and with immense annoyance, turned around and disappeared.

Tim returned back to the deli, and I watched him go until Melinda appeared out of nowhere.

"Adele," she hurried over to me, and with a vicious glare at her I turned around and headed back to the office without a word.

CHRISTIAN

S he wasn't at her desk. It was lunch time now so that led me to assume that perhaps she had stepped out for something to eat, but I was also aware of how wary she had been about leaving the safety of the building, which made me wonder if perhaps she was just on another floor. I stared at the empty chair and was just about to return to the office when the door to the reception was pushed open.

She came in with a stroll, but immediately froze when she saw me standing there. I stared at her momentarily, forgetting what I wanted to say. But all of that didn't matter anyway when I finally noticed the moisture in her eyes. My heart immediately lurched.

"What's wrong?" I asked.

She immediately lowered her face. "Nothing," she replied, and when she lifted her gaze back to mine, there was instead a smile across it. "Nothing," she repeated. "Did you need something?"

"The cops called," I said, as I carefully studied her. "Let's talk in my office."

I turned around, and she obediently followed.

"What did they say?" she asked a few moments later. I was now seated at my desk and she stood before me.

In her haste to pat her eyes dry, she had slightly smudged them dark and didn't realize it. This made it apparent more than ever that something had deeply upset her.

"They've done a sweep of your place," I said. "They'll call you soon to personally give a report but since I'm in constant communication with the officer in charge, I was able to obtain the update from him. He said they didn't find any bugs in your place. They carefully inspected every corner and there were no hidden cameras."

She stared at me, her gaze going blank and for a little while it seemed as though she was no longer in the room.

"Adele," I called, and had to repeat her name a second time before the call even registered. "Thank you," she said, and managed to work up a smile.

She turned around to leave, but then her eyes widened with the realization of something.

"Did you..." she began. "Did you visit Andrew? My ex?"

I momentarily stilled, and pondered on the right response to give. I had expected him to contact her, or even sue, but was hoping for neither since going there had been me losing control of my temper. So right now, and as I watched her, I wondered about just how upset she would be if I admitted to it.

"I wanted to know," I said. "If he was the one behind this."

"By punching him?" she breathed.

I was far from remorseful for this, but a little apologetic to her. "My temper got away from me."

I expected her to storm out, but to my surprise, her gaze softened as she watched me. My mouth moved before my brain could step in.

"I'm sorry," I apologized, but she shook her head.

"Don't be. Don't be. Thank you. I wish I could punch him but I'd probably break my hand in the process so... thank you."

A smile escaped my lips. "I'll teach you," I told her. "You'll be able to do some damage. Next time."

"Thank you," she said. "But I'm hoping there's never a next time, and..."

Her gaze lowered somewhat shyly.

"And?"

She smiled, but it was so sad that the pull on my heart was painful.

"I feel incredibly indebted to you, and with each passing day, it seems like just saying *'thank you'* is not going to cut it anymore."

"You're right," I agreed. "So why not just stop saying it all together? I know you're thankful, and I'm willing and more than able to help. So let's leave it at that."

"How about we..." her lashes lowered once again, hiding her eyes from sight. "How about we exchange favors? For instance right now, I feel so grateful that I want... I want to..."

Her voice trailed off yet again, but her gaze returned to mine. It was intense, and filled with a fondness I had never quite seen in there before. I gripped the edge of my desk as I waited for her to finish speaking, although by now I was truly certain this flirting was intentional, and it was driving me crazy.

"What do you want?" I asked, impatient.

She released a shuddering breath, the corners of her lips curving ever so lightly. "I want to suck your cock," she said.

I stopped breathing.

"You've had a rough morning," she said quietly. "I imagine it'd be great to take some pressure off?"

No words came to my brain as I stared at her beautiful frame, encased in a striped, dark blazer and matching pants.

Seeing I couldn't respond, she began to walk towards me, her movements slow and sensual, and it was so natural that only the responding swell of my cock could register this was happening.

Soon she arrived before me, so I turned in my chair to face her.

Her knees met the floor, and although initially hesitant, her hands soon found their way to my belt buckle. She couldn't hold my gaze so I just watched her, not even bothering to lend a helping hand. She tugged the zipper down, and then reached in to hook her fingers into the band of my briefs.

"What about your boundaries?" I managed to speak, my voice sounding strained and completely foreign to my ears.

"Don't rub it in," she said, yet another small smile tugging at the corners of her lips.

"Well, I guess it's a good thing you're about to rub it out," I said and the air around us seemed to freeze over.

ADELE

I couldn't fucking breathe.

First was due to the joke he'd just made, which should have immediately elicited laughter, but all I could do was stare at him dumbfounded.

And then his lips tilted, as he fought to stop the smile from breaking out across his face.

The smile won, and my brain cells were fried crisp.

As I gazed up at his perfect teeth, the question slipped out of my mouth before I could stop it. "Did you ever get braces?"

"No," he answered, his brows furrowing in amusement at the incredibly random inquiry.

"So, you never needed braces, you're this handsome, devastatingly sexy and you know how to make bad jokes? Are you real?"

"Hey!" he complained. "That was a good joke."

My heart kept tumbling in my chest and after a deep and shaky inhale, my breath released with a shudder.

"It was a bad joke," I said, but thankfully stopped myself from admonishing him to halt his charming antics, because if he did or said anything else as endearing my knees were going to give out from under me.

I turned my gaze towards his door, needing to confirm it was completely locked before I started on him. Just as I made to rise however, all the amusement drained away from his face. With a hand on my shoulder, he gently halted me from moving.

"The door-" I began, but was immediately stopped by the intensity of the desire I found burning in his eyes. His pupils were dilated, gaze heavy, and in an instant I recognized the look. It was the entrancing and almost drugged one he only wore in the throes of his passion, and it was the only time the sharpness of his gaze was dulled.

"It's fine," he breathed. "We're fine."

I didn't need any more encouragement.

With my gaze glued to his, and my insides slowly melting away, I reached into his briefs, past the smattering of hair on his crotch, and grabbed the base of his cock. I heard his breath hitch just as his hand on my shoulder moved to the nape of my neck. He slanted his head, and latched his lips onto mine.

Arousal soaked my underwear wet, my clit throbbing and excruciatingly sensitive against the cotton fabric. I would have fallen over if not for my hold on his knee, because the stroking of his tongue against mine, the suction of his lips, his smoldering presence and intoxicating scent... all of it came together to completely destabilize me.

In the distance, a strangled moan sounded, and I couldn't even tell who the sound had come from. Then he broke the kiss, leaning away to settle back into his chair. However I needed a few moments for my senses to clear. When they did I was almost too afraid to look at him, unwilling to let him see the extent of his effect on me. Instead, I channeled the growing depth of my affection for him towards the flushed head of his erection, covered my lips around the wide crest and felt his body jerk at the contact.

I sucked hard on it, my tongue licking across the sensitive head, and it immediately rewarded me with the first spill of pre-cum. I was obviously smitten because I lapped up every bit of the discharge before slanting my head to run the pad of my tongue up his length.

He was so hard, and thick my confidence slightly faltered in my ability to thoroughly milk him to orgasm. Especially since it was what I wanted to give him, what I needed to give him to express my gratitude and to ensure it remained in his mind for the rest of his day. I wanted him to unravel before me, just as he had done to me in his arms, and for him to think of this every time he laid his eyes on me.

His hand once again returned to the back of my neck, and my lids lifted to see his head slightly thrown back against the chair, the seat of power from which he controlled the entire company, but in this moment, I controlled him. His chest rose and fell heavily, the larynx in his throat bobbing as he struggled to breathe and swallow, his eyes solidly shut and his lips parted.

I returned my lips to the head, and then took as much as I could of him into my mouth.

"Adele," he breathed, and I reveled in the sound of my name on his lips.

Hollowing my cheeks, I began to bob my head up and down his throbbing erection, my hand milking the length in a rapid but steady rhythm.

"Adele," he groaned aloud. "*Fuck!*"

He pulled on my hair, and the sharp pain ripped a dark jolt of pleasure through me. He was squirming and bucking on the seat as I jacked him, my pace increasing and my suction hardening. Once again, I slanted my head and traced the bulging veins along the now slick length before lowering even further to pull his balls into my mouth. They were full and heavy with arousal, and that singular act drew out such a groan from him that for a moment, I was alarmed we could be heard beyond the confines of his office.

Reminded but still somewhat thrilled by the risk of our current engagement, I tightened my fist around him, and deepened my suction, spurred by the urgency.

My eyes watered as I milked him closer and closer to the edge. My jaws hurt and so did my knees but I didn't care. My entire being was currently fully dedicated to gifting him the release that he'd earned and deserved.

"Adele... I-I'm going to come," he grunted and tried to nudge me away but I refused. The pleasure took over then, his awareness dissipating as his orgasm crashed into him. He rocked his hips into my mouth, his cock fucking the snug warmth.

"Adele!" he grunted through gritted teeth as he spilled into my mouth, the stream warm and thick. I tried my best to swallow it all, unwilling to let even a single drop go to waste.

Afterwards I continued to fist him, eager to milk every bit of release he still had in him. He was still somewhat restless from the subsiding sensations, his breathing haggard and his hand pulling at the roots of his now tousled hair.

I pulled away then, licking the dampness off my lips, and my gaze almost unable to look away from the still slightly hardened and glistening length of his cock. *He could take me right now*, was all I could think. He could bend me over this desk and thrust his beautiful cock into me, and it would drive us both wild.

However I couldn't help but be aware it would be pushing whatever grace had kept us from getting caught for this long. Fucking unrestrainedly in the middle of an office that anyone could drop by at any time, and this close to the end of lunch hour? That would most certainly be us courting disaster. So I found the will to pull away, and with my hand on his thighs managed to rise to my feet. My knees were wobbly, but my hand soon moved to his desk to stabilize myself.

The picture I met of him from this height knocked the breath out of me, and I knew it would always remain in my mind. His head, thrown back, his dark hair usually pristine and in place now disheveled, his cheeks flushed and his chest heaving. Then of course his glorious dick, still exposed and hanging proudly out of his still unzipped pants. Once again, the desire to impale myself onto him for a ride gripped me, and if I had been wearing a skirt then perhaps I would have lost my head and thrown all caution to the wind.

However the hassle of slipping out of my pants and now soaked underwear stopped me, so I settled instead for the pleasure of watching him in this most vulnerable state. Eventually I started to move away, but his grip on my hand was immediate and solid.

"Where are you going?" he groaned, his voice still drowsy from the pleasure.

"Lunchtime is over," I replied, and his gaze darkened.

"I need to fuck you," he said, every word thick with intent.

"We'll finish this at home," I said, and with great amusement, fought to pull myself out of his hold. If he wasn't still undressed, he would have probably chased me down but instead he watched me with a searing look of betrayal as I rounded his desk with a wink.

"You're going to pass out tonight" he swore, and I almost stumbled at the promise. Or was it a threat?

It didn't matter anyway because my entire body immediately tensed with anticipation.

"*Fuck*," I swore. "You shouldn't have said that. Now I won't be able to concentrate till the end of the day."

"Serves you right," he said, as he straightened in his chair, swiveling in it to watch my departure.

"You're my boss," I reminded him. "My performance directly affects you."

"Well I don't see myself being very effective either after what you just did to me, so how about we take the rest of the day off."

My gaze at him was incredulous. "You can't do that!"

"I can do whatever the fuck I want."

That conviction and bravado in his tone almost made me come right there. I shook my head to clear it as well as to refuse him.

"We can't," I told him. "You have a crucial conference call with the Boston office."

"Fine," he groaned, and to that I sent him a heartfelt smile.

"See you later boss," I said and walked out of his office.

CHRISTIAN

I couldn't remember ever being as excited to head home.
However when I arrived all seemed the same.

I didn't know what I had expected, but her being nowhere in sight was not amongst it.

It made me wonder if she had even returned. I had left earlier to handle an extended meeting out of the office, so I couldn't confirm if she was still there. I considered heading up to her room, but eventually decided to head to the kitchen. There I poured myself a much needed glass of water and then sent her a message.

I waited, my mind going to our tryst from earlier in the day.

I had gotten blown severally in the past before, but none of it had ever felt like hers. Even the sight of her on her knees, entrancing blue eyes, watching me intently had nearly unraveled me. And then her lips had wrapped around my cock, and every cell inside of me had come alive.

"Fuck," I cursed again, and picked the phone off the counter to check for her response. There was none, so I abandoned the glass of water and headed up. A few small taps on her door later, and her voice floated over to me in response.

I waited, and soon enough the door was pulled open. It was already night time, so the warmth of the light from her room spilled out into the dim hall, basking her in a glow that made my heart soften. She looked somewhat exhausted, and it worried me. However we both just stared at each other, amused, and our gazes were intimate and knowing. Not much needed to be said because we both felt it, the special hour of our afternoon was still very much alive in both of our minds.

"Hey," I greeted, and before I could stop myself, my hand reached out to brush her hair out of her eyes.

"How come you're in here?" I asked.

Her smile was sheepish. "Where else would I be?"

"It's a big apartment."

"It is, but it's not mine," she said, and at my slight frown she quickly explained. "I can't just hang out anywhere. It's more polite to remain in my room."

"Says who?"

She smiled. "The guide book of courtesy?"

"According to who?"

A sliver of her beautiful teeth flashed at her grin. "Adele Walters."

I shook my head, and held out my hand to her. Although she hesitated, she took it and soon we were walking side by side down the hall and towards the staircase.

"Have you eaten?" I asked.

"Mmmm," she replied. "I have a bit of a dilemma about that."

"What do you mean?"

"I thought of getting some food on my way back, but I imagined it would be a little selfish considering =you might not have eaten. I wanted to ask you about it but I didn't want to interrupt your meeting. And I don't think I trust my cooking skills enough to make you something. And I also don't want to just assume it would even be okay for me to do that."

"Why wouldn't it be okay?" I asked.

She didn't give a response to this, and it was only when we arrived at the kitchen that I realized what had been left unspoken.

I smiled. "People without wives also have to eat too."

She was so startled by the statement that her hand fell from my grasp.

"You're my secretary," I said. "And right now you're in my house. So if you want to make something for yourself to eat, or for the both of us, then don't hesitate. The kitchen is already severely underused, and considering how much my mother spent in decorating it, it is quite painful."

She laughed softly. "Alright."

I settled onto one of the stools at the breakfast bar. "So, what are we eating tonight?"

She headed over to the fridge, and when she pulled it open we didn't see much.

"There are some eggs," she said. "Half a carton of milk. Alfredo sauce... no vegetables or meat."

"We should probably order in then," I said, and she shut the door in amusement.

"What do you want to eat?" I asked, as I tapped the app open.

She didn't respond so I raised my gaze, and met her deep in thought.

Her hands were in the pockets of the pants she had worn to work earlier today, and her top was a simple, white, sleeveless blouse. She bit down softly on her lower lip as she pondered, and I watched, mesmerized at the contrast between her sophisticated stance and the cuteness of the mindless habit. *I want to be the one nibbling on those lips,* was all I could think of. And then she turned towards me.

"Nothing comes to mind now but..." she stopped.

I returned my gaze to hers, and no doubt my face had clearly reflected what I had been thinking just a moment earlier.

"You were saying?" I asked, when a few more seconds passed and she still didn't speak.

"Um," she shook her head to clear it, and I couldn't help my smile. The room was so tense and thick with our sexual pull towards one another that you could have sliced through it with a knife. It was only a matter of time before I hoisted her onto this counter and fucked us both numb.

"The deli," she said. "It's not too far away, so perhaps we could get some rice bowls from there. They're really good."

"Is it the same place you get my sandwiches from?" I asked.

"Yes," she replied.

"What's it called?"

"Timbals," she replied and I nodded.

When I was done with the order, I placed the phone aside and looked up to see her watching me. I gave a nod of confirmation, and she thanked me.

The space went silent for a little while, and although it wasn't awkward, I did want to spend the time getting to know her as much as possible. Beyond moments like this, there were very few opportunities, especially at the office.

"Do you remember Marcus Sims?" I asked.

She immediately nodded in response. "I do. You have a meeting scheduled with him for next week."

"Yeah." I said. "Well he brought a proposal to me which I have yet to assign to any department, since all I promised him was that I'd look it over. Their client is relaunching their avocado oil brand in a few months, and wants us to handle the marketing and advertising. Marcus though isn't handing it all to us."

"So it's more like a collaboration?"

"Yeah," I replied. "Which means I have to go out of the norm in bringing together a team to handle this project. I'm thinking of either making an entirely new team, or to pose this as a competition, and allow submissions. The winners can then handle the project."

She nodded, taking in what I had just said, and as she usually did in the office when my words were approved.

A small laugh rumbled at the back of my throat. "I'm asking what your opinion is, not just telling you how I want things to get done."

"Um," her smile was hesitant, but sincere. "Christian. Can I call you Christian?"

"Sure," I replied, and she blushed. I absolutely loved how the warmth seemed to lighten her eyes up even further.

"Alright. You're not just a project manager or a team leader. You're the CEO. I mean, most people would find it difficult speaking to you without getting tongue tied, so you can't just ask me a question that could most likely put my job in jeopardy, and expect me to respond."

"How would it put your job in jeopardy?"

"That's a serious business question, and it feels like a test. You can't try to test me at eight o'clock at night in this kitchen."

"It's not a test," I said. "I really want to know what you think."

She smiled. "I understand, but again, because you're the CEO, I really don't want to appear less than competent so I'm going to keep my opinion to myself on this one."

"What?"

"I'm serious."

"I can see that you are and you should relax. Nothing you say when we're intimately in each other's presence right now will affect anything concerning your position at the company."

She regarded me as though trying to gauge the truth to my words.

"I mean it," I said, my words heartfelt.

Her eyes were dancing with amusement and so were mine, but we both took this assurance seriously.

"Alright" she said and came over to sit by my side. I noticed now too for the first time, she didn't sit two stools away from me, so I turned to face her and she did the same. Our knees brushed against each other's, and I reveled in the innocent but yet charged touch.

"I think that opening it up for submissions would be great. We haven't had one in about a year and a half. The first one I think happened about three months after I started working at the company, and there's been nothing since then."

I nodded. "Alright. I'm also curious to see what hidden talents we have in the company. I'll get the gears moving on it in the morning. I've already mentioned it to Gary but can you set up an official meeting tomorrow so we can hash it out? I'll find a way to slot him in between ten and eleven."

"Quarter after ten," she said. "Your meeting with the CFO is going to bleed into it, so quarter after ten would be great."

"Alright," I replied.

She looked around for a second, and then a frown came across her face.

"I didn't bring my phone," she said, and rose to her feet. "I need to note this down."

She then started to walk away, but I caught her hand and pulled her back to me.

"Christian," she called, in a laughing breathy voice that immediately intensified my desire to have her under me. I brought her to lean against me, a hand going across her midriff till she was stationed between my legs.

"Do it later," I leaned down to bask in the scent on her neck.

It was floral, I realized... perhaps lavender? And it was soft and enticing just like she was.

"I'll forget," she tried to wriggle out of my hold. However there was no way in hell I was going to let her go. So I pressed a warm, heated kiss to the skin just above her pulse, and felt the slight shudder of her body.

"Christian," she called again, but this time her tone had significantly lowered.

I then began to trace the kisses downwards, her grip tightening on my thighs.

"Christian," she called again. "We have food coming soon."

I couldn't think up a response for that as my brain was beginning to shut down, so I continued on.

Soon, I was pulling the blouse out of her pants and over her head. I flung the fabric aside, which revealed her creamy skin and the dark lacy bra that was contrasted against it.

I wasted no time in working the hooks and soon her breasts were spilling into my hands. My lips returned to hers while I fondled the soft, heavy mounds.

She leaned further into me, needing every inch of contact she could get.

The pad of my tongue stroked the engorged bud of her nipples, but I needed more.

So I got off the stool, and swiftly lifted her off the ground.

A squeal escaped her lips at the sudden lift, and it reverberated through the quiet room. I loved everything about it and about her presence here. She was deposited on the counter, her legs wrapping around my back, and then my lips returned to her breasts.

I sucked hard on the pale, pink peaks, until I had her near pulling my hair from its roots.

Her soft moans rang in my ears, and it was pure music. I could listen to her moan forever, and wondered if it would be quite strange to have the sounds recorded. I decided to bring it up, so between brief pauses from my feasting, I mentioned it and she shook with laughter.

"I'd be glad to," she replied as my lips began to trace down her torso. I wanted to eat her out but it concerned me that the food would arrive before I was midway through. I cared little for it now as I wanted to take my time with her and wanted no distractions whatsoever.

So I straightened and returned my lips to hers. The kiss was long and deep, with her tongue licking deliciously into my mouth. We kissed like we had been at it for years with each other, and now needed this intimate tasting of the other to survive. When we finally parted to breathe, my eyes fluttered open however she kept her eyes tightly shut, reveling in the moment.

I needed to fuck her then, and couldn't hold myself back any longer so my hands went to the button of her pants. She leaned slightly backwards, her eyes coming open and I watched her, mesmerized as her hair cascaded down her back.

Suddenly, the front door's bell rang, and my heart jumped in disappointment.

I would have to pause for a little bit, and as I managed to pull away from her, I could see the frustration she too had in her gaze.

"I'll be right back."

"No," she cried, and my insides warmed with emotions that had me stopping in the middle of the foyer. I needed a brief pause to get my brain working, but then the bell rang again. So I strolled to the door, got our food and returned to her.

She was still on the counter, her legs spread out and her hands fondling her breasts. My grip loosened at the sight and the bag fell to the door.

"Christian," she called, slightly startled, but before she could say anymore I was silencing her with a hard kiss. Pulling her pants off took much longer than I almost could tolerate, so by the time the access to her sex was earned, I was starved with need.

Lowering, I spread her thighs even further apart and covered her with my mouth.

A few minutes later, her orgasm came in a delicious stream that coated my lips and tongue. My scalp was sore from all the pulling, but it was a dull ache that was beyond welcome. I loved the way she gripped me, how she threw her arms around my shoulders and crushed me to her, gratitude and adoration flowing from her as she planted kisses all over my face. Then she started on the buttons of my dress shirt and from then on, things spun out of control.

We became frantic, desperate to have our bodies joined so the fabric came off me nearly half torn. Then her hands were on my pants, but I soon took over and stood naked before her. She paused momentarily then. Her chest rising and falling heavily, and her hand flattened just over the space where my heart was lodged. The organ did an excited jump.

"You're beautiful, Christian," she said, her eyes watering. "So fucking beautiful."

"And so are you," I tightened my arms around her waist. I allowed her to go at the pace she wanted, so I watched as she ran her hands down my chest and then her hands closed around my cock.

Her touch made me throw my head back, and as she jerked me, I shut my eyes and leaned completely into the caress.

"Fuck me," she said, reaching lower to cup my ass. Her grin was full of mischief and torment so I kissed her once again, and grabbed my length. I slicked it up with her release, the head pulsing and flushed with excitement. When I finally pushed into her, the snugness and her warmth forced me to go still for a few moments.

Then with a hand underneath her thighs, I gripped her and shoved my dick all the way in.

" What... if you... *mnghh*."

"What if I what?" I managed to ask, my focus on settling my hips into a sweet rhythm, just fast enough for the both of us.

"What if you were short?" she said. "You wouldn't be able to fuck me on this counter."

Somehow, I was able to laugh. "I'd fuck you against the wall," I told her. "Or maybe climb onto the island with you."

She burst out laughing, but the sound was soon cut off when my cock hit a spot inside of her that was particularly sweet. She gasped, her nails digging viciously into my skin.

"Christian!" she cried out, slightly trembling. "Do it again... right there."

I withdrew, angling my hips in the required position and slammed into her. Her ass nearly left the counter, her body twisting and squirming with the barrage of pleasure.

"Holy fuck," she cursed, her face falling into the crook of my neck as I continued ramming into her. She grew considerably louder, and I relished her unraveling till she almost began to pull away from me.

"I can't," she shuddered. "It's too-"

I gripped her even tighter to hold her in place and kept fucking her till the strength began to seep out of my legs.

The race towards both of our releases was now crazed. The room had been cool earlier but now, sweat beaded both of our foreheads and down our backs. The hairs on my body were standing upright, tingling with the delicious emotion of the mind numbing pleasure.

Soon we both neared the peak and it registered that neither of us had remembered any protection.

"I'll pull out," I swore to her, doubtful that she even heard me. However when we both reached the threshold of the orgasm, she grabbed onto my ass and shook her head.

"I need you," she breathed. "I want to feel you cum inside me. I'm on the pill, it's alright."

No further convincing was needed. She soon crumbled, her cry filling my chest with pride as the orgasm ripped through her. I soon followed, emptying my release into her.

"*Fuck*," I shook uncontrollably and afterwards collapsed against her, barely able to keep us both upright as she panted into my neck.

I just needed to call out her name and so I did, over and over again, paying homage to the woman that was reducing me to nothing but a melted heap of sensation and sweet euphoria.

Afterwards we kissed till the strength was completely drawn out of us, and at the end, she completely and wholeheartedly collapsed against me.

ADELE

Eating naked with my boss shouldn't have been normal.

But then here I was, my ass smacked down on his groin, and his naked torso against my back as we ate from the plates spread across the counter. It was the most intimate meal I'd ever had.

He couldn't stop caressing me, and so my duty was feeding the both of us to replenish our energy while his hands went around my body. At some point, his fingers found their way into my sex and in the moments that followed after, I was gone. He finger fucked me till I came yet again, and it was a while after before I was able to move.

"Shower time," he said to me, and I nearly choked on the emotion of it all. My time with past boyfriends had been enjoyable, but I couldn't remember ever feeling like this. Which made me come to realize how much it had to do with the man himself.

I gazed up at his smiling eyes... the slight crease by the corner and his narrow nose. Unable to stop myself, I reached out to tap the tip with the pad of my finger. He laughed softly at that, but it wasn't enough. I met his gaze, and the depth of emotion I saw in them I was certain mirrored mine. So I leaned forward and kissed him, refusing to listen to the voice telling me perhaps I had feared the wrong things from the start.

My concern had been on the impact our rendezvous would have on my professional life, but I had failed to consider the impact it would have on my heart. He guided me in rising as he did the same, and I watched him, his purposeful and controlled movements, the confidence with which he even rose despite the fact he was stark naked. I loved the build of his body... the way the broad shoulders were defined with muscle, and the way his olive skin melded to every slab. Then his ass... it was fair and firm and needed my mouth nibbling on it at some point in time. And then there was his cock, which I suspected I would never get sated off. Right now it was still slightly aroused, his length quite intimidating and his width jarring.

All of him had been inside me, and now I was certain he was on his way to clutching my heart.

"I'm gonna carry you," he said, and immediately I shook my head in protest, running before the option could even become a possibility. He caught me before I could go too far away, and immediately I was lifted off the ground and put across his shoulder.

"Christian," I squealed, but his response was a drawn out chuckle that had my heart tumbling in my chest. When we finally arrived in his room, I was dizzy from being held off the ground and bent over for so long.

I slapped his chest lightly in retaliation, but he took the hit with elation. Leaning down to lightly grab my bottom lip, he sucked softly before turning on the water and adjusting the temperature. He lathered his hands with soap and with his gaze on mine, slid his fingers over my nipples.

Yet another intimate moment. So intimate that I truly wondered how I would ever be able to properly work with him again. Where indeed was all this leading, if anywhere at all? He slowly moved his hands down my body through my sex and stroked me, slick and clean and the sensations made me dizzy until all I could do was hold onto him for dear life.

There was no need to think, I told myself.

Absolutely none at all, at least in this moment because all that was needed was for me to take it all in and bask in the much needed relief and bliss.

It didn't take much for him to have me coming once again, and this time around it was with my legs wrapped around his waist as he pummeled into me, my back knocking repeatedly against the smooth tiled wall. I held onto him until he was spilling into me with an anguished moan.

I relished it all and at the end, was beyond spent and limp and most definitely unable to feel or even stand on my own two feet. I soon found I didn't need to because he rinsed me off, and then took me with him out of the stall.

My consciousness slowly returned as he set me on the vanity counter, and then retrieved a towel to wipe me dry.

I felt vulnerable... and much too exposed, especially in the well lit space. We remained silent in each other's presence, and it should have been peaceful except my head couldn't stop screaming once again about how this was my boss and about how we weren't in any sort of relationship. And so eventually, I began to lower to my feet. He let me, and with a shy smile I took the towel from him.

I saw he wanted to speak, however my mouth moved before I could let him.

"I'll go um..." I pointed towards the door. "My things are in my room."

He watched me, in that knowing way that made me know he understood once again exactly what had come over me.

And so he gave a curt, but kind nod and I scurried out of there.

Just before I left his room however, I looked back at his bedroom, decorated in dark shades, and at his bed... neatly made and as cozy as a dream. I couldn't help but recall then how wonderfully I had fallen asleep in his arms the previous night. Perhaps this is why he had brought me here for the shower instead of my own room. I sighed again and thought to return but then decided against it.

Currently in my life, I had much more severe battles to tackle than this one, but as the days went on and as my dependence on him increased, I couldn't help but wonder if this particular one was building up to a fight I was sure to lose.

Shaking my head, I pushed the concerns as far away as I possibly could, and made my way back to the room I had been assigned.

ADELE

The next morning, a new and very serious dilemma presented itself and that was as to the issue of what I would wear to work. Somewhere, it had been a part of my intentions from the previous evening to find a way to resolve it before at least heading to bed, but the time had gotten away from me courtesy of Christian.

And now it was the morning after, and I was stumped.

My only option seemed to be to perhaps hurry off to find an open store so I could get what I needed, but the very thought of being around town where whoever it was was hot on my heels could approach and harm me was not in the least appealing.

There seemed to be no way out besides perhaps wearing what I had the previous day, however this I was certain could possibly draw the attention of anyone who paid attention. For instance Melinda. There was no way she wouldn't notice if I ran into her, and if she could, then someone else also could. That in turn could add fuel to the already ignited flame of suspicion the entire company had on how and why exactly I was single handedly picked out for a position others were equally and perhaps even more qualified for.

I sighed as I buttoned up my blouse, but then as I began to tuck it into my suit pants, something else occurred to me. I could perhaps… borrow a shirt from Christian?

My heart skipped a beat at the very thought, but then it made enough sense to me. My only concern though was his scent on it which could also possibly give me away, and above all else would be the most incriminating.

I considered this a bit more and then decided to first of all ask if he had something that he'd never worn before.

And so I moved into action and headed over to his bedroom, nervous, but certain he would already be awake. I knocked, and it took a few more seconds with me contemplating on whether to do it again at the now plausible concern perhaps he was still asleep after all. My hand had just lifted to try again one last time, when the door was pulled open.

He appeared, torso bare, but with his pants on but unbuttoned. He had on dark briefs underneath so there was regretfully nothing scandalous to show but all of it was more than enough to fluster me to the point where I even forgot why I had come there in the first place.

"How are you?" he asked, and all I could do was respond with a nervous smile, my heart racing so hard in my chest I could hear it in my ears.

"Do you need something?" he asked, and luckily this was enough to jolt me back to my senses.

"Is it possible for me to borrow a shirt from you? I don't have anything to change into and I'm not quite comfortable with wearing what I did yesterday again. I planned to head home for some supplies but it didn't quite work out the way... I'd planned.

I slowed at his immense concentration at my request, and for a moment my heart squeezed at the thought that perhaps I was pushing things too far.

And so chickening out, I started to withdraw the request, but then he gave a nod and turned around to head into the room.

"Of course," he said. "I'm sure we can find something for you."

I blinked, at how easily he had agreed with no prejudice or reservations.

And so I followed him past the bedroom and into his walk in closet.

He led me over to his rack of hung dress shirts and then turned around to face me.

"Take your pick," he said with a courteous smile and I almost couldn't look away from his beautiful face.

I soon had to however, and so my attention turned back to the rack of clothes. I immediately went for a white shirt since it was basic and was the least conspicuous. Plus I didn't have any intentions of being picky before him.

"Thank you," I said and immediately started to turn around but then he grabbed onto my arm and held me back.

"Don't you want to check if the fit will be alright? We're not exactly the same size."

He didn't need to mention this, and my eyes as well didn't need to lower down to his ripped torso but they did, and it was quite the feat to swallow.

"Beggars can't be choosers," I managed to say and he laughed, his chest shaking slightly at the hearty sounds.

"Wouldn't a t-shirt be preferable?" he asked, and I considered this but then eventually deemed that it would be too casual.

"No," I replied. "This will do. As long as it's tucked properly into my pants, I'll be able to get away with it. Oversized dress shirts for women are not strange. I think."

"You think?" he asked, seemingly taken aback that I didn't seem certain of this.

"I think," I replied, amused. "I'm not really up to date on the trends."

"Alright," he replied.

"Thank you," I said, and then we both stared at each other.

The moments that followed were quite awkward and confusing as neither of us seemed to know exactly how to act before the other. At least I didn't know how to, especially as I gazed at his lips and instantly recalled exactly what they had done to my sex just the night before. The instant jolt of arousal to my core at the memory was sharp and numbing, tearing a thankfully quiet gasp out of me.

That was my cue then to leave, and so immediately I turned around.

He however, and once again, held onto my arm and stopped me. And then he stared into my eyes. "If you need any more help let me know," he said and my heart fluttered so much it nearly flew out of my chest.

I nodded, unable to speak and then his gaze lowered to my lips.

I would have kissed him right then, if he hadn't let go of me, and then turned around to go on his way. I would have leaned in and reminded myself of what absolute bliss felt like.

Instead I shut my eyes, drew in a deep breath and then released it.

Then I went on my way, the ground beneath my feet, mighty unstable.

ADELE

I managed to make it work.

The shirt was tucked into the dark, striped pants I had worn the previous day, while the sleeves were bunched up towards my elbows and then secured on both arms with hair ties. I tied my hair up, was more than glad for the stylish touch my necklace gave it, popped the collar and let an extra button lose along my chest to deflect away from the masculine fit.

It definitely smelled like him, and by relation, so did I and so the moment I arrived at the company's lobby I considered taking the stairs.

However it sounded like suicide as there was no way I could climb all the way up to his floor, so I put the nonsensical thought away and hurried over to the elevators.

As the doors slid shut, I prayed with all my heart that no one else would come in. It was early enough, just a few minutes past seven, and so when it eventually shut, I couldn't help but let out a heavy sigh of relief.

I arrived at our reception in considerably good spirits, with the resolve to stay away from as many staff as possible, but still somewhat pacified by the reminder since Christian was so new as a CEO, not many people could identify him by his scent. It could also be the case that this was my boyfriend's shirt, who was not Christian. However given the current state of speculation about my rise to the top, I doubted that excuse would ever fly.

Regardless, I arrived safely, settled in and then started on work. About half an hour later however, the elevator on our floor dinged the arrival of a visitor and my head lifted up. Soon enough and much to my alarm, Melinda came strolling in and my heart nearly fell into my stomach. She was most definitely sure to notice something.

"Hey," she smiled brightly at me, in a gorgeous teal pantsuit that momentarily made me forget my reservations about meeting her today.

"That's beautiful," I complimented, and a spring was added to her step.

"Right? I got it last week. I've forgotten the brand's name, something about matches but it was on sale and I immediately snatched it up. They're too pricey otherwise."

I touched the fabric as she arrived by my side, and leaned against my desk. It was only then I realized even talking about the suit was sure to invite conversation about my own outfit.

"You look great." she complimented and I smiled, eager to change the subject.

"What are you doing here?"

"The shirt's oversized," she barely heard me. "That's not your style."

With her gaze on me, I knew I had to respond with something else. I shrugged. "It was on sale at Zara, so I decided to try something different."

She took a closer look and I nearly rolled my eyes.

"Isn't this supposed to be something of a dress shirt?"

"Yeah," I repeated. "I didn't have anything else suitable. I have to do laundry tonight when I get home."

"Ah," she replied and then moved on from the topic.

"Anyway, why I'm here is a rumor is going around downstairs that there might be an open submission competition for the CEO's new project? I heard an old acquaintance brought it directly to him?"

I was taken aback. "How di-"

She was amused. "It's true right? I think he mentioned it to Gary."

"Oh," I frowned slightly.

"So..." she urged. "Did he mention it to you?"

My lips parted to respond, but I wasn't exactly certain as to what to say. I mean last night for sure over dinner but officially? Absolutely not.

"He didn't," I replied. "Or rather he hasn't."

Her eyes narrowed at me. "Is that true?"

I feigned offense. "Why would I lie to you?"

She humorously glared at me for a few seconds more, and then she finally accepted I was telling the truth. It didn't feel good.

"Well if he does decide to go ahead with it, you'll be the first to know so inform me alright? And also be on the lookout for any tips that could help us ace it."

"You'll be applying?"

"Yeah," she replied. "I think so, it depends on the brief. I think I want to try my hand at it. I'm so bored of being in the secretary's pool."

"I understand," I nodded and she straightened.

"Will you try to apply, if he does open it up?"

"Of course I will," I answered.

She sucked in her breath, her eyes going around the elegant room. "It seems pretty great to be here. No other troublesome colleagues to deal with, privacy, peace and the most yummy looking man to ever exist within such close proximity at every point in time. Honestly I don't know how you're able to get any work done with him as your boss. Don't you just get distracted and forget you're staring at his lips? Has he ever called you out before about it?"

My eyes widened at her questions and she laughed. "Oh, I just remembered you've actually slept with him before. Oh my God, Adele. How the hell can you get any work done?"

I'd had enough. "If you don't leave right now I'm going to call security."

She laughed, but thankfully and soon after that, she was on her way.

And then Christian came in.

Our greetings were courteous as was usual, but there was no lingering affectionate gaze. Our eyes barely met and although I was more inclined to write this off as his fault, I knew it was untrue because I had refused to look at him. He shut the door behind him and we both continued with our work.

I waited for a few minutes to give him the time to settle in, and then went in with his schedule for the day and to be assigned whatever tasks he needed done.

He looked up as I approached, his gaze less on me but more on his shirt and how I had turned it into a suitable outfit.

I placed the brief of his schedule before him and then straightened.

His gaze met mine then but there was no commentary. Butterflies filled my stomach because there was no way I could look at him and not remember, and so at the throbbing of my clit in awareness, I shifted my weight from one foot to the other.

He picked the folder up and I was so lost in the sight of his big sturdy hands, and how they had cupped me over and over again that it took a little while for it to register his attention had returned to me.

When it did, my gaze meeting his, I was so startled that for a few seconds I didn't know what to say. His gaze lowered before he spoke but I didn't miss the slight lift to the corner of his lips in amusement. I burned with embarrassment, and from then on knew well enough to avoid staring at him.

"Please contact Peterson to shift our meeting just before lunch to later on in the evening or at a different date. I received a call on my way in this morning from an old business contact so I have to take an extra hour during lunch time to see to that."

"Okay," I replied and noted this down on my tablet in hand. He continued scrolling through the file and then with a nod handed it over.

"I've decided to go ahead with the open entry submissions for Mr. Sims project. None of the departments can fully take responsibility for it now anyway so why not create a temporary new team to handle it?"

Just like Melinda had hounded me over earlier in the morning.

I nodded, and he went on instructing me of the details and soon enough we were done.

"I'll draft this and hand it over to IT to get it set up. When do you want it to officially begin?"

"Today," he replied. "And we'll keep it open for three weeks. Marcus will hound me over it if it takes me any longer to give him a response."

"Alright," I replied and turned around to take my leave.

"Will you be applying?" he asked, and I stopped momentarily. I looked at his eyes then and my heart softened at the true concern in it.

"I think so," I replied, not wanting to disappoint his expectation on behalf of my own good. "I'll do my best."

"Alright," he replied, and I wished right then I could go over to kiss him. I wondered if it truly would be too inappropriate for me to just do so, I mean why the hell had I drawn such clear boundaries between us from the onset? I sighed, wishing I could take it back, but decided not to beat myself up over my decision either way. I had been reeling from a breakup, and couldn't have any faith whatsoever that considering anyone ever again would be in my best interest.

I still didn't think there was an ounce of good judgment even now to begin to consider this, especially since it would also be quite presumptuous of me to imagine the option was even available, but I couldn't help but think of it.

And so with a sigh, I turned around and walked away.

ADELE

bout forty-five minutes before the lunch hour began, the announcement went up and it was on my ride up from Gary's department that I got the message from Melinda.

"*It's up!*" she wrote, and I texted back.

"*Yup.*"

"*Jeesh you couldn't have informed me it was actually happening? Earlier this morning you seemed clueless.*"

I sighed as I typed in a response.

"*I was. He put me on it as soon as he walked in.*"

"*What are the odds?*" she sent back and I couldn't help but feel quite the tinge of annoyance at her words.

"*What does that mean?*" I texted back my brows furrowing.

She didn't respond. Instead she sent me an invite to lunch.

"*No,*" I replied back. "*I had a huge breakfast.*"

I hoped this would be the end of our interaction for the day but before I arrived back on my floor, yet another message arrived from her.

"I feel as though you're keeping me at a distance these days. You're not as open as you once were and it almost feels like we're strangers. I don't want to chuck it up to the difference in our positions because I know you're not the kind, but I can't help but feel unhappy sometimes. You were barely hospitable when I was at your desk this morning, and then your messages all seem like I'm pestering you, and that is when you even bother to respond timely. I truly hope we're good because I would hate to lose you as a friend."

The moment I received and read through it, I instantly had a splitting headache.

And thus, I didn't look where I was headed as I reread the message in concern. I was aware some of her complaints were valid, but didn't know how I was going to explain I had become so distracted and withdrawn due to the fact I was being haunted and stalked.

I ran into Christian. His familiar arms sliding around my waist to hold me in place.

"Oh my God!" my heart nearly flew out of my chest.

For the first few minutes, I was disoriented, especially as I stared up at him wondering what had gone wrong.

He soon explained. "I stopped," he said. "I thought you'd look up at me. What's got you so occupied? Is everything alright?"

I immediately heard the concern in his tone, and watched as he reached between us to retrieve my phone that had thankfully not flown away but was instead nestled between us. At the brush of his hand against my chest however I was momentarily struck, awareness jolting me.

"Everything's fine," I replied as he handed it over. "I mean… there's nothing yet from…" He understood.

"Alright," he said and then let me go. "I'm heading out for my meeting."

"Okay," I replied, and then turned around to watch him go. Dressed in his crisp navy blue suit, and a matching, patterned waistcoat within. He looked delectable and at the reminder of his touch around my waist, I couldn't help but find it just a bit harder to breathe.

I watched him until he disappeared out of sight, and then returned my attention to Melinda's text.

I sighed, considering if perhaps I should take lunch with her, but being out of the building once again and being subjected to the near panic attack I had the last time at the suspicion the sick individual that had turned my life into a living hell was staring right at me without me even realizing it was much too much suspense for me to handle.

And so I just called her.

The first time she didn't pick up, and so the phone rang until it went to voicemail. I sighed however and tried again, deciding to give her the benefit of the doubt that she wasn't purposely ignoring me and was probably just without her phone.

Thankfully she picked up, and for the first few seconds after neither of us said a word.

"I was barely hospitable to you?" I repeated her words back to her.

"You were," she replied.

I waited for her to say more and when she didn't I sighed again.

"Melinda, whether I came off as hostile or not, you do know it has nothing to do with you right? Or with my position as you mentioned."

She was silent, and so I repeated the question.

"You do know this right?"

"I just..." she sighed. "I'm sorry. I'm used to us communicating frequently and being quite close, but lately it hasn't seemed like the case. I know you're having a really hard time with the breakup with Andrew, especially with how you reacted to seeing him yesterday. I just... I just hope you'll open up a bit more. I'd love to help you out, but when you don't, I feel distant from you and it just makes me uncomfortable." she laughed softly. "I'm sorry. It's the middle of the day and I sound very dramatic. I just needed to get this off my chest."

And unload onto me, to add to my multitude of existing problems, I couldn't help but think, but then I cautioned myself on being too hard on her. But there was no way I was going to tell her the truth, and neither was I willing to come up with a way of resolving this so I just left it up to her.

"I'm sorry," I apologized first. "I guess I was a bit standoffish this morning but I haven't been sleeping very well and perhaps was just too exhausted. I don't want us to be distant either so how can I make it up to you?"

She went quiet again and I presumed it was to consider this.

"You really can't have lunch with me today?"

"No, Melinda. I'm really sorry but I can't, truly. I have some work to catch up on."

"What about after work then? It's Friday. We could have dinner together and perhaps go out for some fun. I think we both need this."

Absolutely not, was my immediate response but before I could think of how best to word my refusal, she spoke.

"You can't say no to this. You just said you haven't been sleeping well and there's nothing like drinking and dancing to exhaust you and send you straight to bed. Plus you get so drowsy after you drink."

She was right on all counts, however a club or bar like she was suggesting was even more dangerous as it was almost impossible to see or hear anyone clearly.

Before I could work up a tangible enough excuse however she stamped her conclusion on the matter.

"Adele it's settled, be ready for dinner after work."

"Melinda, I have to work late today," I said to her. "Let's do this some other time."

She refused. "We'll skip dinner then and go to Trouble Hatch. The fun starts close to midnight anyway so we can head over late. And you can go home at any time. An hour or two of a little dancing and sweating will be great for us both."

I no longer had any excuses and so I nodded.

"I can't see you," she groaned. "But I know you're responding in some kind of way so is it a yes or a no?"

I sighed again. "Alright," I replied, with no idea whatsoever about how I was going to pull this off.

The call came to an end but my worry about this continued, until the evening arrived and it was time to make a decision.

The only options I had now were feigning an illness or some emergency appointment, but neither of those would fly I was certain.

My gaze was on my computer screen but I didn't see a thing until suddenly there was a knock on my desk. I startled, jumping slightly at the figure that had seemingly come out of nowhere.

"Christian," his name sounded in my mind but then I recalled where we were and rose to my feet.

"Sir," I said and he cocked his head at me. Watchful... concerned.

"This is the second time today," he said, and I was very clear on what he was referring to. My gaze lowered, and I knew I would have to say something, and it was much easier to spill what was on my mind to him than anyone else. Surprisingly, this stranger I had met not so long ago had turned into an unbelievable pillar of strength for me.

"I'm being forced to go out tonight... to a club... and I'm concerned about my safety." he watched me attentively, however I didn't know what else to say beyond this.

"Who's forcing you?" he asked, and I shook my head.

"She's not forcing me… it's just… with everything going on I've been quite distant, especially with me wearing your shirt today and having your scent all over m-" the word halted on my tongue as his gaze lowered, slowly, purposeful, down my torso and then came back up to linger on my chest. I was sure he was definitely picturing me naked, and my cheeks burned.

"You look great in it," he said, his tone smoky and instantly recognizable from the night before. My body reacted instantly… my nipples hardening, and the bud between my legs pulsing. I shifted uncomfortably, trying my best to ease the ache.

"I-I'll make sure to have it laundered before returning it," I said and his gaze returned to mine. "No need," he said. "Unlike you I don't mind your scent all over it."

It took me quite the while to process this, and after it registered I immediately hurried to counter this. "I don't mind your… I mean… I just don't want anyone to catch on… or suspect anything is going on between us."

He smiled and at his amusement, I realized he was just teasing me.

"Christian…" my shoulders slumped but then once again, I realized where we were and straightened. "I mean, sir."

"Drop the sir," the smile left his face. "No one else in this building calls me that."

"That's not true," I immediately countered, and he cocked an eyebrow at me at my defiance.

I refused to be intimated. "I'll ask around. That can't be true."

He smiled, and it made the wings of my heart flap.

"Who's inviting you out?" he asked, and I snapped back to attention.

"Melinda," I replied. "We were very close back when I was in the secretary pool. I mean we still are but because of being so withdrawn these days she's worried we might be drifting too far apart."

His eyebrows furrowed.

"That sounds like a relationship," he said and I was amused.

"We girls take our relationships a bit more seriously." but then I realized this wasn't the truth because even to me, things felt slightly off.

"I think it's because our friendship is really not that deep, or else I should have been able to inform her of all that's going on right?"

"Exactly," he replied. "And true friends don't need to always be in contact with each other."

"I think we just got used to it," I replied. "And plus we've worked together for quite a while so we got pretty attached."

"Understood," he said, and then looked away briefly to think.

"You can't feign some sort of sudden illness to get out of it?"

"No, I've already been completely called out for flaking out on her. Anything beyond showing up at that club with her is unacceptable. I won't be staying long though. It'll only be an hour or two tops, and then I can use the sick card but I most definitely have to show up."

He nodded again, his gaze still focused on the wall behind me in thought.

Eventually his gaze returned to mine, and I was eager to hear what his suggestion would be.

"Go," he said to me. "And try your best to have fun. I think you might need this."

I was taken aback.

"Isn't that dangerous?"

"I don't think whoever this sick bastard is really wants to hurt you. You haven't received any handwritten threats have you?"

I shook my head.

"Either way, I'm going to arrange for security to have their eyes on you. They'll blend into the crowd so you can have as much fun as you want, and I'll ensure you're protected."

I had absolutely no idea of what to say, so I just stared at him.

"That's too much trouble," was all I could eventually say, but he shook his head.

"Having you hurt in any way is the trouble," he said and my heart slammed against my chest. However it wasn't because I was touched, but because I felt fear.

Because he said it so casually, without thought or contemplation and in a way that indicated without the shadow of a doubt he meant every single word he was saying. And all I could feel was fear we were going too deep... becoming too close. He was my boss. I was supposed to stay away from him and not get entangled. That had been the whole plan from the beginning. Instead he had somehow wormed his way into my life and now, I didn't want him to leave.

Perhaps speaking to Melinda after all would be a good idea so she could warn me about keeping my head. But then I remembered she had encouraged our union from the beginning, and I couldn't help but doubt any warning whatsoever would come from her when it came to Christian.

"I don't think there's any need for that," I said, my gaze lowering. His response however was simple.

"I'll be the judge."

CHRISTIAN

Restlessness slowly invaded my mind.

With every minute that passed, I received the crippling urge to reach out to her. To confirm she was truly okay, however, I held back.

So as not to push her away.

So it wouldn't be too much... for her at least.

Solely for her.

For me... it wasn't even near enough.

The needed security had been assigned to her, and I had stayed back in the office, simply because it was closer to the club. If I drove fast enough, I could be there in thirteen minutes. The house however was a different case. It wasn't too far away but this was downtown on a Friday night. Maneuvering through the traffic was sure to drive me mad before I even arrived.

But that was in case she needed me.

For the umpteenth time I looked away from my computer screen, which I had long stopped seeing, and at the reminder that I had seen her doing just the same quite a number of times, zoning off into her thoughts I couldn't help but smile.

But as I looked down at the screen of my phone, which was very clear with the message one of the hired security had sent to me saying she was doing alright, my heaviness returned.

Perhaps I should have discouraged her from going... prioritized her safety on her behalf. But she needed this.

Or at least I hoped it would do her some good, and get her colleague friend off her back.

I had seen the colleague in question around a couple of times, and knowing she was her friend I couldn't help but pay special attention to her. However what I felt towards her now was something akin to loathing.

It wasn't her fault for not knowing about the dangers currently plaguing Adele, and selfishly dragging her off to such a crowded place but still, I couldn't help but be annoyed.

I picked up the phone... my heart once again racing.

I wanted to be there, which was ironic given I hadn't been to a club in years. Outside the rare business meetings in restaurants and bars I had more or less chucked any nightlife desires out of my system. It had been more or less the purge needed so I could pour all of my time and attention into proving myself and climbing up the career ladder.

However, for what had to be the thousandth time at this point, I didn't want to be her boss. I wanted to be over there with her and protecting her. Making sure no one and nothing dangerous came within even an inch of her.

These feelings were no doubt ludicrous, but I refused to question them. Instead I allowed them to run free through my mind... telling myself it was just for tonight... and it was okay to worry and be vigilant... so I didn't lose her.

I swallowed, a sudden and humongous lump appearing in my throat, however when even that appeared to be quite the feat I picked up my phone. I wasn't exactly certain what I was doing but when my thumb scrolled past Adele's name and instead searched for Stacy's, I had a pretty good idea.

She picked up on the third ring, and sounded so surprised for a moment I almost completely forgot why I was even contacting her in the first place.

"Holy shit!" she exclaimed. "Why are you calling me?"

I sighed, amused. "I spoke to you two days ago."

"Yeah but you texted me. No one ever calls, especially not you. You're so impatient," she laughed. "Anyway what is it? You better be okay."

"I'm fine," I replied. "I just wondered what you were up to." I looked around at my quiet office and then rose to my feet to head over to the tall windows behind.

"Not much," she said, and my heart slightly deflated. I didn't know how to ask about what I wanted afterwards.

"Actually, that's not true," she replied. "I am up to something, and I'd hoped it would be something worthwhile but it's just a fucking disaster and I'm pissed."

"What happened?" I asked, and she went on to tell me about the date she was currently on... the first with the guy, which was turning out so far to be torture.

"He slurps his food, and he can't fucking answer a question of mine without first asking one back. It's like I'm in fifth grade all over again and competing with Harvey Dick for top student.

I laughed. "Harvey Dick? That can't be his real name."

"Harvey is his real name," she replied luckily. "Dick is because I can't remember his fucking last name."

I smiled again, truly amused. "That's fair enough. What's this guy's name?" I asked. "The one you're currently on a date with."

"I don't fucking care," she replied. "As far as I'm concerned he doesn't exist anymore."

I laughed again. "So why are you still there?"

"I want us to split the check. This is a fucking small world and I don't want to forever be the girl that chose the pricey restaurant and walked out on him midway through so as not to have to pay for it."

"You could head over to the cashier to pay for your half?" I suggested, but she refused.

"It's fine. I've heard this place has the best Tiramisu known to man. I want to have a bit of it before I leave, because I won't be spending my money here again. Plus they might take it off the menu at any time. This place is quite unnecessarily spontaneous with their menu."

I felt light again, my chest filling with humor.

"How much longer do you have left on the date?" I asked.

"About thirty minutes, if he ever decides to finish eating. Have I mentioned he slurps his food? I'm in the bathroom now because I couldn't stand the sounds he was making from his pumpkin soup. It's fucking pumpkin. How the hell do you slurp that?"

I heard her inhale deeply, and then exhale.

"How about I come get you?" I asked. "How far away from my office are you?"

She seemed a bit surprised. "Um, about thirty five minutes?"

"Too far," I said. "Are you absolutely sure you want nothing to do with this guy? Eating habits are not that big of a deal if you truly connect."

"Christian," she called dryly. "I have nothing in common with him."

"Got it," I replied. "Do you know Trouble Hatch?"

"Of course I do," she replied. "It's downtown."

"Can you get in a cab immediately and meet me there?"

"Um… sure. Is something happening?"

"No," I replied, calming my tone as I realized how urgent I was making this seem. I mean it was but I didn't want her to know this.

"Nothing's happening," I replied. "I um…" I cleared my throat, knowing I'd have to reduce the gravity of my desperation with a little lie. She was too smart to not catch on otherwise.

"I'm wrapping up with a meeting here, but I'm considering staying a bit longer. Who better to do it with?"

"Oh my God, are you saying that we're going dancing?"

I laughed at the unmistakable excitement in her tone, but couldn't help but feel slightly guilty that none of this was the truth.

"I'm not dancing," I informed her. "But I will watch you... happily, and perhaps take some videos."

"Declined," she said. "If I'm going to have fun by myself then why should I come over?"

"Please?" I said, and just as expected, that was all that was needed.

"I love you too much to say no," she replied. "Plus my goal now is to get you drunk enough so you're not even aware enough to notice it when I drag you to the dance floor with me. "

"I never get that drunk," I replied, but her mischievous chuckle told me she had already taken it up as a challenge.

I sighed, arranged our meeting place and then put an end to the call.

I thought of Adele and wondered if she would be unhappy at seeing me there. Probably not, or at least I could stay in the shadows and not let her know of my arrival? That I would most definitely do.

All I needed was to have my eyes on her, so nothing went wrong, because only after she left the club and returned home would I be able to breathe easily.

ADELE

I was already on my third drink for the night, but I had sworn to myself it would be the last. And so when Melinda ordered yet another glass of their Troubled Leaves cocktail, I refused to join her.

"Oh my God we haven't been out in forever!" she leaned forward to yell into my ear. "Have fun… loosen up a little."

No thank you, I thought but didn't bother voicing this.

"I don't want to wake up with a headache tomorrow," was what I said instead, but was certain she didn't hear me. She blinked a large smile on her face and then straightened up on her stool.

I looked around, perusing the dark space, flashing strobe lights, and sandwiched bodies. Thankfully we were away from the chaos, and enjoying the less crowded arena of the bar, and it was the only thing that made me somewhat calm. I had ensured to take the last seat at the end of the line, so I wouldn't lose my mind from being suspicious of whoever came to sit beside me. For all I know, the bastard could take the opportunity to sit beside me and I wouldn't even realize it. Just the thought made a cold shiver run through me.

"Let's go dance," Melinda said, as she drained her glass and set it down. "There's a guy I've been ogling over in that corner."

I watched her flirtatious smile at the dark ahead, and didn't bother trying to figure out who she had spotted. I was a bit worried for her though, wondering if perhaps by association, the bastard that was after me would also harass her.

"Be careful," I said, but then she grabbed my hand and started to pull me along. I immediately shook my head, and pulled my hand out of her grip. "I'm too exhausted, Melinda. Go ahead."

"Oh come on," she whined. "You promised we'd have a good time together."

"Oh no," I wagged my finger, and then pulled her in so she could hear exactly what I was going to say, because in a little while I was going to leave.

"I promised to come out with you and that's it."

With a pout, she gave me a sour look and then began to head into the crowd.

I watched her go, and tried to cheer her on but at my slight whoop, she turned around to give me a pitiful look. I concluded she would be fine, but still kept my gaze on everyone around her. I also paid attention to my sides, just in case anyone suddenly approached me.

All of this caution was draining to say the least, and so all I could think about was returning to Christian's house and settling in for the night. Perhaps even with him, I dared to dream and had to lower my gaze in order to hide my blush from myself. I wondered what he was currently doing.

I had stayed a little while longer in the office, and then taken a cab over here to meet up with Melinda. He hadn't left when I did, and it made me worry he was still there and working.

I'd texted him of my departure, and he had texted back to say he'd hired two security men to be with me. They would stay out of sight but would keep their eyes on me at all times, and so there was no cause for me to worry.

My throat had clammed up with emotion at this, and I had found it hard to breathe. I had wanted to head back into his office to thank him, but all of this now was beginning to feel like equally dangerous territory and so I had simply done that through text and gone on my way.

However, now I truly wanted to show him my gratitude. I wanted to be with him the way I had been the previous night, and God it made me overheat in the fairly chilled room just thinking about it.

However, since I wasn't in the office, I allowed myself to think about it, allowing it to occupy my thoughts and keep my mind company even as my eyes remained watchful.

Pangs of pleasure, reminiscent of the previous night, battered into my core... the exquisite sensation of him filling me up and stretching me tight... his hand digging into my ass and his lips closing around my nipples. And then his kiss... I recalled his taste on my tongue, the lush slides of his tongue against mine, and could barely breathe.

I most definitely needed another drink in order to cool myself down, so I went ahead to order it. Melinda suddenly returned though, and it made me realize I needed the space and privacy to cool the heat on my cheeks and the lust currently simmering through my body. And so I set my feet on the floor from the stool, and informed her I would be right back.

"I need to use the bathroom."

"Oh, me too," she rose as well, and I was quite taken aback. Almost annoyed even until I realized this would mean I wasn't alone which was great.

I told the bartender to hold my drink until we returned and away we went.

In the bathroom, I went straight into an empty stall before she could look too closely at my face, and spent quite a while in there.

"Adele?" she called.

"Still here," I replied, as I heard flushing from a few stalls away.

"You're still here," she giggled. "I'm washing my hands."

"Alright," I replied.

"I can't believe you wore that huge blouse here," she said. "It's like you're completely over men after Andrew."

I was perplexed. "What's the correlation?"

"You don't care about being attractive," she said, and I truly didn't want to talk about this in a space where other strangers could be listening. But still, I proceeded to speak, not quite willing to leave the safety of the stall yet.

"I have quite the number of buttons released in case you didn't notice," I said.

"That's not enough," she complained. "It's too dark to see any way. You could have at least pulled the tails of the shirt out of your pants and tied it around your waist. You know what, that's exactly what we're going to do when you get out here."

"Not going to happen," I said, and finished up.

When I got out, I met her waiting but warned her with a glare.

"I will splash water on you if you come within an inch of me."

She laughed.

"C'mon, live a little. I know none of the men here are up to our boss's standard but that man is an Adonis. I still can't believe you've slept with him."

Okay, this was going into uncomfortable territory, and so with a frown at her and a glance at the stalls behind, I returned my attention to washing my hands. Just then however, I heard a flush behind me and sighed. Now I was going to face whoever that was, but then I just decided not to speak again so they wouldn't know whose voice had been who's.

"So…" Melinda wobbled slightly as she turned around to lean against the wall, watching and waiting. "How was he really? You've never given me details."

I sighed.

"Oh c'mon, you've been the worst sport all night. If you really didn't want to come out you should have just told me so."

"I did tell you so," I said, but ensured to keep my tone low.

The stall opened then, and I shut the tap off. With my wet hands, I moved over to the dispenser on the wall. Melinda was leaning against it so I nudged her out of the way. She laughed as I pulled the paper towels out, however I was just about to announce I would be leaving in twenty minutes when I heard my name.

"Adele?" my heart nearly stopped in my chest.

My gaze instantly went to the mirror, and in it was the reflection of Christian's little cousin.

Her eyes were widened in surprise at seeing me, while mine were widened in shock and mortification, especially at what Melinda had just been saying came to mind.

"Oh my God," I gasped underneath my breath.

Her face however had a massive smile on it. "I am so happy to see you," she said. "I didn't know when I would again after-"

I panicked and instantly stepped in, my voice louder than it needed to be.

"I'm happy to see you too, how's your mom doing?"

At the sudden pitch of my tone, my gaze went to Melinda and hers followed. Thankfully, she understood.

"Mom is doing great," she replied, and headed over to the sink.

"He's here," she replied, a smile on her face, and my eyes nearly popped out of my socket.

"What?"

"Yeah," she replied. "Do you want me to tell him I ran into you? I'm sure he'd be happy to know."

It took me a little while to get myself back together, especially as I didn't know how to relay to her he most definitely knew I was here, which made me wonder if he had indeed come over because of me. My bones turned to butter.

"Um…" I started to blush again. "No need."

"Alright," she said. "It was great seeing you again."

"It was great seeing you too," I replied, and then turned around to walk away before Melinda could ask any questions.

It was only after we returned to the corridor leading back to the dance floor, that I was able to breathe. "Jeesh, could you have gotten me out of there any faster?" she asked, and I could tell once again, she had found something to be offended about.

"She's a friend's sister," I said. "I'm sorry we have a bit of history… I mean with her sibling… so, I'd rather not make any more connections."

"Wow, how much don't I know about you?" she laughed, and I decided I wanted to leave. But then Christian was here. How could I?

I was going to see him when I arrived back at his home, but still, I wanted just a little glimpse of him here in this environment before I left. Even if it was just briefly. At the knowledge he was here my whole body had come to life and was now brimming with so much nervous excitement that I could barely contain it.

And so I nearly grabbed at my waiting drink the moment I returned to the bar.

Melinda began to go on about how disappointing and handsy the man she had approached on the dance floor had been. I picked up my phone as I listened to past tales of handsy men she had met on a dance floor, and eventually made up my mind. I mean, who knew where I would be in another week or month, or if Christian and I would ever get this chance of a nightlife together. And just like that, I knew exactly what I wanted with him. I wouldn't ask, but still I needed to at least say hello. And so I sent him a message.

I couldn't recall his cousin's name which sucked, and so I just used her title.

His response came a few seconds later, and my heart was near racing out of my chest.

"Yeah, she told me," he replied. And then nothing else. I was a bit disappointed. Perhaps he truly hadn't come here because of me? Perhaps I should have asked his cousin.

I shook my head then, deciding to try again but a message soon came in from him. My stomach flipped.

"*Having a good time?*" he asked, and I blushed.

"*Absolutely not.*"

But then I realized he probably had eyes on me, and my breathing caught in my throat.

"*Can you see me?*"

It took a few more seconds for him to respond, and it made me want to claw at my skin.

"*Yeah,*" he replied. And that was it. I couldn't tell if he was purposely teasing me, or if he didn't want the conversation to continue. Slightly frustrated, I allowed only a bit of my unhappiness to show, and set the phone down. Then I returned my attention back to Melinda who was about to order her... I'd lost count of what drink number she was on and so I stopped her. "Get some cranberry juice, or some water," I told her. For a moment, she looked like she would argue but then she nodded in agreement, thankfully.

My phone pinged with the notification of yet another message, but I didn't want to seem too eager with checking it, since every cell in my body was now aware that his eyes were on me. I however didn't want to be disrespectful, because I currently owed so much to him. So as soon as Melinda was stable, I picked up the phone.

"*You don't want to dance?*" he asked, and my heart jumped.

I couldn't stop the smile then from spreading across my lips.

"*Do you?*" I asked.

His reply this time around was immediate.

"*I don't dance,*" he said, and the answer was so typical I couldn't help but laugh.

"*Alright,*" I replied and was about to place the phone down when yet another message arrived.

"*But I would with you,*" he wrote and I froze.

I stared at the message, forgetting to breathe until Melinda interrupted me.

"Do you want to go somewhere quieter?" she asked. "It's too loud to talk in here."

I agreed, but I didn't exactly want to talk to her.

"Just a second," I said, as I tried to think of what to say to Christian.

Nothing however seemed apt, and so all I could do was delete what I typed over and over again.

"*I can get us one of the private rooms on the second floor,*" another message suddenly came in from him.

I looked up to see the tinted glass walls of the extended, private rooms that protruded towards the dance floor.

"*We can see out of them, but they can't see in,*" he said. "*We could dance there for a little while.*"

My heart lodged in my throat. But thankfully, I recovered enough to respond.

"*What kind of dance?*" I asked, and nearly gasped as the memory of his dick slamming into me came to mind. I was so screwed I realized, literally and figuratively.

"*You decide,*" he texted back and I nearly lost my mind. I placed the phone down and wondered if another drink was called for. I decided however I couldn't wait for it, and before I could stop myself I was rising to my feet.

"Bathroom," I announced to Melinda, and her eyes slightly widened. "Again?"

"Yeah, I'll be right back," I said and wobbled away on shaky legs. At the back of my mind, it registered that I was still in danger but for once, I didn't really care as all I could think about was heading over to someplace secluded so he could join me. I headed over to the elevators leading to the second floor, but I wasn't allowed any further. So I nodded patiently and waited against the wall, safe since the bouncer's gaze was on me, no doubt wondering why I was still standing there.

I wanted to explain to him I wasn't going to be a problem, and I was just waiting for someone but I shut my mouth and waited.

A few seconds later, I felt him before I saw him.

"She's with me," he said, and I didn't bother looking back as his hand closed around my arm.

I went willingly as he pulled me away from the wall, his hand then moving to the small of my back.

"*Fuck*," I swore underneath my breath, and headed up with him.

True to his words, there was a private room reserved for us and it made me wonder if he had just done this, or if the arrangements had been made ahead of time. He shut the door, and at the sound of it closing, the question fell out of my lips.

"I just made the reservation now," his response came from behind me as I stared out towards the glass wall.

"It's lucky they had one of these available."

"Not lucky," he said. "I paid extra for it."

My breathing hitched.

"How long do we have?"

His body arrived then, pressing into mine, and I immediately began to melt. His arm then came around my waist to hold me in place, while mine went behind and curved around the back of his neck. Moving my head to the side, I rested against his shoulder, giving him complete access to the crook of my neck. He breathed me in, and at the heat on my skin, I felt myself go woozy.

I could feel his hardness pressing against my ass, and it made me quiver. Between my legs was now so soaked that it was near uncomfortable and more than anything, I needed his hand right there, stroking and soothing the ache that was about to drive me crazy with lust.

"So…" he began as he pressed a kiss against my skin. Goosebumps broke out all across it.

"What kind of dance?"

My eyes fluttered shut as I truly pondered on the question. I mean, was I willing to solely grind against him in the privacy of this room, or was I ready to fuck him? And what would that do to our relationship, or whatever this was between us? And how would it affect his perception of me that I could be so wanton?

At the back of my mind, I knew none of this was important to care about, but I couldn't bring myself not to, and I didn't want to examine why.

And so I couldn't respond.

I couldn't help but to grind my ass against his hardness, loving the feel of him against me.

We moved together to the rhythm of our own music, and although I was certain neither of us knew what it was, we were perfectly in tune to it. I needed to kiss him, and so my lips parted, leaning towards his and in moments, his were latching onto mine.

They were so soft and sweet, and I couldn't get enough of them. I sucked on his bottom lip and then the upper, before sliding my tongue in.

At the lushness, I felt even more strength drain out of my legs, and so my hand tightened around his wrist, unconsciously pleading with him to keep me stable. He held on tightly, so I was free to focus completely on the kiss as it fragmented my mind into pieces.

It seemed to go on forever, but yet I couldn't get enough. Going even deeper than ever, and allowing it to be just a little sloppier because I wanted to taste even more of him.

"Christian," I heard myself whimper as his hand moved upwards and closed around my breast. The resulting jolt to my core was just as painful as it was sweet, and for a moment, it destabilized me. Especially when his hand then slipped into my shirt, and connected directly with my overheated skin.

I moaned, grinding harder into him as his hands molded around my breasts, and stroked my nipples.

At this point, I needed the ache between my thighs to be relieved in any way, and so my hand left the back of his neck and stumbled its way towards the button of my pants. I tried my best but was quite clumsy, and not until his hand left my breast and moved downwards to take over, did I have any hope that the damn pants would ever be undone.

He made quick work of it, and then his hand was sliding into the barrier of my panties and through the coarseness of my crotch. He felt around in the puddle of my slickness, his fingers stroking lightly against my clit, feeling me up oh so intimately.

"Grab me," I breathed, and he wasted no time whatsoever. His hand covered my sex and in the next moment my legs were nearly lifting off the floor.

The pleasure was exquisite, but then he began to circle against my bud once again, his pace quickening, and I could barely catch my breath.

He then curved over me slightly, and then I felt his fingers slide into me.

My mind was made up then, because there was no way in hell I was going to leave his arms without a release... whichever way I could get it.

His fingers began to thrust in and out... carefully but I needed more... I needed to be filled.... needed him to hit that depth inside of me only he could reach. The ache was almost driving me insane, and so I tilted my head to the side to find his gaze.

However he kissed me before I could speak, and I melted into it. By the time it ended, I had almost forgotten what I had intended to ask, but then I didn't even need to remember because the rhythm of his stroking had increased. Without thought, and now solely driven by need, I hooked my hands into my pants, and pushed them down my hips to give him all of the access he needed. Then I pulled out the excess fabric of his shirt, however I couldn't ignore the crowd that was right before us.

"They... they can't see us right," I breathed... almost surprised the words were able to form.

"They can't," he rasped out, and my eyes shut. I leaned into him, relishing the pleasure that now seemed to have replaced the blood in my veins.

"Fuck me," I gasped into his mouth as a particularly good stroke pierced my core.

"Please... I can't..." I grabbed onto the back of his neck and ravaged his mouth hoping that it could somehow convey the hunger I was no longer capable of vocalizing.

"Are you sure?" he asked as he wrenched his lips from mine, and trailed the kisses down my neck.

I was taken aback, and so I pulled away to look into his eyes, mine agape with shock. He smiled and I realized then he was most likely teasing me.

"We can take this home," he said. "Right now. It'll only take twenty five minutes."

My response was immediate. "No! I can't wait that long."

And he surrendered.

He glanced at the wall before us, briefly causing me to follow his attention.

"Against it?" he asked, and my heart slammed against my chest. I took a moment to look around, noting the stretch of lounge chairs in the room. Any one of them would be more than suitable for him to fuck me on but... I considered his proposition once again.

"Yes," I nodded and even his brows raised in surprise. My face burned, and for a moment I almost changed my mind but then he began to lead me towards the glass and soon my hands were flattened against it.

I looked down at the flashing, colored, lights, and the horde of people dancing on the floor and wondered if I could see Melinda from up here. I sure hoped not, but then a part of me had already lost its mind and was now clearly driving my actions, evident by my agreement to this, and the entertainment it could possibly cause. But then Christian pulled my pants the rest of the way down to puddle at my feet, ripped the strands of my thong off my hips, and once again palmed my slick sex as he leaned down to place another kiss against the racing pulse in my neck.

"Ready?" he asked and I turned to look into his eyes.

It was then however, I finally noticed the camera on the opposite end of the room, tucked into a nook of the wall.

I almost screamed out as I plastered my body against his.

"Camera," I shook, and he looked behind to see what I was referring to.

"Taken care of," he said. "You have absolutely nothing to worry about Adele."

I wanted to trust him, but then again the tragic reality of my current life came to mind.

I was currently being stalked by someone I didn't know… and yet I was willing to be this vulnerable with him?

The realization jarred me to my very bones.

"You're covered," he said to me, and I looked down to see what he was referring to. The long, oversized tails of his shirt were hanging way past my groin while my backside, although slightly exposed, was completely shielded out of sight by his hips.

The moment I realized this, I let out a shaky breath.

"Don't be scared," he lowered and kissed my lips before my brain could even process anything else.

"I'm here."

I stared into his eyes one more time, and felt my heart do several flips within my chest. My eyes burned with tears, and then I nodded, giving him the go ahead. Before any more of my troublesome emotions could be revealed, I turned towards the glass and tried my best to relax.

In no time the thick head of his cock was sliding between the lips of my sex, intensifying my arousal to the point it resulted in a headache. Or perhaps it was triggered by the drinks that I'd had earlier? I couldn't tell.

And it didn't matter, especially as his dick eventually made its way to my entrance and then he was pushing into me.

I moaned aloud, unable to hold back.

"*Fuck,*" I heard his answering curse just beside my ear in response, and couldn't help my smile.

"Go faster," I wanted to tell him, however my mouth wouldn't work and so I waited… relishing the shallow intrusion as much as I could, and the feel of his hands as they settled against the sides of my hips.

He held onto my overheated skin and I knew what was coming. In one swift thrust he rammed into me, all the way to the hilt, and my moan increased.

I absolutely loved how thick he was, and how he filled and stretched me until it was all I could be aware of.

His hips then began to roll and in response I undulated mine, and raw, torrid pleasure blasted through me.

"Fuck me," I pleaded, unable to stand even one more moment of being unsated.

And he complied. His thrusts began shallow, but it didn't stay that way for very long. In little time, he was ramming breathlessly into me, my hips solid in his grip.

He pummeled deep, the satiny smoothness of his dick scraping deliciously against my walls. My hands were flattened against the glass to keep my balance, but I could no longer feel the floor underneath my feet. Regardless and in those moments, falling was the last thing on my mind.

Our copulation was urgent, and frantic and when coupled with the ambience surrounding us of the booming music and possible exposure before the crowds, the intensity of it all seemed to triple.

Unintelligible noises escaped my lips as perspiration dampened my skin, and behind me I could feel the exertion of his breathing.

It all felt wonderful, but at the same time uncontainable, to the extent that my cries turned into pleas.

For him to go even harder and faster, but whether he did or didn't I couldn't tell because suddenly I was coming... *hard*.

For a moment my entire body went numb, and then the pleasure was crashing through me in powerful waves.

My toes curled and my limbs quivered, and then his arms were wrapping around me. I could feel him everywhere and I never wanted him to let go.

"*Fuck*," I heard him shudder, his hips bucking into mine as he too found his own release.

"Adele," he called my name over and over, but I couldn't form any words to respond. So I sunk into his strength and warmth, unable to remain standing on my own, and it was a good while later before either of us recovered enough to even turn for a look at each other.

His eyes were hazy, and so were mine I was certain, and at first it was tender but as the ambience from around returned, and it finally dawned on us just how much we had lost our heads, amusement ensued. He laughed softly and so did I, my already flushed face burning even redder as I couldn't believe I had just fucked overlooking a sea of strangers.

He held me even tighter, and at the kiss he pressed to my lips, I felt him push his way even further into my heart.

CHRISTIAN

I still felt quite shaken.

And so I kept her in my arms, holding tight and with my cock still inside her.

She didn't complain, and so I kept my face buried in her neck, inhaling her scent, which I was now certain I would forever turn at. I wasn't quite sure when it began, but as I stood there unwilling to let go, it began to dawn on me I truly cared about her. The steps I took to ensure that she was safe... and the concern that filled my heart every time I caught the worry in her gaze.

It was such a shame she had warned me of this... of us, in this way... and so with a sigh, I finally loosened my arms from around her.

However she held on... almost automatically, but it was so brief that for a moment I wondered if I imagined it.

"Do your legs work?" I asked, and the shyest smile spread across her face. "They do but..." her gaze lowered to the pants puddled at her feet. "I think I'll have to hold on to you so that I can get those."

"I'll get them," I said and her hands grabbed onto mine. In no time I was pulling the pants back up to her hips, and then tucking my shirt back into them.

I loved the way she looked in my shirt and especially how she had tugged the sleeves up to gather around her elbows.

She squirmed however as my hands went round her ass and crotch, tucking in the fabric, and so I couldn't help but be amused.

"I'll do it," she said, but I refused to let go until eventually she grabbed onto my wrist and pulled out of my hold. I watched her scuttle around and away and then began to put my own self back in order.

Soon we were both decent, and I pulled her to me once again for a kiss.

I savored her taste and the sweetness of her lips until once again she began to pull away.

I let her, and she stared into my eyes. "Do you want to stay a while?" she asked.

"Here?" I replied.

"No I mean the club?"

I shook my head. "It's been a long day so I'll head home. I have an event to attend over the weekend in New York, so I'll have to make preparations."

"Oh," she seemed somewhat surprised to hear this.

"Do you need any reservations booked? You should have let me know… it's my job."

"Your job," I corrected her. "Is to organize my affairs within the context of the company and its affairs. I wouldn't want you doing more than is required and outside of work hours."

She nodded. "I love that you're so considerate but truly… I'd love to help as much as I can. You've been so incredibly good to me, and I want to at least thank you somehow. Is there anything that you currently need that I could handle for you? Like your flight ticket for instance? Hotel reservations? Or do you perhaps already have a place there since you lived there for so long?"

"Adele," I caught her hand, and it was only then she stopped. "I'll be fine. I'm more than capable of handling my own itinerary."

"Alright," she smiled, and then quickly tucked something into her pocket. I didn't need to look too hard to see that it was the underwear I had ripped away earlier.

"Do you want to remain here with your friend?" I asked, and she once again glanced down at the massive window.

"I don't," she shook her head. "But I will have to share an Uber with her since my home is on the way to hers. She might become suspicious again otherwise, and I don't think I particularly want to be dragged out at night again to prove that our relationship is still intact."

I huffed in amusement.

"Alright," I replied, and soon we were out of the room and on our way back down the stairs. Before we parted though I reached out to grab her arm. She turned, slightly startled.

"I'll drive behind your Uber," I said. "So after she leaves we can head back to my place."

She seemed a bit taken aback. "You would... I mean..."

I had a good inkling now of why she seemed surprised. "That will be stressful will it not?"

I shook my head. "Not at all. The added drive will be good for me."

"What about your cousin?" she asked, and for a moment I was stumped at how to respond.

"She'll head home."

ADELE

Just as agreed, Christian drove behind the Uber and never had I been happier that Melinda was too intoxicated to notice this. She still had her faculties intact, but was finding it quite hard to remain awake. So when the driver finally noticed the vehicle following us, I was able to allay his concern about it without her noticing.

"It's fine," I told him, and he gave me a peculiar look.

In no time, we arrived at Melinda's and I managed to pull her out of the car.

She came awake then, surprised to see we were at her place instead of mine.

"I didn't want to leave you intoxicated and riding home alone," I told her, and led her in with the keys I found in her purse. After making sure that she was settled in bed and with a glass of water by her side, I stroked her hair and bid her goodnight.

She barely noticed, mumbling what I took as a response and soon the door was closing behind me.

I was then able to breathe easier. I locked up Melinda's house and took the key along with me to be returned next week at the office. She had a spare of her own, and wouldn't miss it.

I met Christian waiting at the base of the building's stairs for me, and joined him in the car.

I half expected to see his cousin in the backseat, but it was empty. I looked towards him for an explanation as I put my seat belt on.

"Uber," he said and I nodded.

"I feel apologetic," I said. "She must have really wanted to spend time with you today. I barely got a chance to even say hello to her properly."

"She's fine," he brushed away my concern as he pulled out of the parking lot.

The silence between us then became extremely loud, but yet it wasn't uncomfortable. I was just very aware of him... of the way that he smelled... of the confidence with which he maneuvered the wheel. All of our memories thus far began to come to mind, and it made me feel like I was walking on clouds.

"Do you need some supplies from home?" he suddenly asked, and I was returned back to earth. Back to the fact I should have been thinking about my survival and grabbing at the opportunity he was with me now to get what I needed from back home.

It was disheartening to realize just how incredibly distracted I had become, and as a result my mood began to plummet.

"Adele?" he called, making me realize I hadn't even responded.

"I do," I turned to him. "Thank you for reminding me."

"No problem," he replied kindly… softly… and I sighed again.

Once again I returned home, and he came in with me.

Turning the lights on to what used to be my home but was now a borderline nightmare, hit me more than I had expected it would.

I looked around, wondering if the cameras or whatever had been used to capture me were still present. The police had done a sweep of the entire place and found nothing, and it made tears burn in my eyes now as I looked around and wondered when all of this would come to an end.

I tried my best to keep them away, but then I felt Christian come up behind me and the moment I felt him, the dam broke.

I employed all of my will to keep them soundless, but in the silence, he heard it all and his arms wrapped around me. He didn't say a single word, and in that moment I loved him for it. He simply just held me, close and tight and I found the refuge I hadn't even realized I needed. Soon enough, I was able to bring my emotions under control and when he noticed this, there was suddenly a pressed cotton handkerchief before me. I opened my soaked and reddened eyes to see it, and my heart melted. It almost started another round of water works, but I managed to keep myself under control and wiped the moisture off my face.

I couldn't quite face him after that, and so I went through the motions of getting a small suitcase and packing up the clothes that I would need for the next week because I didn't intend to live the way I currently was beyond the following week. And I was determined to make this happen in any way that I could.

Afterwards, I checked my fridge and found two long forgotten containers of prepared dinners now gone bad. I emptied them out along with a few bananas, and then went on my way.

Our ride back to his home was once again quiet and comfortable. I loved being in his presence I realized, and was even more astounded by how in tune he was to my mood. He seemed to just understand me...when I needed him to hold me and when I wanted him to be out of the way or assertive. I tried my best in the dark to subtly watch him but on one of those occasions as we came to a stop at a traffic light, I was caught. I immediately turned away and he didn't ignore it. He laughed softly, kindly and my entire soul warmed over.

I couldn't remain quiet then.

"Thank you," I told him, and before he could brush this away I hurried to say all I truly wanted to.

"Those words I realize will never be enough but... thank you, with all my heart. Someday I'm going to find a way to pay you back, but until then, I'll just be the best secretary you could ever need."

My mind went to our relationship beyond the office, but there was absolutely nothing I could say regarding that.

Afterwards, I breathed easy and then he turned to look at me. I however was now too shy to meet his eyes.

"There is one thing...." he said and my attention immediately perked up.

"One thing?"

"Yeah, that you could use in paying me back."

"What?" I asked incredibly eagerly. Anything, absolutely anything he demanded even if it was somehow beyond my reach, I would ensure to make available to him.

However, what he requested shocked me so much I couldn't speak, even after the traffic light turned green and the car was back in motion. Eventually though, and just before we arrived at his home I was able to speak.

"You- you want me to come with you to New York?"

"Yes," he replied. "It's my former colleague's engagement party and it would be nice to not be alone."

I couldn't help but to glance at him. "Why would you be alone if your former colleagues will be there? Wouldn't it instead be a great chance to reconnect with them? I wouldn't want to be in the way."

At this he smiled, nodding. "Great point. Well, I guess you caught me then. I want you to get out of the city for a bit. So you can truly relax without having to look over your shoulder. Even if it's only for a couple of days. You'd be at home anyway and I wouldn't want that. Unless you just want to rest?"

Wow, was all I could think to myself. I had just spent the last hour feeling overwhelming gratitude towards him, and pleading for a chance to pay him back, but yet he was even offering me more.

I didn't want to say yes, because it felt like I was always taking and taking, but on the other hand I felt as though he would be truly unhappy if I didn't. Soon we pulled into the underground parking lot, and after he shut the engine off, we remained there in silence. I knew he was hoping for a response, and the last thing I wanted was to disappoint him. So I just said the truth.

"I don't want to be more of a burden than I already am."

At this he turned to me. "And how exactly would you be a burden?"

I gazed into his eyes. "Wouldn't I be encroaching?"

"And how exactly would you be encroaching?"

"Stop…" I couldn't help but laugh, however underlying it was an undeniable sadness.

"You stop," he says. "This is a favor to me. You just said you wanted to repay me."

I sighed as I stared at him. "We both know this is you helping me again," I said and he shrugged.

With another sigh I turned away and faced forward. And then, because I wasn't shameless enough for the words to so easily roll out of my mouth, I nodded.

"Okay… and thank you."

CHRISTIAN

I t felt somewhat like a business trip, and it made me feel unhappy.

All through the morning, our interactions with each other were cordial with her saying all the right words and smiling as appropriate. Soon enough, we arrived at our boarding gate to wait, right on time, especially because she had ensured not to be late or to be an inconvenience in any way.

The moment we sat down, she pulled out her phone and kept all her attention on it, reading something I presumed.

I did the same, and pulled my iPad out. I pretended to review some of the department reports I had gotten the previous day, before it finally truly hit me what was happening.

Here we were on a trip intended to pull down more of the walls between us, and yet I was allowing her to lead the way and to keep us both at arms length with each other. I refused it and so I set my tablet down and looked towards her.

She didn't look up, but at the quick shift of her eyes, I realized she was very aware of me. And so I couldn't help but smile.

"This is a vacation," I said, and although at first she pretended not to hear me, she eventually took her gaze away from her phone and looked up at me. Her smile was sheepish, and although it was quite the feat, I tried my best to keep my expression neutral. Seeing I had set my tablet down, she too put her phone away and turned to me. I felt good, because at least I had overcome one hurdle but then what was next? She waited, but soon realized I didn't have a plan and so she laughed.

"This is a vacation…" she said. "Okay. And?"

I knew how to proceed then. "Let's actually spend time together and forget about L.A. and everything else going on."

She looked around. "Well, we're still technically in LA."

"Imagine that we're not," I said, and she laughed again, making me realize perhaps this was a good thing. It was good to see her laugh.

She looked around once again, and then back to me.

"What is it?" I asked, wishing somehow I could read her mind.

She hesitated for a moment, but then and to my relief, she responded.

"I can't wait for us to get out of here."

I was a bit surprised to hear this.

"Really?" I asked. "You're excited to go to New York?"

She laughed again. "I am, but I'm more excited to be safe again at least for a little while, unless of course whoever it is manages to follow us all the way."

I was speechless for the longest time as I stared at her, and as she noticed this her smile faltered.

"I'm sorry," she applied. "That was a bit dark wasn't it?"

"Don't apologize," I said, pained at how worried and yet burdensome she felt. "Your concerns are valid."

She smiled again, however I could still see the apology in her eyes. "I'll try to put it all behind me this weekend. I promise."

"There's no need to make a promise to me," I replied. "Just try your best to relax and rest, and if the concerns ever get too much then remember I'm here."

She nodded, and for a moment my heart began to race in my chest thinking perhaps she would lean forward to kiss me. But then before I could find out, there was an announcement made over the PA system, and we both stilled.

Or perhaps we weren't even moving towards each other like I had imagined. Perhaps it had all been in my head.

"That's our flight," she said, and I was forced then to pull my eyes away from hers. She rose to her feet and so did I. Soon we were cleared and heading towards the plane.

Our seats were business class, and although I had booked them I hadn't specifically asked her which she would prefer, the window or aisle. So we stopped awkwardly when we arrived and looked at each other.

"Do you prefer the window seat?" I asked. I wasn't expecting her to tell me the truth so I watched, and the moment I saw her hesitate I held the small of her back and led her in.

"Wait," she laughed but I didn't listen until she all but fell into the seat. I took her carry on from her, placed it in the overhead compartment and soon took my seat. However just before I plopped down into the seat she made an objection.

"Wait, I want to use the bathroom." I started to get back up but then I realized there was more than enough space for her to pass through and so I remained seated.

"Christian," she called, and I smiled, nudging my head to indicate she could go through. I wanted to make her smile, and I hoped at least this would help.

She started to go past, and I didn't exactly make it easy for her by trying to get out of her way. Eventually, she was able to pass through, laughing softly, and it took all of my willpower to stop me from just watching her go.

I waited, somewhat excited for her return, and when she did, I allowed her to come in. But then just before she could go through, my hand went around her midriff, and she fell right on top of me.

Thankfully, she wasn't too loud about it, and when I turned to the seat across, I met the smile of an elderly woman.

"You're a beautiful couple," she said to us, and before Adele could deny it I sent over my thanks.

"Christian," she scolded, and I let her go as an announcement for our takeoff came in. She headed over to her seat, and it made me extremely happy when she smacked the side of my arm. I relished the sting and soon enough our seatbelts were on, and we were ready for takeoff.

We both settled in, the silence between us quite comfortable. She stared out of the window as the plane took off the tarmac and we stabilized in the air. I couldn't take my eyes away from her. I realized the extent of my attachment to her was spiraling out of control.

She turned suddenly, and I didn't even bother turning away. I needed her to stare into my eyes and to see what she had warned me from the onset not to say aloud.

And so I decided I was going to show it, in every way I could.

She smiled as she met the intensity in my gaze, but her gaze slowly faltered and I hoped just like mine, in that moment, her heart had also slammed hard against her chest.

ADELE

I had never been to New York before.

Right after college, I had considered moving and had even applied for certain internships, but then life had steered me in a different direction.

Now however, I was visiting, but I had to admit the majority of my excitement had more to do with the man I had come with than the city.

Throughout the flight, I had remained quite shaken, and I wondered if he'd noticed.

After the way he had looked at me in the moment after take-off, I had felt something I had been holding desperately onto within me just completely unravel.

I didn't know what it was just yet, but there was an ease and comfort that it seemed my heart had permitted me to have around him.

We checked into the magnificent hotel, and although I was now extremely excited, I couldn't help but feel slightly unhappy when we arrived at the front desk and discovered not only had he already paid for the rooms, but he had booked two separate ones. Most probably for what I was certain he presumed would be my preference.

I couldn't outrightly show my displeasure for the latter, but on our way up I couldn't help but voice my displeasure for the former.

"I'll reimburse you for the room," I said to him as the elevator doors closed before us.

He turned to glance at me and I boldly met his gaze.

"You don't have to. I invited you on this trip."

I was beginning to feel quite frustrated. "You already paid for the tickets."

He went quiet for a moment and I turned away, slightly unhappy because although I didn't want to become an actual leech, I also didn't want my unwillingness to accept any more help from him to become aggravating.

And so I softened my tone.

"You understand me right?" I asked as the elevator kept rising to the eighty-sixth floor where our rooms were located.

"Take it as a business expense," he said and I turned to him again.

"I work in said company and I know you're going to write it off as a personal one."

He sighed.

"Fine, take it as a personal expense then. It's an expense I'm choosing to incur to someone that I romantically desire."

As soon as the words left his mouth, our elevator suddenly came to a stop. My gaze snapped up to the display monitor, to see we were still just at the fifty-sixth floor and so I wasn't surprised when the doors pulled open and two men walked in.

They rode up with us, and thus Christian and I didn't say another word.

Which was all well and good, because even after we arrived at our floor I still had absolutely nothing to say. And so we each walked to our doors which I found were opposite the other. I glanced back at him as he slid the card into his lock and counted the seconds until he disappeared into the room ticking away in my heart.

I wanted to call out his name, so we could have a proper conversation but nothing came to mind and so I slid my card in, and by the time I pushed my door open I heard his shutting behind him.

I turned around to watch the shut door and wondered if I had annoyed him. I didn't think so... because surely he understood me. I sighed and thought of what to do, and couldn't help but recall how much of an effort he had put in so far into ensuring I loosened up... so we could both have a good time. I decided I wasn't going to let this fester and so I turned around and headed over to his door. I knocked, once... twice... and then on the third and what I had decided would be my final try, it clicked open.

He appeared and for a few seconds, all we did was stare at each other.

"Are you mad at me?" I asked and suddenly realized we were relating as though we were actually dating. He turned around and walked into the room.

"Oh," I couldn't help but exclaim at the gorgeous and neutral decor. "It's beautiful"

"It's the same as yours," he said, and headed over to his refrigerator to grab a bottle of water. I immediately shriveled inside because I knew how overpriced those were, but he of course had no reason to mind. I on the other hand did, however it seemed as though I was beginning to mind too many things.

"You understand me right?" I asked once again, and his brows furrowed.

He sent the question right back. "Do you understand me?"

I was stumped. I also couldn't move. He headed over to the bed and took a seat, his eyes on me as he lifted the bottle to his lips.

I didn't know what to say.

And so after he completed the drink and screwed his cap back on he spoke.

"Adele. You've let me know your stance on where you want things to be between us. Admittedly, we have crossed some lines since then but for the most part, I'm still trying my very best to be respectful. However I'm also human and you have to be aware I am truly interested in you. So when I ask you to come on a trip with me, yes I'm going to do my best to make sure we're lodged in as nice a hotel as I can afford. Because I want you to truly rest and relax, especially with all you're going through. However, I don't want to constantly argue about this with you. I understand you don't like to ask for help or be indebted to anyone, and I accept this. But I do hope you can also cut me some slack and accept that paying for a room for you in this hotel makes me happy. I'm not asking for anything else from you, I'm just asking you to allow me to cover the expenses from a trip that I invited you on. Is that too much to ask?"

At his words, I was once again speechless, and for so long all I could do was stare at him.

And then I just began to nod.

"Alright," I said and before I could talk myself out of it I added. "But can I suggest a concession?"

My heart began to race in my chest, especially as his attention perked. I knew the look that came into his eyes because I had seen it so many times back at the office, when whatever was before him was crucial.

It made me nervous and I couldn't help but hesitate.

"What concession?" he asked, and I looked back at his door before returning my gaze to him. "Why- why don't we split the bill then?"

My question made absolutely no sense, but I hoped he would be able to understand what I was saying without me needing to spell it out. He cocked his head, his gaze going to the door and then back to me.

And then he smiled.

My heart almost collapsed with relief.

"You want us to share this room?" he asked, and my face burned.

"I mean I can afford mine, it's just... since you don't want me to pay, I'd feel better if you only paid for one. And besides, it's just two days."

He smiled again, but didn't say another word in response and I couldn't help but shyly lower my gaze to the floor.

CHRISTIAN

A few hours later, we both decided on a French restaurant that was just about a fifteen minute walk from the hotel for a late lunch.

However when we arrived, I wasn't quite sure she would be taken with the ambience of the space.

Her eyes roved all over the room as we took our seats. The lush flowers all round, the mirrors, the red upholstery. It was a gorgeous space, a bit too dark for my taste but she seemed to appreciate it and so I was pleased.

I was also especially pleased by the fact she had somehow gotten the both of us to share a room, founded solely on logic and necessity rather than frivolity, and from an outsider looking in her reasons where quite valid. I hadn't thought it would be possible to like her any more than I currently did, but after her little cohabiting stunt, I could barely take my eyes off her.

For one she looked absolutely gorgeous, dressed simply in a white frilly blouse, a dark short skirt and a pair of heeled sandals that kept my gaze constantly returning to her legs.

Her hair was pulled up and wrapped into a neat bun on the top of her head, with soft wavy tendrils framing her face. I was mesmerized.

"When is the engagement party?" she asked, smiling, and it made me realize I had been staring too much.

"Later tonight. At around eight thirty."

"Mmm," she nodded. "We have a bit of time left. So after this we can head back, perhaps rest a little and then get ready?"

I nodded, my mind instantly filling with all the ways we could spend it, however the waiter soon arrived with our beverages and I employed all of the self-restraint I possessed to keep me from once again just outrightly staring at her.

"Have you been to this restaurant before?" she asked and I shook my head. "It's my first time but I have heard good things about it in the past, especially of their soufflé. I've heard it's the best in the city."

At this she laughed. "Well, I guess we'll see if that's true."

"We will," I replied. "But what I'm truly interested in is their burger au poivre. One of my colleagues here used to rave all the time about its creamy St.-André cheese topping. I never got the chance to try it."

Her look on me softened. "You were too busy working?"

I smiled. "I was too busy with everything else to think about food. I always planned to try it someday, but I just never got around to it, and then I had to move to LA.

The waiter reappeared then with our meals, and we both turned quiet as we dove into them.

From time to time we exchanged glances with each other, and shared our wine, and it was such a relaxing time to just be.

"Do you have any ideas yet for Mr. Sim's pitch?" I asked.

Her gaze lifted to mine, eyes slightly wide. "I do," she responded cautiously and it made me wonder why.

"Do you want to run them by me?" I asked, and her eyes nearly blew out of their sockets.

"I can't do that… that's unfair."

"How?" I asked, perplexed.

"I mean, it's unfair to the other applicants."

"I'm not the one judging it. The company is going to vote and then we're going to recommend the shortlisted options to the client."

"I know," she said. "But if your input comes into this then, isn't it truly an unfair advantage against the other company staff?"

"How exactly will it be an advantage?" I asked. "You're not assuming I have the best ideas do you?"

At this she laughed out, and it warmed my insides like a candle.

"Don't you?" she asked.

"I do not."

She kept her smile on, but then there was one more question that I wanted to ask. "What if we were married?" I asked. "Would you still be unwilling to discuss these things with me?"

"If we were still in our current positions, then yes."

At my mention of marriage, she truly didn't flinch, and it made me wonder if the word had just flown over her head, or perhaps she truly didn't care. Either way, we continued on with our meals and were soon done.

The soufflé arrived, and although I hadn't previously felt any excitement over it, seeing how she shut her eyes briefly to savor it, nearly moaning from the exquisite taste gave me immense pleasure.

I could watch her forever, I realized.

"It's amazing," she cooed and I nodded, pleased and relieved at her review.

Afterwards, we both split the check which I was unhappy about, but I understood her, and so after insisting a few times and meeting with her refusal, I let it go.

ADELE

We had arrived at the restaurant in a cab, however since the hotel wasn't too far away, I went on to ask if he would mind walking back with me. He was open to the idea and so afterwards we walked side by side on the lively street. There was so much to look at and admire, and I was distracted enough to not notice it when he suddenly took my hand.

The moment it registered though, my heart jumped, and never had I been so grateful people couldn't read minds otherwise, I just might have fainted from the embarrassment of revealing just how much effect his touch had on me. I held onto his hand, the late afternoon breeze of the city air washing over me, and putting me at extreme ease.

"I just might never leave New York," I said to him and he smiled.

"There's so much to explore and enjoy about the city, but sadly it only becomes truly enjoyable when you can afford to live here."

"Yeah," I replied. "Perhaps I'll work even harder on this pitch and get selected. Maybe then I'll get a promotion and be able to afford a month or so out here?"

At this I could hear his soft, kind, laugh and couldn't help but turn to look at him. He returned the gaze and this time around, I held it boldly. Then my eyebrows did a thing I hoped at least came across like a wiggle, otherwise I was certain I probably looked deformed there for a moment.

He laughed, and the concern instantly vanished. "What's that for?"

"Will winning the pitch come with a promotion?"

"Now you want executive insight?" he asked, and I blushed.

"I guess I'm a hypocrite," I said and he heartily agreed.

"You sure are."

We came to an intersection and stopped, and I couldn't help but once again sneak a look up at him. When he began to turn towards me, I moved my gaze away and turned around to hide my smile. His hold on my hand tightened.

"If you do that again I'll kiss you," he said, and my stomach did several flips. I tried my best to hide my smile but it was to no avail.

And so I bit down on my lip. The pedestrian crossing light turned green, and I couldn't help stealing a quick glance at him. It was time to walk so there was no way he would pause long enough in all the foot traffic to deliver on the threat, or was it a promise?

The moment our gaze connected he smiled, and before I could take my next breath, he was leaning down. His lips latched onto mine, carefully but hard and a few seconds later I was left dizzy.

When we finally parted, I was so dazed all I could do was hurry along with him across the street before the light turned red.

When we arrived back at the hotel, I was so horny I was about to lose my mind.

However I didn't know how to just come out and ask for what I wanted. We got into the room quietly, with my limbs still tingling from the cool outside breeze and his heated kiss. I still had his taste in my mouth, sweet and intoxicating, and the goosebumps that had broken out as a result I could still see dotted over my skin.

"Do you want to take a shower first?" he asked. "Because I want to take one."

I burned as the opening I had been seeking was delivered to me.

And so I lifted my gaze and stared into his eyes. "Why don't we take one together?"

His eyes were immediately huge and I couldn't help but tease him. "That's quite the excitement you're showing," I said as I began to unbutton my skirt. "It's just a shower. The main purpose is to save time."

"We'll save time alright," he replied as he too began to unbutton his shirt. We watched each other, mischief gleaming in our eyes as the other undressed, however I stopped when I was in my underwear. He however stripped all the way down, and although I tried my best not to look, it was hard to not see just how aroused he was.

My mouth slightly parted, and at this he laughed quietly. Shaking his head he turned around and strolled away while my knees wobbled.

I soon followed and after stripping completely in the bathroom, walked into the stall to join him.

All I did for the first few minutes was watch him as the heated water drenched his entire body. His skin glistened with warmth and his movements seemed to be a reel in slow motion before me. I watched him until he eventually brushed his hair out of his face and turned to see me staring.

"We're going to be late," he said, and I could hear the cockiness in his tone despite the fact he was feigning total unawareness of what he was doing to me. And so with a scowl, I stepped forward and pushed him out of the way with my hips. Then I shut my eyes and let the warm stream fall down on me, and it was beyond soothing to say the least. I felt safe and treasured, and couldn't believe I had almost rejected this trip.

L.A. and its demons seemed so far away, and all that existed was my bliss and contentment in being in this man's presence. I felt him come towards me, and then his groin connected with my ass. At the sharp thrust of his hips, I couldn't help my smile, my hand shooting out and flattening against the wall before us to keep me stable.

"I thought you said we didn't have time?" I asked as his face angled, and his lips connected with my neck.

His arms wrapped around me, and I allowed my frame to melt into his like butter.

"I never said that," his voice washed all over me like a song.

My breath then caught in my throat, my core clenching and unclenching with anticipation as his flattened hand against my stomach began to inch downwards towards my sex.

"What I said..."

He nibbled on the lobe of my ear.

"Is that we're going to be late."

I trembled at the dark promise, and couldn't help but completely give in then, a hand going behind to stroke and guide his cock to exactly where I needed it to be.

He let me, and soon enough I was parting my legs, and rubbing him through my slickness. And as both of his arms tightened around me in the sweetest embrace, unintelligible moans began to escape my lips. He kissed me and every contact seemed to sear my skin, with the heat going straight to my heart.

I especially loved his equally intense groan when I nudged my opening with the sensitive crown of his shaft.

"Ah," he breathed as I sheathed him, inch by delicious inch, and I was rewarded with his hand finally reaching the juncture between my thighs and grabbing me.

A gasp tore out of me as he began to stroke the aching bud between my folds, and it soon became impossible for me to remain still. My entire body writhed and twisted in his arms as I began to rock against him, and in seconds, my awareness of all beyond the wild pleasure that was overtaking me, was lost.

I rocked into him with abandon, completely giving in to the affection, intimacy and safety that this moment awarded me.

He nibbled on my chin, and kissed along the curve of my shoulder as we screwed each other to a rhythm that only the both of us seemed to know and it was one of the most beautiful states I could ever remember being in. The urgency to simply reach the peak was minimal, but instead all I wanted was to continue to bask in the moment, and in this secluded space with him forever.

This could not be the case unfortunately, as the ecstasy eventually reached uncontainable heights. I cried out as his pace quickened and could do nothing more than try my best to hang on as he rammed over and over into me.

I felt dazed and formless, and was certain his firm grip on me was what kept me upright until the end. My eyes tightened shut as he released into me, while I trembled violently as the mixture of our pleasure spilled down my thighs. I relished the sound of his breathless groans in my ear as our bodies spasmed and jerked together, and eventually became the sweetest, most affectionate smile I found on his face. I stared at him, mesmerized and then leaned forward to kiss him with all of my heart.

~

I still felt somewhat intoxicated by the time we arrived at the dinner party.

All of my tension and stress seemed to have been completely drained out of my body by Christian's dick and presence, so I found that he constantly had to hold onto me to keep me upright. I giggled at everything he said and couldn't keep the smile off my face. I also felt as light as a feather, and coupled with the way he looked at me, I couldn't remember ever feeling quite so beautiful or desirable.

We arrived at the venue late, just as he had promised, and as we rode up to the rooftop bar, I couldn't brush away my concern at this.

He kissed me for reassurance that the celebrants wouldn't be offended, but I no longer trusted him to tell me the truth if it would even in the least bit upset me.

We soon arrived and although the venue was a bit chilly, I found I loved the magical ambience of it courtesy of the striking views of the city's lit skyline.

I love New York, I couldn't help but think as I took in the stylish elegant people and setting, but then as I felt Christian's hand settle on my waist so he could speak to me, I couldn't ignore the fact that most of the charm of it all was attributed to the man by my side.

"I'll get you a drink and then begin the introductions," he said and I nodded.

"Find us a seat?" he said, and then kissed me.

I was glad for the chance to roam about freely for a bit. I found us a table and then sat down to watch the clusters of people around. Soon, he arrived with the cosmopolitan I had asked for, and I kissed him in welcome. But then I felt slightly alarmed because we were in the midst of his former colleagues and we hadn't yet decided on how I would be introduced to them.

"Oh I'm sorry," I said, eyes slightly widened. "I'm supposed to be your secretary."

"No," he refuted, and leaned forward once again to kiss me. In L.A. you're my secretary but in New York... you're something else."

"What am I?" I asked, but couldn't get my response because just then, there was a deafening and excited call of his name.

"Mr. Christian Hall!" A tall bearded man appeared out of nowhere. Christian wore a polite smile across his face.

They shook hands, and I couldn't help but notice the look of wonder and surprise on the other man's gaze.

"I can't believe you made it," he said. "It's so great to see you."

"It's great to see you too, Bob," he replied, and then turned to me.

"This is my girlfriend Adele," he said just as I was rising to my feet, and I stopped mid way. Thankfully, I was soon able to recover enough to straighten.

"Wow! Finally! I guess it's true what they say about L.A. It does force you to slow down. You're extremely beautiful Miss Adele."

"Thank you," I said, my cheeks hurting from smiling so hard that I couldn't wait for the man to be on his way.

"Where's Nicolas?" Christian asked, seeming to want to keep him there for as long as was possible.

"Oh he just stepped out with his fiancé. They'll be back soon. Andy and Martinez are here and of course Carol. I will send them your way. They will be so stoked to see you."

"Alright," he said.

"I can't believe it man," he said once again, and then went on his way.

I turned to Christian and he returned my gaze, cooly and unruffled.

"We're in New York," was what he said in explanation and I couldn't believe him. "You heard what he said. They're happy I'm slowing down. What a loser I'd look like if I were to say that you were my secretary."

I was still shaking my head.

"You don't want me to look like a loser do you?"

I continued to glare at him, but he leaned forward once again to kiss me. I moved my lips away but when his hand reached down to link mine in his, I didn't make any move whatsoever to move away. I was about to return to my seat however, when we heard the excited call of earlier mentioned friends as they headed over, now four in number.

"Yikes," he said, and moved his hand to hold me around the waist. I told myself to relax, and to just enjoy this insight into his previous life.

"I'll accept the title for tonight," I told him. "But on only one condition."

"Which is?" he asked.

"I want all the gossip on everyone."

"I am the wrong person to be asking that," he said and I sighed as I understood why. How could he possibly be aware of any of it?

Still, I allowed him to hold onto me, and it was the most exhilarating feeling to know and feel for the night like I belonged completely to him.

ADELE

New York was a dream, but soon enough the next morning came and we made our return back to L.A. We were starving by the time we arrived in the afternoon, and since there wasn't anything either of us could put together for a quick dinner, I was more than excited to order in my favorite rice bowl from the deli close to our office.

Christian had immediately headed straight up for a nap, and it amused me how tired he was. I was the same, but I needed to run to the store for some urgent feminine supplies that I truly didn't want him to be aware of. I was certain my period would be arriving any day now, and I didn't want to have to be concerned about it at the office for the rest of the week. It was also a great opportunity to get some groceries for us so we could at least have decent meals for a few days. I couldn't help my excitement because I at least wanted to give him this for the remainder of my stay here, so he wouldn't have to eat out constantly. Plus, I didn't want to spend any more money than I currently did on takeout, and neither could I just cook for myself. So my hope was he would be able to join me.

So I waited for the delivery, and was glad once again to see it was Tim.

For some reason, I always felt quite happy to see him, and looked a bit closely at his face to see if the bruises from his scuffle with Andrew had healed.

He was quite shy around me, which was endearing. I offered him a drink, and a few minutes of rest with me in the kitchen but he refused, and soon enough was on his way.

I too got in my car, although I was quite nervous, looking with every spare moment at my rearview and side view mirrors for anyone who could potentially be trailing me.

When I arrived, I checked the car was locked properly, pulled my hat low on my head and hurried in. In the store I felt a bit safe as I was surrounded by people, and so I quickly moved through the aisles, grabbing what I needed, and the time ticking away in my head of how quickly I needed to be out of here.

My urgency and fright nearly made me choke up as I stood in line at the checkout counter, staring at everyone near and far from me. Every sudden or lingering eye contact made me wary, and it pained me at the thought of how long I was going to keep living like a fugitive.

I was going to speak to Christian about this, I decided. So we could come up with a concrete plan of how to solve this once and for all, because I could feel all of the fear and caution, feeding an anxious disorder within me, one I had never had in my life.

And so I hurried over to the car and got in, not even bothering to put the groceries in the trunk but instead in the seat next to me.

I shut the door and was able to breathe easier, at least for now I was safe. I began to back out of the lot, and had just pulled out onto the road when I finally noticed it.

My heart slammed into my chest as I gazed at it, until a sudden honk from nearby startled me. I returned my gaze to the road, and tried to stabilize my breathing.

It however remained haggard as my heart continued to race. However I couldn't stop.

My gaze strayed from time to time to the envelope, and for the rest of the trip back, I prayed it would fly off the windshield wiper. *Maybe it wasn't what I was assuming,* I tried to console myself. Perhaps it was just something promotional that had been attached to the blades, but it was the same kind of envelope I had received earlier. White, plain, unsigned.

It remained on my windshield until I arrived back at Christian's building, and for the longest time I just remained in the car. At first, I ignored the envelope and just sat still. And then I turned towards it, furious but trying my very best to remain calm. It terrified me what I would find this time around, especially because I hadn't been at home. And that was where I had been monitored wasn't it? Or..."

I gasped and immediately grabbed the groceries and got out of the car. It dawned on me then just how secluded this underground parking lot was. I retrieved the envelope, locked the car behind me and was soon hurrying over to the elevators.

In there, I felt terrified that if it stopped on the way, then perhaps whoever was haunting me would join me in it, and I wouldn't be the wiser. Thankfully it wasn't the case and so by the time I arrived on Christian's floor, I was weakened from the tension. I hurried to his apartment, looking to every side and the cameras that were in the hallway.

There was no way they'd ever made their way here right? It was impossible. Perhaps these were old pictures. As soon as the door was unlocked, I hurried in and shut it, twisting the lock in place and dropped the groceries. Afterwards, I leaned against it and tried my best to calm down. However I couldn't, and so the tears restarted until I suddenly heard Christian's voice.

I immediately pushed away from the door, wiping the tears off my face, just before he arrived.

"Adele," he called, but I couldn't look at him.

"Hey," I replied, and hurried past him but he caught my hand.

"What is it?" he asked, but I couldn't respond either.

"I'll be right back, I just need to use the bathroom."

I pulled this hand away and then hurried up to my room. Instantly I headed into the bathroom and locked the door behind me. Then I sat on the toilet seat and after taking a deep breath, retrieved the pictures from the envelope.

My hands were shaking as I pulled them out, but I was determined to see what they were.

And I did.

I gazed at them for the longest time, and felt my entire body go cold.

I would never know how long I remained in that position... staring, but then eventually I was startled.

The stack of photographs fell out of my hands, spreading all over the floor.

"Adele?" I heard Christian call, and turned towards the door.

"Adele?"

He called again and I could hear the immense worry in his tone. "Open the door. Please?"

I couldn't bear to torture him anymore, and so I rose to my feet and went over.

I unlocked it and met his face downtrodden with concern.

For a while he just stared at me, his gaze widened at the state of my reddened eyes and damp cheeks. And then without saying a word, he stepped forward and pulled me into his arms.

It was just what I needed, although I didn't want to acknowledge it, and so when he held on even though I tried to pull away, I eventually gave in. I broke down in his arms and he refused to let go.

CHRISTIAN

I took her to bed and she came willingly with me.

In there, I tucked her in under the covers, and held her to me as she sobbed. I didn't say a word, and didn't need to ask any questions either because I had seen the photographs strewn across the floor. She had received yet another one, and although I was dying to know what had been captured in them this time around, especially since she had been in my care I couldn't bear to leave her yet. And so I waited... petting her softly until eventually I was certain she had fallen asleep, exhausted from the fear and her sobs.

I took an extra half hour to ensure she was deeply asleep, and as a result fell asleep with her. I woke up later on with a start, and then moving as carefully as I could, tightened the covers around her and then headed into her bathroom.

I picked the photos up from the floor, and then took a seat on her toilet bowl and began to peruse through. They were no longer of her in her apartment which was relieving but now, they were of her everywhere else. At the office, at grocery stores, with Melinda... and to my horror... the club. Of us entering and leaving... and of course, of the private room but thankfully from the dance floor. From the outside the wall was tinted alright, but if I looked just hard enough, I could make out the outline of us fucking against the glass wall.

Of her in the underground parking lot of this complex, of her entering and exiting but thankfully there was none of her inside the apartment. This relieved me, but then I kept moving through the photos and saw one of our exact front door. It was closed shut and that was it. But the message was clear. That whoever this sick bastard was knew exactly where she was and he would continue to haunt her. Perhaps it was also a matter of time before he would find a way to also record her inside of the apartment.

I took a deep sigh and made up my mind that enough was enough.

ADELE

I woke up alone, and all over again the panic rushed towards me like a storm.

My sleep had been restless, and although there were fragments of a nightmare reaching out, eager to clutch onto my now conscious mind, I couldn't quite clearly make out any of it. I instantly got up, looking around at the now empty room, but well aware Christian had been here, and I had fallen asleep in his arms.

It had darkened outside, and as I recalled the fact that I needed to get ready for work the next day, I instantly got up and went in search of him.

I didn't find him in his room, and so I headed towards the stairs. The corridor was dark but as I headed down the staircase, I could see the lights were on across the ground floor. I could also hear voices, but they were indistinct.

I wondered if it was his family that had come to visit, and if this was the case, then I had no interest whatsoever in seeing them. I didn't even want them to be aware I was still living in his house.

And so I treaded down the stairs carefully and watched. Soon the voices came closer, and when I stopped to look, I found he was escorting two men from the kitchen, towards the foyer. A few minutes later they were on their way, and then he turned around.

He came over to the base of the stairs, and looked towards where I was hiding in the shadows.

"Hey," he called out, his voice soft and kind, and I couldn't help but to go towards him. He held out his hand just before I arrived, and I took it. Together we headed towards the kitchen, and I was led to sit on one of the stools the men had just vacated.

I wanted to ask him about them, but I knew he would explain so I just focused on calming my nerves and trying to relax.

I was in his presence right now, I reminded myself. I was safe.

And so I simply watched as he retrieved a platter of food from the refrigerator, and then placed it into the microwave. He then brought it over to me, and I saw that it was the meal from the deli that I had ordered for the both of us earlier.

"Did you eat yours yet?" I asked and he shook his head.

"No, I was waiting for you."

I was surprised to hear this, and unhappy. "Why? You should have just gone ahead without me."

He came around the counter then, his own plate in his hand.

"I wanted to wait," he told me as he took his seat by my side. "I had a sandwich earlier so don't worry, I didn't starve by waiting."

This was somewhat amusing, and it surprised me I could even find it in me to smile.

We began eating, and I thought at some point he would bring up the men but when he didn't, I imagined perhaps he wasn't sure exactly what my state of mind was, and if I even wanted to hear anything about them. And so I proceeded to ask.

"Those men... who were they?"

"Private investigators," he replied, as he began to eat and once again my tension spiked. "We're going to get to the bottom of this, faster."

"Oh," I replied, my tone quiet because at this point, I had no clue if it was even possible.

"They made a suggestion when they were here," he said and I looked up from the meal I could barely taste.

"What suggestion?"

"They want you to take a leave of absence from work."

At this, I stilled. "What?"

"Yeah. Whoever this person is right now, he's in the shadows and we need to lure him out. So if he gets his kick from stalking you and letting you know it, then perhaps it would be best if you don't give him the opportunities. From the pictures sent to you today, it is quite obvious that although he might have access to the surrounding areas, he doesn't have any access whatsoever to this house. If he doesn't have any access to you for a little while to harass, then perhaps this will frustrate him enough to become sloppy just so he can reach you."

"So my absence will be used as bait?"

"Yes," he replied. "If you keep being out and about as usual then it will keep going until, who knows."

I smiled, bitterly. "Until he hurts me."

At this Christian went quiet and so I lifted my gaze to his. He met it. "I don't think he wants to hurt you," he said and I was perplexed.

"What?"

"I think he's just trying to get your attention. Otherwise if he knows this much about you and truly wanted to hurt you, then he should have known to send those pictures to the office… and get us both exposed. He should know this is one of your biggest fears. And moreover there's no note… there's never any note or demands."

"So what do you think is the purpose of this?" I asked.

"I have no clue," he responded. "But we have to find out immediately."

At this I sighed and returned to my meal. "This leave of absence… how long would it need to last?"

"Let's start with a week and see if this makes him restless enough to make a mistake."

My eyes widened at his suggestion. "A week?" he smiled.

"I knew you were going to react like that. But Adele, this is your safety so I think you should hope it is for just a week. That would be a miracle."

"I don't want to," I replied, my insides incredibly conflicted.

He sighed. "Adele, please cooperate with me on this. Give me a week from now, and let's try our best to fight this thing together."

At this, I felt tears sting my eyes once again.

"Who's going to help you at work?" I asked and he smiled. Reaching forward to stroke his hand against my cheek. I felt the touch all the way to my heart.

"I'll get someone from the pool, and don't worry, your position will be secured. This is just temporary."

It took me a little while longer but in the end, I really didn't have a choice and so I nodded and began to mentally work on the leave of absence request I would be sending over to the human resources department the following day.

"It'll all be fine," he said to me, his arm going around my waist to console me. "I'll get to the bottom of this. I promise,"

I appreciated him immensely and so I allowed myself to lean into him and to accept the embrace.

ADELE

By midmorning Monday and just as I had expected, Melinda was already informed. I had debated on what to tell her, over and over again, and whether the truth was the way to go or otherwise. I didn't want to keep lying to her because truly there was no need for it and she had so far been a good friend to me.

So when her message came in midway through the morning, I stared at it and revisited my decision.

"You're taking a leave of absence?" she asked. *"Are you alright?"*

"Yeah," I texted back. *"I just need a little break and so I'll be going to see my parents."*

"Oh," she replied, and I could tell again by the way I'd handled it I made her feel distant from me again.

"I'm sorry I didn't let you know in time but I think the breakup with Andrew, and the workload has taken more of a toll on me than anticipated. I just need this week to recharge."

"*I understand,*" she texted back. "*Now I feel sorry for troubling you last week.*"

"*It was no trouble,*" I replied, feeling even worse. "*Your complaints were valid.*"

"*Yeah, I wish I could have seen you before you left.*"

"*Don't worry,*" I wrote back to her. "*I'll be back before you know it.*"

"*Alright,*" she replied. "*Have fun, and rest. Maybe I'll follow in your footsteps soon and do the same.*"

I smiled and then the texting came to an end.

I looked around the kitchen and at the fruits before me I had brought out to make a smoothie. I couldn't remember the last time I had been off work in this way and it didn't particularly feel comfortable, especially given the circumstances demanding it.

I imagined Christian at work and wondered who amongst the secretary pool had been chosen to take my position. I thought about asking him, but then I didn't want to interfere. I'd even offered earlier in the day to come in to train the temp, however he'd refused, not wanting me out of the house for any reason whatsoever.

And so I made my smoothie and began research on the oil brief.

By lunch time however, I couldn't stand it anymore and I sent him a text message.

"*I could always do a video call with your new secretary if they need me for anything.*"

Afterwards I put the phone aside and tried to get to work, but couldn't help picking it up after every two minutes.

Eventually and to my immense relief, his response came however it wasn't as a message.

It was a video call.

I was startled as the facetime call came, but thankfully, was soon able to recover enough to respond.

I quickly ran my fingers through the messy tendrils of hair framing my face, and then his gorgeous face came into view. I felt all the warmth and admiration for him curl in the pit of my stomach.

He stared at me for a few seconds intently, and it was awkward to say the least.

"What is it?" I asked.

"Are you just generally an anxious person or you do not know how to take a break?"

I was stumped at the answer, so much so that even when my lips parted to speak I couldn't find anything to say.

"All is well here," he then proceeded to assure me. "If we need anything I'll call you. Now please Adele, relax."

I smiled then.

"Can I at least order you lunch from the bistro?"

"The temp will handle it."

I sighed then, and nodded. He gazed fondly at me.

"Take a swim," he said, "that might calm you."

"I will."

"If you're not calm by the time I get back let me know. I know other ways of getting the tension worked out of you."

The moment he said this my cheeks flushed a bright red, as I didn't need him to be any more explicit to understand exactly what he was referring to.

"Have a nice day," I said as I looked away to hide my smile and he laughed.

Afterwards, I took his advice and indeed went for a swim, needing to be calmed since I was no longer plagued with worry.

ADELE

"Can I come see you?"

It was an emotional phone call, one that I hadn't been looking forward to having... ever. But it was nearly two weeks later and my sudden leave of absence could no longer be explained away to Melinda as an extended visit to my parents.

I didn't owe her an explanation but for the lies and distance so far, I truly wanted to come clean and to share my frustrations.

However I didn't want her to come to Christian's home... just in case I was being watched. Since I was no longer out and about, to be freely stalked and harassed, I didn't want Melinda to somehow be dragged into all this. And this was what I told her the moment I walked into the coffee shop.

I was on high alert and so a quick perusal around the shop and I instantly spotted her. Attired in a dark green blazer and a pair of jeans, she waved and I headed over.

After we had spoken and I had revealed as much as I could she sat there, speechless.

"Oh my God."

I lifted the glass of iced tea to my lips, my gaze darting around the room in search of anything or anyone whose gaze on me lingered. My heart began to race in my chest because I considered perhaps I should have informed Christian. However, he had gone over to his mother's house that morning and the last thing I wanted was to bother him in the midst of his visit.

My gaze returned to Melinda and the tears that had gathered in her eyes. I couldn't help but feel my heart squeeze.

"Please don't cry," I said to her. "It's under control. We're getting things under control."

"How?" She asked. "Have they identified who he is?"

"They're narrowing down suspects," I replied. "Christian has yet to inform me of anything."

She looked away then to wipe the tears from her eyes.

"I can't believe I was hounding you so hard and, I can't believe you kept all of this away from me."

"I'm sorry, but I didn't want you to be concerned."

"No, you didn't want me to judge you for getting intimate with Christian again. And it's my fault, because of my stupid remarks at the beginning. I made you defensive and I am so sorry you couldn't even speak to me or rely on me."

"Melinda," I sighed, looking to see how her reaction was drawing much too much attention to us. It made me feel scared, and so I couldn't help but to rise to my feet.

"I'm going to go to the bathroom for a little bit. Do you want to come with me?"

I was hoping she would say yes, but instead she shook her head pulling a handkerchief from her purse.

With a squeeze to her shoulder, I got up and hurriedly escaped to the bathroom.

On my way, I pulled my phone out of my pocket and as soon as I got in, thought about perhaps texting him. Just to let him know why I wasn't at the apartment in case he returned before I did.

I was just crafting the message when I heard someone come in, so I moved out of the way and pulled up his contact.

"*Christian*," I sent. "*I'm-*"

There was a sudden blow. It was blunt and hard and it made my vision spin before me. I saw stars, and wailed, because it felt as though my head had been split in two. But then I felt a hand clamp around my mouth... and everything went black.

ADELE

The first thing that registered when I came to, was the splitting headache. Absolutely nothing else could register beyond the vicious soreness at the back of my head.

What was worse however, was I couldn't hold onto it. I couldn't do anything. Couldn't move my arms or legs, and when I realized they were both spread out, my heart nearly gave out. I tried to pull my eyes open and my vision spun. It took a while but soon enough, my gaze cleared enough to be able to look around the room. At first, I wasn't certain what I was seeing, but as the seconds ticked by, it soon became clearer, leaving me in shock.

All around the room were my photos. Some of them I could recognize as they had been sent to me, but there were also others I was seeing for the first time. And they were everywhere and in varied sizes plastered to the walls.

I swallowed, my gaze darting around and so when it came across a very familiar pair of dark green underwear, my heart slammed viciously against my chest.

I couldn't breathe, and so I began to struggle, my hands and legs kicking against the ropes around my wrist that had bound me like a starfish to the bed. The only positive so far was the fact that my clothes were still on. Never, more than now had I been relieved at the fact I had worn jeans. I was still intact, and had to get out of here by any means. I couldn't scream, or call for help in case it alerted whoever this sick bastard was but yet again I couldn't do anything else.

Tears pooled in my eyes but I tried my best to stop them, to not fall apart before I could clearly understand what was going on and appropriately respond to whoever was doing this.

They however began to slide down the corners of my eyes, and so I shut them... *tight*.

And that was when I heard it. The push of the door as it was pulled open, however I didn't hear any footsteps, the person was too quiet, or perhaps the carpet the floor was covered with muted his steps.

I waited, trying my best to remain still, but my body began to tremble and I was forced to open my eyes.

They were at the foot of the bed but I couldn't look directly at them... at least not yet.

But that was until the person spoke.

"I'm sorry," he began, his voice small.

I was confused. My eyes shot open and when I saw who it was, I gasped.

"I'm sorry," he repeated but all I could do was stare back in shock.

"T-Tim?"

"I didn't want to do this…" he began and then began to pace restlessly. "But I didn't have a choice."

"I-I wanted you to notice me," he began rattling off. "I tried everything… well," he stopped, his shoulders slumping.

"I tried everything except asking you, but how could I?" he turned back to me, his smile shaky and sad.

"You're too good for me. You would never have given me a chance."

I was stunned. More tears escaped my eyes.

"What?"

"I made you afraid," he said to me. "I'm sorry, I didn't mean to but then… you made me afraid. I waited… I waited till your relationship ended with that other idiot. But then you started up with your boss and I knew you'd never look at me. What is it with you?" he seemed to lament. "Why couldn't you just remain available so I could get a chance? These men don't love you… but me, I was ready to give you everything I have, everything you needed, but you never even looked my way."

I closed my eyes because truly, I didn't know how to process any of this.

"I'm not going to hurt you Adele. You are kind, but I'm just going to show you what I have to offer… what we can be together, and then afterwards you can make your choice."

'Show you what we can be together?'

I couldn't believe this. My heart was now pounding so viciously in my chest it was almost more than I could bear.

"Please don't do this," I said to him. "Please let me go, or at least untie me so we can talk."

"You won't talk to me," he huffed and I heard the foot of the bed depress as though his weight had come on it. "You're too good for me. But I can show you... I swear I can show you. If I can only show you then you will believe me."

And then he was moving onto me.

"Tim," I cried, now mercilessly trying to wrench my hands and feet away from the ties, because in this position I could do absolutely nothing to set myself free. Never in my life had I felt so helpless.

"Ti-Tim!"

And then suddenly, he was above me. The sick smile on his face came above mine, and then his hands grabbed onto the lapels of my shirt. He tried to wrench it apart, struggling until the buttons popped off and I was exposed.

And then I *screamed*.

CHRISTIAN

I hoped with all of my heart I wasn't too late. And I hoped even more I wasn't wrong or else I was going to lose it.

I drove as fast as I could towards his house, and Melinda's voice kept repeating in my head.

"We can't find her. She left to go to the bathroom and... she never came back. I looked for her all over the shop. And she couldn't have just left because her purse and car are still here."

I slammed on the steering wheel as I was forced to come to a stop at the traffic light. *Fuck!*

My phone began to ring, and when I saw who it was I immediately picked up.

"How close are you?"

"We're about eight minutes away from his house," the response came. "Jordan and Kyle are about ten minutes from his deli. If he isn't there, they'll find out about his family immediately and track them down."

"Fuck!" I cursed again.

"When you get to his home, can you wait for us before you go in?" he asked. "It could be dangerous."

I ended the call, not even bothering to respond because he was out of his mind for the suggestion.

How could I wait for them to arrive when a second's delay could mean life and death for her? They were fucking idiots, and so was I for not arranging a protection detail sooner. I had been able to feel her growing restlessness from the previous days, and was planning to discuss with her about returning back to work since so far, no more harassment had been made. However, I had waited too long.

I was mad at her for leaving without even informing me but then again, I hadn't told her she couldn't. I had even been the one to try to convince her perhaps the bastard didn't want to hurt her at all. But now, he had taken her and I didn't know if I would ever be able to forgive myself if anything hurt her or worse.

It seemed to take forever, but soon enough I was arriving onto his street. I slowed down and parked a few houses away and then began to run over to his home. I was cautious as I approached the small old bungalow... going around to see if there was a way in. All the doors were locked, as well as the windows and for a moment I imagined he wasn't home. But then I found his van parked out in front.

He most definitely was.

I had my gun in hand, and was able to jump over the fence to his small cluttered backyard. In there, I found his patio door was also locked, but the glass could be shattered. I hesitated, knowing if he heard the intrusion, and she was truly in there with him, then it could most definitely put her in harm's way.

However as the seconds ticked by in my mind, I realized it was either now or never and I had to move fast.

And so with the back of the gun and four hard blows, the glass surrounding the door handle cracked and shattered. I pushed my hand in, barely feeling the cuts and scrapes that followed and in seconds, the sliding door was unlocked. I pushed it open and ran in… my eyes roving around the small and empty living room and adjoining kitchen. The place was a mess… dark and musty and dilapidated.

I hurried down the hallway, and it was then I heard her scream.

It pierced through the quiet of the room and then I heard something shatter. A few curses, and then everything went quiet.

My heart stopped in my chest. I hurried over then, pointed the gun at the door and then said a little prayer in my attempt to save her, I wouldn't instead put her in harm's way.

With one vicious kick, at the handle, it broke splintering away from the door and then the door was pushed open.

At first all I saw was his bare back and jeans riding low on his hips, and then her, under him, struggling but with her cries muffled. I realized he had gagged her.

He turned, sweat beading his forehead, and eyes reddened and widened with shock at the sudden intrusion.

"How the hell-" he began but then saw the gun in my hand and scrambled off the bed. A quick glance at her to see if she was alright, and her state broke my heart. He had torn off her shirt, and had her chest exposed, but thankfully, thankfully things hadn't gone very far.

She cried and struggled... and I returned my gaze to his. I felt anger and hatred with an intensity I couldn't remember ever feeling before. And so as he scrambled against the wall, hurling insults at me for breaking into his home, I considered letting him go, but I just couldn't. And so I lifted the gun and aimed for his knee.

I didn't miss, and the shot was so deafening it shook the house. His scream of pain seemed to be a thousand times worse. I put the gun away and hurried over to her as he bled in the corner. In no time the restraints were off her, and I had her in my arms. She couldn't stop sobbing.

"Get me out of here," she cried over and over again, and with one last glare at the wailing bastard in the corner, and the room plastered with her photos, I turned around and took her away.

A dele

I came to with a headache.

My eyes felt strained and sore from all the tears, and my throat was parched.

It was dim, but as I looked around I realized I was in the hospital. There was a chair in the corner and on it was a very familiar figure. He was slouching in it without even a blanket and my heart ached as I watched him.

I tried to recall all that happened and it came rushing back to me, and through it all I couldn't look away from him. I didn't think I could ever be more grateful to another person especially as I thought of how he had arrived just in time.

My eyes burned once again as the thoughts returned of how my options had narrowed to death in my heart as Tim had prepared to violate me. I knew I would never have wanted to survive that, and even if I had, I dreaded the kind of scar it would have left on my soul forever.

The gunshot went off again in my heart and I jumped at the sound. Even though Christian had been the one holding it, I had still been so nervous he would end up being the one to get hurt. Not until he had brought me outside with him and taken me into his car to await the cops had I managed to find an element of calm. But I could still feel the fright coursing through my system, and realized it would take quite a while to completely work the tension out of my system. He had insisted on bringing me straight here, and I had complied, willing to go anywhere as long as I would be with him and not alone.

I thought of Tim, his shy demeanor but yet the madness I had seen in his eyes in those moments. I trembled once again as I tried to wrap my head around the fact he was the one behind it all. I thought about it long and hard and the more I did, the more it made sense, but then it didn't. Nothing did at all and once again I couldn't wait for Christian to get up.

I needed him, I realized. And this too made me hurt.

For quite a while he had been the only one I had to lean on during this nightmare, and now that it was over, I wondered if his absence would create a massive void in my life. I wanted him in my life but not in this frightening desperate way I currently felt.

I felt dependent and vulnerable, and needed to know what was going to happen to Tim.

Tears were sliding down my face once again, and I didn't even realize it until it became difficult to breathe. I was however conscious of the fact he was probably bone tired, so I turned my face away and tried to muffle the sounds so they wouldn't wake him. I shut my eyes and tried to calm myself down.

I thought of all our times together, the evenings and mornings and even our earlier days of being awkward with each other. It all made me wonder if without him I would have been able to survive this. I knew the answer, and couldn't but be grateful once again that Andrew had broken up with me which had led to me meeting Christian.

I was so grateful, and once again I couldn't wait for him to get up so I could appreciate him with all my heart for just being there for me in so many ways, and yet again here in such a crucial way. I turned back to the chair and my heart lurched.

He was awake and staring at me, and although our eyes met, he didn't move for the longest time.

My lips parted as I tried to speak and call out to him, but no words would come out. He rose to his feet and I tried to get up.

"Don't," he complained softly but kindly. I needed to at least hold on to him so I managed to raise my arms and hold them out.

With a smile on his face, he walked right into my embrace and lowered so receive it fully. I held him tightly, and buried my face in his neck, breathing in the sweetness and warmth of his scent.

I loved him, I realized, and it made me cry even harder because I didn't know how I was ever going to repay him.

Eventually, he managed to pull out of my embrace despite my reluctance.

His eyes went all over my face, and his hand lifted to gently begin to wipe the wetness off.

"You fell asleep this way," he told me. "And now you're waking up in the same way?"

"What way?" I managed to mutter.

"In tears," he replied, and I saw the unhappiness in his eyes at this.

"I'm sorry," I immediately apologized, and he shook his head as he lifted my hand to place a kiss on the back.

"You have no need to be. I'm the one who is sorry for criticizing you. It's alright to cry for as long and as hard as you need to. But I hope you can do it out of relief you have me by your side, and all of this is over and will never occur again. It's all under control so don't cry out of fear or unhappiness.

I'm here. I promise. And I'm not leaving. You'll get through this."

Unable to say another word, and with quivering lips I pulled him back into my arms.

I would never know how long I held him for, but eventually I had to let him go because he began to shift uncomfortably and I realized how painful it must be for him to remain bent in that way.

He laughed softly the moment I released him, and he pulled the chair towards my side. He didn't let go of my hand as he took his seat, and I was more than grateful to be as close as possible to him without falling off the bed. We stared at each other for a while, and I asked the questions that I wanted to.

"The police took him away right?"

"They did," he replied. "For good. They will begin his prosecution immediately. He won't get away with this, I promise you that."

I continued to stare at him. "How did you find me?"

At this, a slight smile curved the corners of his lips. And then his gaze lowered as he stroked my fingers and retreated into his thoughts.

"I never suspected him at first," he said. "But then when I knew what to look for it made sense he was the one. Talk about hiding in plain sight. It started when you received the last set of pictures a few weeks ago. There was one among them of my door. That was all he could get as he had delivered food to us there, it would have been impossible for him to get a photograph of the interior as he's never come past the foyer. Plus the building's security is top notch, so when I requested the surveillance, I was able to see we'd never had any strange visitors except for Tim. Well he wasn't exactly strange, but he was my only lead so I hired the private investigators to watch him and told the police of my suspicions."

"They've been keeping a close eye on him but nothing seemed untoward so we gave up a few days ago and started searching in other directions. Until I received the call from Melinda yesterday that you'd gone missing. Because of what you'd explained to her, she was scared to call the cops so she'd immediately contacted the office and they'd put her through to me. I took matters from there."

I smiled, but as I thought back to the scene once again and its progression, I couldn't help but shudder. He leaned in and began to rub up and down my arm affectionately.

"It's alright," he tried his best to assure me. "You'll be fine."

"I'm sorry," I apologized yet again, but he shook his head.

"No need."

I looked away briefly and the contemplative silence dragged on between us. And then something else occurred to me. "Where did you get a gun?"

"I've always had one," he replied. "I got it a couple of years ago. Why do you ask?"

"You seemed to be a great shot."

"Well I do visit the shooting range from time to time."

"You do?" I replied, eyes widening in excitement.

"Yes, it's pretty cool. You should come join me sometime."

"Can I get a gun too?" I asked, and he looked at me for longer than was needed before responding. "Sure they have guns."

"Not what I asked you."

He laughed and when the amusement subsided, turned serious once again. "Alright we'll see what we can do."

I looked at him and was so happy to see the smile on his face that it brought tears to mine once again.

"Adele," he called softly as he leaned forward and took me in his arms.

EPILOGUE

ONE YEAR LATER

Christian

"I can't believe you were able to get them to close this place down for the evening."

I looked up from the myriad of congratulatory messages I had snuck off for a bit to go through, as the familiar voice floated over to me.

It was gentle and beautiful and quite possibly the only sound in the world that made my heart instantly soft.

I watched as she strolled over to me, graceful and breath-taking in a pale pink halter neck dress that clung to her body like a second skin. The body I had now come to know even more intimately than she probably did herself.

She was now in my life, indefinitely although the change from her being my secretary to now being placed in one of the marketing teams had been a bit of an unsavory transition for me. She'd gotten second place in the competition, and I'd managed to convince myself and all the other executives the first three places all had great ideas that the client was open to incorporating.

And so all three employees had been drafted to work on the new project, while I'd managed to poach a few more experienced employees from the other teams who were eager for growth to lead them. And thus a new and complete marketing team had been formed. I looked forward to having her lead one of her own projects someday, as there was very little comparable to seeing her trying to navigate a challenging project.

She was dedicated and relentless and creative.

I sighed as I once again lifted my drink to my lips, overwhelmed at how much I loved everything about her. I then set the glass down as she arrived, my hand immediately reaching out, and my legs spreading wide open to accommodate her.

From my perch on the stool, I looked into her eyes, the crowds of well wishers all around fading into the background.

"You have my mother to thank for that," I said as I leaned forward to nibble on her lower lip and she giggled.

"I thought you handed it over to Stacy."

"They worked on it together," I replied. "At least that's what I heard."

"But it was your idea? Wasn't it?" she asked.

"Well, they did ask for my input, and where better to have our rehearsal dinner than at the very bar where we first met?"

She laughed, leaning down once again to give me a proper kiss. "I have my ears open in case anyone comes up to me to say they know I was a drunk mess when we met, and you had to save my ass and take me home. So far no one has, so this wedding is still on, but the night hasn't ended yet so don't relax either."

I laughed... "Don't worry, I kept the story simple. We met, we drank, we fell in love."

"That is the truth... the whole truth and nothing but the truth."

She kissed me and my heart felt too full to remain in my chest, and then we stared into the other's eyes.

"I still can't believe this is happening. I want to pinch myself."

At that, my gaze lowered to her stomach. "I'm the one who still can't believe this is happening." My hand lowered to it, trying to feel any movement whatsoever but shyly, she looked around and smacked my hand away. "Hey! People are looking."

"They'll find out soon anyway."

"I know, but I want this wedding to solely be about us."

"Sure," my arms wrapped around her waist.

"Adele," there was a sudden call, and we both looked up to see Melinda coming through the crowd excited and clearly tipsy.

"*Refill,*" she squealed and placed the glass on the counter for the bartender to handle.

"God I'm having a blast!" she exclaimed, leaning forward. "And um... I don't have to call you sir when we're not in the office right?" she said to me. "We'll basically become family tomorrow."

I smiled, my heart warmed. "You don't have to call me sir anywhere. Christian is great."

"She still calls you sir though," Melinda pointed out, and I couldn't help but stare at my fiancée.

"She doesn't even talk to me at the office," I replied. "But I'll win the battle. I have time now to fight it."

Adele laughed, her arms smacking mine. "Okay, I better head off as I can see my mom laughing a bit too loudly too."

"She's having so much fun," Melinda said. "Wait for me, I'll come back with you.

She kissed me, before she left, and reluctantly I let her go. I watched as she moved and then she turned around.

"I love you," she mouthed, and it left me breathless.

The End

Chapter One
Amber

As much as I loved my staff and how busy the bakery got during peak hours, I reveled in the silence of the afternoon when we shut down for the day. The staff usually left by three and then I spent an hour working on the business side of things. I gave the counters another wipe, though Joe, our cleaner, did a pretty awesome job.

From the corner of my eye, I noticed a blond-haired woman trying to open the front door even though there was a large sign that read 'Closed'. I tried to ignore her but she tugged at the door again. With a sigh I left the counter and unlocked the front door.

"I'm sorry, but we're closed." There were always customers who came after we had closed and as much as I hated turning people away, we really did have to stick to our closing hours.

Something about the woman's face seemed familiar and I narrowed my eyes and tried to place.

For her part she stared at me without speaking, before her eyes widened, and she let out a cry. "Amber Davies! Oh my God. Wow! I can't believe it's you. Heck you haven't changed one bit." She grinned and the picture of a pretty, curvaceous girl sprung to my mind.

It was my turn to shriek. "Jesus Christ! Julie Watson!"

She was one of my closest friends in high school before she and her family moved away. We'd communicated for a short while, but slowly drifted apart over time.

"What are you doing here? Are you back in town?" I asked her.

She nodded eagerly. "Yes. I moved back here a couple of months ago and I went looking for you in your old neighborhood, but there was someone else living in your old house. I couldn't find anyone who remembered you or me. I thought you'd left town."

"No. My parents passed on a few years ago and Timber and I sold the house," I told her quietly.

The grief had lessened over the years leaving behind a dull pain. Whoever said that you never got over the loss of a loved one was correct. It didn't help matters that our adoptive parents had been the only children in their families. Once they were gone I had no other relatives other than my older brother, Timber.

I noticed the stricken look that came over Julie's features. "I'm sorry, I never heard."

"It's okay, it was a long time ago." It dawned on me that we were still out on the street. "Come in."

She saw the closed sign and made a comical face which made me laugh. "Oops, I'm sorry I didn't see that."

"I'm glad you didn't or else we wouldn't have met," I said, feeling giddy with a rush of happiness. Julie and I had always believed that we would be friends for life. She had been the closest thing to a sister I'd ever had.

I never did forge that kind of friendship with anyone again, even in college. I had friends but they were not that close and establishing the bakery had taken a lot of my time and energy.

"How are your parents and sister?" I asked her, leading the way into the bakery.

"All well, but back in Washington," she said, looking around. "This is really cute. You work here, of course?"

"Yes, Timber and I own it." I couldn't help the tone of pride in my voice. I loved my little bakery.

I co-owned it with my brother, but he was a silent partner and usually only helped out when he was in between his photography assignments.

Color bloomed on Julie's cheeks. "Uh, and how is he doing?"

A giggle escaped my lips. Julie had been hopelessly infatuated with Timber. I'd loved teasing her about it and each time she denied it, but whenever she was home and Timber was around, she would follow his movements with lovesick-puppy eyes.

Julie burst out laughing. "I made such a fool of myself. Did he know?"

I shook my head. "I don't think so."

"What happened to Josh," she said. "The guy you swore you'd marry and have many babies with?"

We spent the next fifteen minutes reminiscing and giggling, reminding me of how much I'd missed having a close girl-friend. The years melted away and we were young girls again.

"I've missed you," Julie said with tears in her eyes.

"I've missed you too." Impulsively, I went to her and pulled her into a hug as if the last decade hadn't happened.

We drew apart after several seconds and laughed self-consciously.

"I'm glad you're doing so well," she said, her eyes moving to the counter.

"Thanks," I said. "Want some cookies? On the house."

Her face sobered up suddenly as if she just remembered something sad. "Cake. I want cake. I had a lousy afternoon. My fiancé just broke up with me and moved out of the apart-ment we share. I need a big fat slice of cake to cheer me up."

I tried to imagine the pain she must be feeling. I'd never been so in love that I was ever heartbroken the way literature and movies showed it. When my last relationship ended, I'd actu-ally been relieved. I'd gone out with Carson for a year. It had been nice at the beginning, and I'd loved having a man so obsessed with me that he even watched me sleeping and texted me almost a hundred times a day.

Yeah, I'd been that naïve. It hadn't taken long to realize that Carson had a problem. He didn't want to be my boyfriend. He'd wanted to own me.

"Oh, I'm so sorry, Julie," I said sincerely.

Tears swam in her eyes.

"You need more than cake," I decided. "You need a drink. Can I treat you to a drink?"

"Yes please," she said gratefully. "I'd love to catch up."

"I just need to close up and then we can go."

Five minutes later, we were in an Uber headed to one of the trendiest bars in town. I loved it for the anonymity it offered and the band that played on Fridays and weekends. The residents of our middle-sized town in New Jersey were a mixed group of all ages but the majority were young people.

We chatted casually in the Uber, catching up on mutual friends we'd known back in the day.

It was a little early for the young professionals who frequented The Oyster Bar, and we got a nice table at the far end of the room.

"I've missed New Jersey," Julie said after the waiter had taken our orders for drinks.

"New Jersey has missed you," I told her, still amazed by how suddenly she had walked back into my life and it was as if no time had passed.

"I was contemplating returning home to Washington but now I'm having second thoughts," Julie said. "I just found a job that I love, and I hate the thought of leaving it."

"What do you do?" I asked her.

"I'm an interior decorator," she said. "I just got a job in an architectural firm, and I love it."

"Then stay," I urged, excited at the prospect of living in the same city with Julie again and strengthening our friendship.

Our cocktails were served and before I knew it, we'd drained our glasses and were ordering more. It was the best evening I'd had in a long time. I laughed more than I had in the last six months, and I told Julie stuff about Carson that I'd never told anyone.

"He was a bastard and I'm glad you finally got rid of him," she said.

"The court restraining order got rid of him," I said, my voice louder than usual. The five cocktails I'd taken were doing their work. Julie and I laughed uproariously.

A sad expression suddenly came over her features and even in my tipsy state I knew that she was thinking about her ex-fiancé. She needed a distraction. Something to help her forget about him even if it was only for one night.

"I know what you need," I announced.

Julie leaned forward and stared at me expectantly.

"A one-night stand," I said and stood up to get a better view of the people in the bar.

Julie laughed. "Are you serious? Is that your solution for my broken heart?"

"I read that the fastest way to heal from a broken heart was to sleep with another guy. What do you have to lose?"

"I will if you'll join me," Julie said with a twinkle in her eye.

I was glad to see that she still possessed the wild side she'd had in high school, but I wasn't really in the mood for a man, let alone a one night stand. I looked around disinterestedly. My eye was caught by a group of four men standing in a semi-circle at the bar. One of them, a dark-haired, utterly and totally edible looking man stared right back at me, holding my gaze.

My heart pounded in my chest and my legs turned to jelly. Heat pooled in my pussy and spread to the rest of my body. Lust burned a hot pit in my belly. My breath came out in gasps, as if I'd been running. I'd never been that physically attracted to a man. Maybe it was the alcohol talking.

I shifted my glance back to her and struck out my hand. She placed hers in mine. "Deal," I said.

Her attention was also drawn to the four guys. "They are hot," she said softly. "I can't remember the last time I admired a guy."

"Me neither." I didn't admit that I'd never had a one-night stand either. I'd wanted to, after Carson and I broke up, but I never worked up the courage. The idea was solely tempting.

I noticed movement at the corner of my eyes and when I turned the hot guy was headed our way. He moved like a panther, fluidly, unhurriedly, but full of suppressed power. All the air left my lungs as he got closer. He was seriously ripped, with his shirt stretched out across his wide muscular shoulders and chest.

I grabbed my glass and took a large swig of my drink. When I looked up, he was standing over me, a panty-melting smile on his panty-melting face.

"Hi ladies," he murmured in a warm deep voice.

"Hi," we both echoed back.

"Would you like to join us for a drink," he asked.

Julie and I exchanged a glance, communicating without words, just as we had when we were younger. We both stood up.

He led the way to the bar counter where his three friends were. They were friendly and welcoming. Introductions were made all round. The only name I heard was panty-melting Brody's. Brody. Oh my. That was a name for a cowboy. Well, he could have passed for one. He was soooo gorgeous.

Brody and I managed to move a little to one side, in essence secluding ourselves from everyone else. I didn't mind. He said something that I couldn't hear over the music. I moved closer. A mixture of sage and manly scents wafted up into my nostrils making my lust go a notch higher.

I had never been that physically affected by a man. Ever. He towered over me and stood so close; his breath fanned my face.

"I've not seen you here before," he drawled.

I tilted my head up, my gaze zeroing in on his lips. They were full and yet so masculine. It was easy to imagine him lowering them to mine. I didn't recognize the person I'd become with a few drinks in me.

Meeting Julie had awakened my hibernating wild side. In school we had been known as the opposite twins. Julie had been the crazy one and I'd been the one who tempered her wild side. Alcohol usually brought out the wildness in me. I was feeling so brazen as Brody and I feasted on each other with our eyes.

We chatted and had another round of drinks.

Then the band played a slow song that I loved, and I dragged Brody to the dance floor. Julie and one of the guys had beaten us to it and were wrapped around each other.

Brody slipped his hands around my waist and drew me close. I let out a sigh as I draped my hands around his neck and rested my head on his chest. God, it felt good to be held by a man.

My nipples hardened under my top, and I was sure he could feel them pressing against his chest. Unable to help myself, I caressed the hard flat muscles of his shoulders as we moved to the music. Brody's hands roamed my back too, increasing my need to kiss him.

I raised my head and as if he had been waiting for me to make the first move, he brought his lips to mine. Our mouths moved against each other, licking, discovering, before I parted my lips, and he slid his tongue in.

He tasted of heat and whiskey. A combination that made me dizzy with arousal. We kissed as if we had been practicing for years, without any awkward moments like scraping of teeth.

Heat poured through my body as Brody deepened the kiss and pressed me tighter against his body. I wanted more than making out on the dance floor. I wanted sex with a stranger. Someone I would never see again in my life.

A warning went off in my head. I'd promised myself to stay away from men after what happened with Carson. But I wasn't looking for a relationship, my brain countered. Just one night of fun.

That was all.

Then tomorrow, I would go back to my normal life.

Chapter Two
Brody

I couldn't believe Amber agreed to go home with me.

Was it really true what they said about red-haired women being crazy and wild? Dylan and I discreetly exchanged our apartment keys before I drained the last of my whiskey.

I watched Amber whisper something to her friend on the dance floor before she made her way back to me. With a slow smile I took her hand, and we left the bar together. I felt as if I'd won the lottery or better. Money couldn't compare with the feeling I had at that moment.

It was rare that I scored that fast with a woman as beautiful as Amber. The chemistry between us as we made out on the dance floor had been explosive. Her body had been like a liquid, molding against mine, making my cock so hard it had throbbed painfully in my pants.

The first thing I'd noticed about her was her smile as she spoke animatedly to her friend. She had the kind of smile that made you smile back for no reason at all. The way her heart shaped face lit up as she gestured with her hands.

I'd never been so mesmerized by a woman, and I'd watched her for hours before making my move. Talking to her had been like having a peek into heaven. There was nothing pretentious about her. She laughed with her whole body, throwing her head back, caring little for the impression she was making.

She wanted me as much as I wanted her, and she made no secret of that fact. She touched me when we spoke and held my gaze, telling me without words that the attraction between us was real.

I had to have her.

A cab was waiting right outside the bar, and we got in and I gave him Dylan's address. Unable to help myself, I pulled her towards me and kissed her, sucking on her lower lip before plunging my tongue into her mouth.

She moaned loudly as if we were already in the privacy of home. I loved a woman who didn't care for other people's opinions. Amber was clearly a woman after my own heart. We got to our destination too fast, just as we were really getting into it.

The cab driver didn't bat an eyelid as I paid the fare. He'd seen his fair share of half-drunk couples making out in the back of his car. I held Amber's hand and led her to the entrance of Dylan's building.

It had never made me uncomfortable in the past to pretend that Dylan's place was mine, but that time, as I pushed the door open to the apartment, I felt a twinge of guilt. There was a good reason for it, I told myself.

Except that Amber didn't seem like the kind of woman who would fixate on me because I was wealthy. But what did I know about her? We had hardly spoken in the bar, as we'd been too focused on our physical attraction.

"Nice place," Amber said, looking around Dylan's living room.

She was less tipsy than she had been in the bar and a wary look had come over her features. A shadow of fear went through me. What if she decided that she didn't want to do this after all?

"Thanks," I said and closed the distance between us and pulled her into my arms. "I've been wanting to get you alone from the first moment I saw you," I whispered to her in between kisses.

She moaned and I felt her body relaxing in my arms. I kissed her until her lips were swollen.

"Let's go to the bedroom," she said. "My legs can't hold me up any longer."

"They don't need to," I told her and easily lifted her and carried her down the hallway.

Her giggles of surprise bounced off the walls and I peppered her with kisses all the way to Dylan's guest bedroom. I was relieved that the bed was already made. Once, I had brought a girl and the bed had been unmade. Talk about a mood killer, having to make the bed first.

I laid her on the bed and crawled in after her, draping my body over hers. I went for the curve of her neck and sucked it before turning my attention back to her mouth. I teased her lips, licking and sucking before I lowered my mouth to her exposed cleavage.

I kissed the skin above her breasts and dipped my tongue in the valley that had teased me all evening. Her skin was soft and tasted of honey. I inhaled her sweet scent of vanilla and let my hand stroke the bare skin of her arms.

My cock lurched when I pulled her top over her head, leaving her only in her bra.

"Perfect." My words came out in a pant as I stared down at her round, full breasts.

Amber brought her hands to her bra and opened the front clasp that held it together. She shrugged it off and I helped slide it off her shoulders. Her nipples were large, hard and inviting. I took one into my mouth and teased it with my tongue and then sucked on it.

Whimpers left Amber's mouth as I showered attention on her sexy breasts. I lowered my kisses all the way to her navel. She raised her hips and I slipped off her pants and lacy panties. I wanted her completely naked.

I dipped a hand between her legs and let out a sharp breath at how wet she was. I stroked her folds nudging them open. Then Amber locked her thighs, imprisoning my hand.

I met her gaze.

"I want you naked too, Brody," she whispered harshly, her eyes gleaming with passion. She loosened her thighs and I got off the bed.

Her eyes didn't leave my body as I unbuttoned my shirt and threw it on the floor. One of the benefits of being a firefighter, even on a voluntary basis, was that we worked out a lot and my body showed it.

I unbuckled my belt and slid my pants zipper down. My cock bulged obscenely inside my briefs and Amber's eyes widened as she looked at it. My lips curved into a smile. I loved the reaction from women when they first saw my cock. Amber's reaction was no different.

I pulled down my briefs and stepped out of them. When I stood up, letting Amber see my cock, she let out a gasp. I wrapped my hand around it and gave it a few strokes.

I rejoined her on the bed and spread her legs apart. I let out a growl as I took in her glistening pussy, wet with arousal juices. I dipped my head between her legs and fanned her folds with my breath.

Impatiently, she raised her hips, and clasped the back of my head.

"Don't tease me Brody," she said, her tone harsh.

"I wasn't planning to," I said with a chuckle. I swiped her slit and she cried out. "I love how wet you are."

I swirled my tongue over her sensitive clit, teasing it and watching it swell by the second. She thrashed her legs and kept my head in place with a firm hold on either side.

I growled as I licked and sucked, loving her taste and the wild, loud noises that she was making. I'd never been with a woman as sexily noisy as she was. She said my name over and over again, making me feel like the greatest lover who ever lived.

I fucked her with my tongue, moving faster and faster until she screamed that she was about to come. I shifted my attention to her clit, clamped my mouth on it and sucked. Then I pushed a finger in and pumped in and out.

I felt it when the orgasm rocked her body. Her pussy walls clenched against my finger and her whole body trembled as if a tsunami had swept through her. I didn't wait for her to recover.

I reached for my trousers and dug for a condom in my wallet. I sheathed myself and returned to the bed. I met her gaze with a questioning one.

She nodded with a smile. "Nothing has changed Brody. I want you."

Pleasure swamped me as I gently spread her open and ran the tip of my cock up and down her still wet folds. I did this several times, spreading her wetness everywhere before sinking inside her tight pussy.

We both groaned loudly at the intense pleasure as I pushed my cock in until it filled her completely. She clamped her legs around my hips tightly and dug her nails into my arms. I pulled out almost all the way and then plunged back in.

Amber let out a series of moans and gripped her thighs tighter. Fuck, she was sweet. Her pussy was like a vice, gripping my cock and milking it with every thrust. I looked down at her and almost creamed myself at the sight of her full breasts bouncing and her lips slightly parted.

"I'm going to come, Brody!" she cried.

"Do it!" I growled, pounding my cock into her deeper and faster.

She came with a scream as her whole body convulsed. She jerked her head from side to side, her thick red hair flying as she did so. She was a vision to behold, and I couldn't hold my release back any longer.

I cried out in pure pleasure as I came in a rush of hot cream. My orgasm was sharper, more intense and drawn out. It was a different experience from other women. I couldn't define it but as we lay next to each other, waiting for our breaths to return to normal, I knew that Amber was a special woman.

I had a good feeling about her. I wanted to see her again.

She was the first to stir, sitting up and swinging her shapely legs to the side of the bed. She got up and padded stark naked out of the room, probably in search of the bathroom. I was in awe of her confidence as she strode off.

By the time she disappeared through the door, I had another massive hard on. I grinned like a fool, feeling as if I'd struck gold. She returned several minutes later. I made space for her on the bed.

Instead of getting back into the bed, Amber sat on the edge and reached for her panties. She straightened them and proceeded to put them on. She gathered the rest of her clothes and put them on as well.

"What are you doing?" I asked her, propping myself up with my elbow.

She turned to look at me. "Dressing. I need to go."

My brain unscrambled. "But I thought we would spend the night together." I felt like a complete fool as those pathetic words dropped out of my mouth. They were so not me.

She raised an eyebrow. "Why would you think that? We're strangers who met in the bar and decided to have sex. I don't want to see you again and I'm guessing you don't want to see me again either."

I opened my mouth to speak then promptly shut it. To be brutally honest, that was usually my line. I'd thought what I'd felt had been mutual.

Clearly not.

She finished dressing, got up and grabbed her purse. She smiled at me, and it hit me again how beautiful she was. It was a shame that she was colder than a fish inside.

"See you around," she threw over her shoulder casually before she disappeared from my life.

Want more?
Please pre-order the book here:
The Fire Between US

ABOUT THE AUTHOR

Thank you so much for reading!
If you have enjoyed the book and would like to leave a
precious review for me, please kindly do so here:

Surprise CEO

Please click on the link below to receive info about my latest
releases and giveaways.
NEVER MISS A THING

Or
come and say hello here:

ALSO BY IONA ROSE